PUFFIN BOOKS

The author of *WAGs' World* loves shopping, travel, fashion magazines and Italian designers, though she is still undecided on the subject of latex leggings. She lives in the UK with her husband and kids.

Also Available:

WAGs' World: Playing the Game

WAGS' World

Knowing the Score

By Anonymous

PUFFIN

PUFFIN BOOKS

Published by the Penguin Group
Penguin Books Ltd, 80 Strand, London WC2R ORL, England
Penguin Group (USA) Inc., 375 Hudson Street, New York, New York 10014, USA
Penguin Group (Canada), 90 Eglinton Avenue East, Suite 700, Toronto, Ontario, Canada M4P 2Y3
(a division of Pearson Penguin Canada Inc.)
Penguin Ireland, 25 St Stephen's Green, Dublin 2, Ireland (a division of Penguin Books Ltd)
Penguin Group (Australia), 250 Camberwell Road, Camberwell, Victoria 3124, Australia
(a division of Pearson Australia Group Pty Ltd)
Penguin Books India Pvt Ltd, 11 Community Centre, Panchsheel Park, New Delhi – 110 017, India
Penguin Group (NZ), 67 Apollo Drive, Rosedale, North Shore 0632, New Zealand
(a division of Pearson New Zealand Ltd)
Penguin Books (South Africa) (Pty) Ltd, 24 Sturdee Avenue, Rosebank,
Johannesburg 2196, South Africa

Penguin Books Ltd, Registered Offices: 80 Strand, London WC2R ORL, England

puffinbooks.com

First published 2009
1

The moral right of the author has been asserted

Set in Sabon MT 10.5/15.5pt
Typeset by Palimpsest Book Production Limited, Grangemouth, Stirlingshire
Made and printed in England by Clays Ltd, St Ives plc

British Library Cataloguing in Publication Data
A CIP catalogue record for this book is available from the British Library

ISBN: 978-0-141-32581-1

www.greenpenguin.co.uk

Mixed Sources
Product group from well-managed
forests and other controlled sources
www.fsc.org Cert no. SA-COC-1592
© 1996 Forest Stewardship Council

Penguin Books is committed to a sustainable future
for our business, our readers and our planet.
The book in your hands is made from paper
certified by the Forest Stewardship Council.

To all the non-footballers in my life. Keep on shopping.

1

If there was one thing Amy was sure she wouldn't miss about living in a football manager's mansion in one of the most exclusive parts of London, it was the motley crew of paparazzi that seemed to permanently hang around outside, desperate to catch her at her worst.

Because of them she could never just throw on her old Juicy Couture tracksuit, pull her hair back in a scrappy ponytail, forget her make-up and run down the road for a pint of milk or a paper – not without it leading to appearances in the 'Fashion Police' pages of several major magazines.

Of course, she never exactly needed to leave Caseydene in a hurry, since everything was delivered without her even having to ask for it. She mostly only left the mansion for luxury shopping sprees and spa sessions, spending far too much time getting ready first. But after a bad start her pictures now nearly always got the style magazines' seal of approval. With her boyfriend's football career in the spotlight, and thousands of sixteen-year-old girls in the country who would do anything to swap places with her, Amy was relieved she was finally getting it right. There was practically a whole alternative league table based on how wives and girlfriends dressed, and loads of pressure. But really it was sort of fun being a WAG. It sure beat last summer's endless days working as a lifeguard at a water theme-park back in Stanleydale.

There was no doubt that a lot of her fashion success was thanks to Rosay, the team-manager's step-daughter, who had helped her transform her wardrobe. But Amy was also becoming an expert at putting together fabulous looks all by herself. Yes, Amy was definitely no longer the 'Fish out of Water – sweet (and clueless) sixteen-year-old girlfriend of hot new Royal Boroughs FC winger Damien Taylor' getting photographed in another fashion no-no.

Amy sat back on the leather seat of the Mercedes and resisted the urge to wind down the tinted windows and wave a cheeky goodbye to the paps as the car glided past them on the short journey from Caseydene to the flat she'd be staying in for the next two weeks.

Two weeks. That was all that was left of her idyllic summer with Damien before she had to return to reality, back to West Yorkshire to start her A-level courses. Mind you, there were various problems to face up to first. Things Amy was trying hard not to think about.

Like the Josh thing, and the credit-card thing.

Damien, sitting beside her, fixed his gorgeous dark eyes on her and squeezed her hand. 'You all right, Ames?'

She nodded, pushing those thoughts out of her mind. She leant over and gave him a quick kiss. Everything would be fine, and the next two weeks were going to be perfect – she was sure of it. She'd spent hours on the phone yesterday clearing the move with everyone: her two best friends from home, her new friend Rosay, Rosay's mum, Barbie, and her own parents.

They'd all tried to talk her out of moving – especially her dad, who rated Damien's manager, Carlo di Rossi, highly. But she'd stood her ground. Now she was going to be seeing more of Damien, and that was bound to make things easier than they'd been so far.

Damien smiled at her. 'I'm chuffed that we sorted it so we could move straight away. It's going to be brilliant to have our own place, away from that lot. I'm not going to miss all the craziness.'

'I know what you mean,' she said, thinking about Big Carl stomping around moaning about how disruptive the players' wives and girlfriends were, and his wife Barbie's foghorn voice. 'Well, I might miss the pool. And the wardrobe space,' she laughed.

'Honestly, you love that pool more than you love me!' Damien teased her.

'No way.' She kissed him again. 'But as for the wardrobe space . . .'

He pretended to be offended. 'I'll get you for that!'

But all he did was wrap his arms round her and kiss her even more. They barely noticed when the car drew up outside the block of mansion flats where'd they be staying now. Kylie Kemp, the girl whose room Amy was taking over, called it Spooky Towers. She'd supposedly come up with the name because the address was 13 Elm Street, plus she said the residents of the other flats always stared like zombies at her and her flatmate, ex-pop singer Paige Young. Mind you, Kylie Kemp was the footballers' girlfriend who all the gossip columns liked to call 'the ultimate beautiful airhead' so she could be relied on to come up with some strange ideas.

The driver opened the passenger door and cleared his throat pointedly, a sound that was accompanied by a familiar barrage of clicks. Amy looked up into the faces of several paparazzi, busy snapping away and shouting out.

'Keep kissing him, Amy! That was a great shot!'

'Come on, give us a kiss for the front page!'

She sighed and moved away from Damien. It looked like they hadn't escaped the paps after all, and this time they didn't have the benefit of Caseydene's wrought iron gates to keep them at bay.

There was also an audience inside the flats. Curtains twitched, the main door opened and, just as Kylie had warned them, a couple of neighbours stood and openly gawked at the new arrivals. Amy and Damien waved a friendly hello, but the man and woman just nodded a grim acknowledgment and kept staring. Amy smiled apologetically and wondered how her parents would react if they had the media camped out on their doorstep every day. She just hoped the paparazzi weren't so fixated on her every move once she went back to school. She was sure her twin bezzies, Susila and Asha, would protect her, but it wasn't going to be easy to return to normality now.

Damien shifted uncomfortably under everyone's gaze as the driver began to unload their luggage. He'd been out on a run when the driver had loaded up the car earlier, and he'd said he felt bad about not having helped more with the move, even though he didn't really have much stuff. 'I don't want to be like those rich people who forget how to do anything for themselves,' he'd told Amy. 'Apart from anything else, you know my mum would never let me hear the end of it!'

Amy had to admit that was true, though she secretly loved quite a lot about the lifestyle she'd experienced since coming to London.

Damien couldn't stand it any longer. 'Cheers, mate, I can take it from here,' he said politely to the driver. He picked up two cases, peered into the large boot and gave Amy a surprised look. She knew he'd been about to say something, but he wouldn't because he'd been repeatedly warned by his publicist not to speak in front of the press unless absolutely necessary. He was constantly baffled by all the media attention and hated Amy showing him gossip magazine and newspaper articles about them. 'I'm just another football player,' he always said. 'I don't understand why they're so interested in me.'

Amy understood, though. Not only had Damien recently been signed up to a Premier League team in a million-pound deal but also, at eighteen years old, he was the latest boy wonder to enter the game. And there was no denying he was total pin-up material, too. She watched his strong muscles ripple as he carried the cases effortlessly to the main door. Yes, Damien was definitely super-fit in every sense of the word – gorgeous, toned, athletic. In fact, this summer he'd trained so hard for Boroughs that it had caused a pretty bad rift in their relationship. It was all set to change now, though – Damien had promised he would spend more time with her, and she knew now that she could totally trust him.

After another trip to the car and back, with Amy joining in and doing her share of the carrying, Damien finally shut the two sets of doors between them and their unwanted audience. He eyed the row of matching Louis Vuitton cases next to his large sporty holdall and finally said what was on his mind.

'*How* many cases have you got, Amy? And where did these all come from, anyway?'

She shrugged. 'They're Rosay's.'

'But didn't you have your parents' suitcase when you travelled from Stanleydale? I remember you asked me to buy you a new case and I got you that instead.' He smiled, pointing at the delicate Tiffany necklace he'd given her when he'd first moved to London in May.

Amy fiddled with the heart pendant and glanced around their new home. It was enormous, but a total mess. 'Well, yeah, I did have Mum and Dad's case. Rosay said I could borrow hers for this move, though.'

'Why? What was wrong with the old case? And I know it was pretty big, but how did you manage to fill all of these?'

Amy shrugged. 'I told you, it's weird. I get loads of freebies now from shops and designers who want me to wear their stuff. They keep giving me things.' That was true, but it was only part of the story. She'd also bought quite a lot of the clothes herself, and she'd largely stopped thinking about the cost. In most of the boutiques she went to, the clothes didn't even have prices on them.

Amy wasn't quite sure why she wasn't telling Damien the whole truth. It had something to do with the mounting panic she felt whenever she remembered how much she'd been using her credit card – the card her dad had given her 'for emergencies only'. She didn't think her dad would consider Amy's shopping sprees much of an emergency, and she was fairly certain Damien would agree. Not that Damien minded spending money – he'd bought her some amazing jewellery in the last few weeks, especially when Amy thought she'd lost her ultra-special pendant. But Damien had never understood why Amy liked shopping as much as she did, and he definitely wouldn't approve of her charging anything to her dad's card.

'And nothing's wrong with the old case,' she added – another half-truth. The monster suitcase was great for family holidays in Spain, but, as Rosay had told her, it didn't quite fit her image now. Rosay had been in the middle of trying to persuade Amy to stay with her at Caseydene when she'd noticed her struggling to squeeze all the new clothes into her old suitcase. She'd taken pity on her friend and offered her indefinite use of a beautiful luggage set with matching extras.

'I can get more,' Rosay had laughed, referring to the fact that she had unlimited access to funds from Barbie and Big Carl again, now that she'd cleared her name of an old scandal. 'It's good to be back!'

Rosay really was back, too – her tan was deeper, her make-up was stunning and her hair had been transformed from dark and short to blonde and extended, all after one day's intensive beauty session at one of London's most exclusive salons.

Amy pulled one of the iconic patterned cases towards her, not meeting Damien's eye.

'I just fancied using Rosay's cases instead of my one,' she explained.

And this wasn't exactly true, either. Technically, she was using her case *as well*. It was still at Caseydene, full of her old stuff – clothes she rarely wore now that she couldn't be caught wearing the same things time and time again. She'd collect it another day. She had her new clothes now. If only she didn't have to worry about paying off her dad's credit-card bill.

Damien gave her a long look. 'I could never be like you,' he said.

'What do you mean?' said Amy, her heart pounding. Had he guessed what she was thinking?

'You know, the amazing way you can fill three suitcases when you've only been here two weeks.'

She looked at him uncertainly, but he smiled and she realized he was teasing her.

'And the way those clothes people are so desperate for you to be seen in their stuff that they let you have it for free. And the way you always look completely fantastic,' he said, looking deliciously deep into her eyes, 'so it's no wonder they all want you to model for them. Hey, maybe we can go out in a bit and explore some of the London shops. We could actually *buy* you some clothes, for a change!'

Amy made a great show of clutching her heart, splaying her freshly manicured nails and staggering about in the black Marc Jacobs shoes she'd worn for the move. 'You're offering to go *shopping* with me today? You? The founder member of the "I Hate Shopping Club"?'

Damien looked at her earnestly. 'Look, I'm going to be the best boyfriend in the world from now on. I mean it, Ames. I hated it when we broke up before.' He grimaced. 'There's no way I'm ever letting it happen again. I can't believe the nerve of Josh, thinking he had a chance with you!'

His eyes flashed with fury at the thought of the team's trainee sports psychologist who'd asked Amy out after advising Damien to give his relationship 'space'. Amy looked away.

But he recovered quickly, grinning again and grabbing Amy's hand. 'Yeah, we can go shopping, then we can get something to eat – maybe those chips you promised me, or how about if I take you out for dinner? And tomorrow you can meet me at the club after training, or I'll take you out somewhere nice. And Wednesday . . .'

Amy smiled at his enthusiasm. 'Hang on, Damien, don't overdo it! I've got plans, you know. I can't make it this afternoon, for a start. I'm seeing Susi and Asha off at the station.' Amy's twin best friends were heading back to Stanleydale today and Amy was going to miss them like crazy. They'd been amazingly supportive and had come down to surprise Amy when she'd had a disastrous start to her summer holiday. Now they were a day late going home because their London uncle had begged them to stay and help out a shopkeeper friend who was doing a stock-take and was desperately short-staffed.

'But you said we were spending the whole of my next day off together, and we wasted yesterday making plans for this move. So that leaves today! You promised me chips!' Damien pouted for a second and then laughed. 'Just kidding! Course you've got to see the twins off. I'm just glad you decided not to leave with them. I'm glad you came to your senses and remembered I'm the perfect man for you. Cos I really am, you know.' He grinned, then he took her into his arms and whirled her round, nearly knocking over a row of glass pug-shaped ornaments that must have belonged to Kylie. There weren't many signs that Kylie had actually moved out yet, and the flat was covered in dog hairs from Poshie, her pet pug.

'Hey, watch it, Mr Perfect,' Amy tried to say, but her voice was muffled as Damien pulled her closer and kissed her passionately, taking her breath away.

'Oh, you've arrived, then.' The voice came from behind them and Amy and Damien jumped apart.

It was Paige, flicking her highlighted hair over one bare and prettily freckled shoulder. She looked great in an off-the-shoulder summer dress, but was definitely paler and thinner than the last time Amy had seen her. 'Don't mind me,' she said good-naturedly. 'I just live here. I could say "get a room", but Kylie tells me you're renting two of them already.' She smiled.

'Oh, hi,' Amy said, flustered. 'Sorry. We were just –'

'Amy, it's OK. I don't want you to feel uncomfortable in your new home.' She laughed sadly. 'Just because I'm all bitter, twisted and heartbroken.'

Damien gave Amy a worried look.

'I'm really sorry about what happened with you and Scott,' Amy said quickly. Poor Paige. As if her break up with Scott White hadn't been bad enough, it had all been so public. For the last few days, the papers and online gossip sites had been crammed with sordid details about the Boroughs striker cheating on her. Everyone was talking about it.

Paige shrugged. 'I'll get over it. Or I'll get even. Or I'll get him back. One of those things, or maybe all three.' She smiled brightly, but Amy could see her make-up, no matter how perfect it looked, was covering up the shadows under her eyes. Paige carried on, 'Honestly, don't worry about me. I can take care of myself. Speaking of which, have you got a minute? Can we sit and talk about something?'

Amy and Damien nodded and found the sofa, pushing piles of fashion magazines out of the way to make space. Amy plucked at the dog hairs that were getting stuck to her new

DVB skinny jeans. She had a feeling she knew what Paige wanted to say.

Their friend perched on the edge of a plush red armchair opposite them and confirmed Amy's suspicions. 'Look, it's great having you two as flatmates, and so soon, too. I agreed to it because I like you both a lot and I know we'll have a laugh. But . . . I hope you know that I don't need, you know, a nanny.'

Damien started to say something but Paige added quickly, 'Don't try to deny it! I can see right through Kylie. I know she asked you here to keep an eye on me. But she's stressing about nothing. Diabetes isn't serious. I can totally handle it and I'm completely fine.'

Amy looked at Damien. She didn't know what to say to that – and judging by his silence, neither did he. Paige was right about what Kylie had said. But recently Paige hadn't shown much sign of handling her condition well. Some of her symptoms – like shakiness and slurring her words – had been noticed by the press, who accused her of having an alcohol problem. Both Amy and Damien had only found out the truth by accident – Paige was desperately secretive. She was worried about what the need for special treatment would do to her image, and she thought it was the reason Scott had lost interest in her. Then one awful night Paige had collapsed from hypoglycaemia and Damien had rushed her to hospital. Amy knew that since that night he'd felt kind of responsible for looking after her.

She kept talking breezily. 'Anyway, moving on. I love Kylie to bits and I don't mean this the way it sounds, but I'm glad she's moved out. The truth is she's a total slob and I'm practically a neat freak.'

Amy's face must have shown her shock as she stared at a lo-calorie health bar wrapper on the floor.

Paige laughed. 'See, that's the kind of thing I mean. So I'd just like to lay down a few ground rules, if that's OK, now I have a chance for a clean break. Literally, you know. Number one. The cleaner comes three times a week and there's a laundry service, but in between . . .'

Amy's phone rang in the cute Bottega Veneta bag she'd borrowed from Rosay. She opened her bag and glanced at the display. Claudette.

Her heart sank. Claudette was the self-appointed head-WAG who'd ruthlessly tried to bribe Amy last week. But Amy had stood up to her. What did she want *now*?

''Scuse me a sec,' Amy said. 'I'd better take this in my room, out of your way so I don't, er, interrupt you, Paige.'

Damien gave her a quizzical look and she shrugged and smiled as if it was nothing – as if it was Asha or Susi calling to make arrangements for the afternoon.

Paige laughed and called to Amy's retreating back, 'You're not getting away with it that easily! I'll make sure Damien tells you the rules! So, listen . . .'

Amy shut the door firmly behind her and answered the phone quickly before it rang off. 'Yes?'

'Oh, hi, Amy baby,' came Claudette's trademark drawl. 'Are you all settled into your new place, playing cute couples with that sexy young winger?'

Amy resisted the urge to hang up straight away. 'Claudette, why are you calling me?' Her voice echoed in the near-empty room and she was sure her heart was hammering loud enough to be heard too.

'Because, sweetheart, I'm concerned about you. When I found out earlier on that you'd moved out of Caseydene, I thought you'd decided to run away and hide from the scandal! But Barbie told me you haven't gone far, so I'm assuming that means you've told Damien your sordid secrets now? And he's fine with it, am I right?'

Amy tightened her grip on the phone. She couldn't think what to say, and Damien definitely didn't know anything about what Claudette was referring to.

'You see, Amy darling,' Claudette continued. 'I just wanted to check it won't be a problem that several magazines are *clamouring* to print the story I've come up with. Honestly, it's the scoop of the season.' She paused. 'Once everyone sees that marvellous snap of you kissing Josh, they'll know Damien's innocent sweetheart is really just another silly little girl, won't they now, Amy *baby*?'

2

Amy clutched the phone to her ear. On Saturday night at the start-of-football-season party, she'd stood her ground with Claudette. Today shouldn't be any different, even if right now her heart was pounding so fiercely that she thought it might burst.

She tried to relax. She had nothing to hide – there was nothing going on between her and Josh. She just needed to find the right time to explain to Damien that someone must have altered the photo of the friendly kiss Josh had given her, so he knew there was nothing to worry about if he ever saw it in print. He should understand; after all, he'd recently been the victim of gossip and lies in the tabloids too, when they claimed he was cheating on her with Paige Young. True, Amy had ended up believing it, but Damien wouldn't fall for the same trick – they were past that now. They totally trusted each other. Claudette could go ahead and send the picture to any magazine she wanted.

'It's a wonderful story. I can't wait till everyone sees it.'

The sneer in Claudette's voice was getting on Amy's nerves.

'And the picture's so clear,' Claudette continued. 'You can

really tell you're standing outside one of London's most romantic restaurants.'

Amy worried for a second about how she'd explain *that* to Damien. She couldn't exactly deny that she'd gone there with Josh, and even at the time she'd worried that the atmosphere was pretty date-like. But she didn't know anything about London's restaurants or what it was going to be like until she got there. He'd understand that.

She took a deep breath. 'Go ahead and print it. I told you I could deal with it, and I can.'

'Oh, I believe you,' Claudette purred. 'I just wondered whether you'd given any thought to the extent of the damage a story like this will cause. It's not just about you and your cute little love triangle with Damien and Josh, you know. I'm talking about the bigger picture.' She paused dramatically. 'Carlo di Rossi could be forced to resign as manager if we go for the angle that he hired an unqualified member of staff. One who *abused* his position to *seduce* a sixteen-year-old girl!' She tutted and then laughed. 'It won't be good news for Royal Boroughs, that's for sure. There's bound to be a shake-up, if you know what I mean. People losing their jobs across the board, including the players . . .'

Amy frowned. 'But won't that affect Danny?' Claudette's husband was the Boroughs' captain. Wasn't Claudette worried about him?

'No, Danny's safe – after all, he was there before Big Carl took over as manager. Besides, another club would take him in a heartbeat, and for big money, too. He's an England International. No, really it's the newest players that are at risk – the ones at the start of their careers.' She laughed again. 'Their *short* careers. The season's only just started and some players haven't even had a chance to show their worth to other teams. Like . . .' She paused as if she was thinking hard. 'Oh, like your Damien! And didn't the sports pages make a fuss about Big Carl taking a huge gamble on an inexperienced teenager when he was signed?'

In the silence that followed, Amy could hear Damien talking and joking with Paige in the living room. She wished she was out there with them, instead of in here, listening to this and worrying.

Was Claudette telling the truth?

Could Amy take that chance?

Could she live with herself if it was all over for Damien's football career, and the career of the manager he respected? Especially if he found out that she could have prevented it?

The heart pendant Damien had given her felt heavy and cold around her neck.

'Claudette, what do you want from me?'

Claudette gave a fake laugh. 'That's the spirit! I knew you'd come around. Listen, I'll let you off for the terrible things you said to me at that party. If you really think I don't care about the gossip, if you think I only want to get one over on the other girls, you couldn't be more wrong! Well, I obviously didn't make myself clear enough. We were all too distracted by the strange events, weren't we?'

Amy gave a vague reply, wishing Claudette would just get on with it. She wasn't agreeing to anything yet, she told herself. She was just finding out what this was all about. It must be pretty important for Claudette to make such a fuss.

'Anyway, darling, I'm not asking for anything major. It's really just the kind of thing I told you about before – keeping your ear to the ground and reporting any gossip, especially to do with Trina Santos. She's getting rather fond of making grand announcements nowadays. I don't want her finding a platform on the set of that reality TV trash she and your little friends are involved in, so it would be good to hear more about that.'

'You mean *Bandwagon*?' Amy wondered what Claudette was getting at. Even though her friend Rosay and her flatmate Paige were both in the new 'battle of the bands' reality show, she didn't think she'd get to hear much about it. They'd been pretty secretive so far. And Amy didn't know much about Trina, who'd just returned from Brazil to be the lead singer of a band created for the show. Except that at Saturday's party, Trina had stunned the crowded room by confessing to the crime that Rosay had been accused of the year before. But then Claudette had told Amy that she'd as good as put Trina up to it, strongly suggesting that Trina would do anything she wanted her to. Surely there was no need for Claudette to worry about Trina?

'Yes, *Bandwagon*. Believe me, you really won't regret this and you might even enjoy it. First things first, I'd like to introduce you to my PR guy, who has sorted it all out for you. We've been discussing it all morning. I have to go away for a while, and you're going to take my place on the gossip-management frontline. Meet me at his place this afternoon and we'll tell you exactly what we have in mind.'

Amy chewed her lip. 'But I have to see my friends off at the station this afternoon. Asha and Susi, you know, they helped to organize the party . . .' Amy realized she was babbling nervously. 'So I can't make it. Maybe another time?'

'No. It has to be today because I'm needed . . . elsewhere. What time are you meeting your friends?'

Amy told her.

'Meet me an hour before. Should be plenty of time. I'll text you the address.'

'OK,' Amy mumbled.

'Good! I knew you'd come through for me.' Her voice softened. 'Everyone trusts you, Amy. The other girls can be so terribly back-stabbing but we all know you're not like them.'

Amy thought she sounded almost . . . sincere and grateful. Almost *nice*. But she changed her mind when Claudette added, 'Oh, and Amy? Don't you go talking about this to anyone, OK? Not even those charmingly earthy twin friends of yours. If you do, I swear I'll find out about it and things will get difficult for them too.'

Amy closed her eyes and resisted the urge to ask 'How?' Asha and Susi had nothing to hide. Asha had gone out with boys in secret when her mum didn't approve, but no one except Amy and Susi knew that, and school-level gossip definitely wasn't the sort Claudette was hinting at.

Claudette must have sensed what Amy was thinking because she added, 'Believe me; my PR guy is great at digging up – or should I say *making* up – dirt, and spreading it widely. A lot of people could get hurt. I know you understand.'

She hung up before Amy could reply.

As Amy paced the room and waited for Claudette's text to arrive, she listened to Paige and Damien's conversation filtering through from the living room.

Tears sprang to her eyes and she felt sick with worry. Finally she was close to Damien again, but Amy didn't think she'd ever felt so alone.

3

Since arriving in London – and not counting those horrible few days when they'd split up altogether – Amy had got used to the fact that Damien was hardly ever around. Big Carl expected a lot from the boys – mornings of physical training, afternoons of talks and therapy, and frequent 'bonding' evenings out. Even when Amy and Damien did spend time together, he was often distracted, as if he'd left half of his brain on the football pitch.

But now that he'd promised to spend more time with her, getting away to meet Claudette without raising suspicion proved to be a lot harder than Amy had expected.

First they spent ages unpacking – or rather, Amy did. Damien went to his room and emptied his suitcase in ten seconds and then offered to help Amy, which she definitely couldn't complain about as it seemed to consist of hanging up one outfit, kissing for ten minutes, then hanging up another one. It meant there were quite a few delicious moments where all thoughts of Claudette and her threats flew right out of Amy's head. But then reality would flood sickeningly back and ruin the moment.

They were about to open the final case when Amy looked at

her phone to check the time. 'Oh, um, I've got to go and see the twins off now,' she stammered, even though she wasn't due to meet them for well over two hours. She casually picked up her clutch bag, her heart beating faster at the lie.

'OK! I'll come with you,' Damien said, jumping up beside her.

Amy was so on edge that she almost shouted out 'No!' but managed to control her reaction. 'Oh, um, I – no, it's OK, you know what we're like! We'll be chatting away, and if the train's late we might even hit the station shops or something. Asha will probably spend half an hour in Tie Rack faffing about whether or not to buy a scarf.' She remembered too late that Damien had already offered to take her shopping more than once lately, so this wouldn't necessarily put him off the way it would have done in their Stanleydale days.

Sure enough, Damien grinned. 'I don't care. I just want to spend time with you.' And then he kissed her again and another ten minutes flashed by. In the end, Amy had to mumble something about how she really had to go, and he should stay and do something fun with Paige now that they were flatmates. She asked Damien to call her a cab, distracting him before he could notice that she was encouraging him to spend time alone with the very girl they'd split up about, less than a week ago.

Amy grabbed her shades – the only 'disguise' she occasionally wore these days, given that she couldn't go anywhere without being followed. She said goodbye and rushed out of the flat before Damien could demand to come with her. It took her another few minutes to get past the new crowd of resident paparazzi, who weren't fooled for a minute by the sunnies. She ended up posing for a photo or two in the hopes that it would speed things up. She plastered a smile on her face and tried to make it look convincing.

Luckily, the taxi arrived quickly and there wasn't much traffic on the way to the address Claudette had given her, so she arrived in plenty of time. She glanced up and down the side street, checking instinctively for paparazzi, but she only saw a couple of people heading for a glass-fronted cafe across the road.

Then she double-checked the instructions in the text, pressed he entry-phone button labelled 'Spencer Greene and Miranda Jessop Associates PR Consultancy' and, without having to say anything, was buzzed in. She climbed up two flights of wooden stairs and pushed open the double doors at the top to be greeted by a heavily made-up girl sitting behind a desk, tapping furiously at her keyboard.

The girl looked Amy up and down intently, as if she was studying her and she'd be tested later. Amy couldn't help feeling nervous and self-conscious. She was still wearing the DVB jeans and low-heeled shoes that she'd selected for moving house, so this was by no means the outfit she would have chosen for meeting with Claudette if she'd had a chance to change.

'They're not ready for you, Amy Thornton,' the girl said. Her skin had an orangey, streaky hue that suggested she'd had a bit of an accident with a bottle of cheap fake tan. 'Take a seat.'

Amy muttered her thanks. She glanced at the girl's computer screen on her way to sit down and noticed that she was playing a game of online bingo. The nameplate on the girl's desk read 'Emily Elliot, PR Assistant'.

The girl caught Amy looking at it. 'Oh, that's not me. Emily's on honeymoon. I'm Lauren, and I'm just a desperate temp. Desperate to work here, I mean.' She laughed, then she looked down at her screen and frowned. 'This game is a con. I think I'll try playing Hearts instead.' She looked at Amy again. 'I've been begging at the agency for months, you know, dying for a placement like this.'

'Oh,' said Amy, trying to be nice despite her nerves. 'Is it good working here, then?' It didn't sound like Lauren was doing much work at all.

'Yeah, it's good round here, you know – sometimes you get to see famous people across the road. You know, in Coffee Coffee?' said Lauren. 'I go there every lunchtime just in case.'

Amy must have given her a strange look, because Lauren added, 'Oh, you mean the job? Yeah, it's all right. But that's not what I'm here for. I'm investing in my future.'

'Oh, so you want to work in public relations?' Amy asked politely.

'No, of course not! I want to do what you do.'

Without thinking, Amy blurted, 'You mean take A levels?' She decided not to mention her plans to go to university and study to be a physiotherapist, because Lauren was already laughing.

'What are you talking about? Why would you want to work and study and stuff when you don't have to?' Her face straightened. 'I mean I want to be a WAG, of course! I've been following the advice in this book but it hasn't worked yet.' She held up a red book with glittery lettering that said *A Wannabe WAG's Guide to Scoring a Footballer*. 'It's really good, have you read it? It tells you how to do all the make-up and the hair and the clothes . . .' She trailed off and slapped herself on the forehead, leaving a smudge mark in her foundation. 'Gawd,

I'm so stupid. Why would you need to read it? You obviously already know all this stuff! You've bagged yourself a Premier League boy, and you must be rolling in it. You've made it!'

Amy felt a bit indignant. 'Oh no, it's not like that,' she said. She fully intended to pay her way with Damien at every turn. She even considered telling Lauren that she was probably in major debt right now, but it was none of her business so she kept quiet and seethed inwardly.

'Yeah, *right*! Don't forget I work for Miranda Jessop! I've got some idea of the requests Damien Taylor's been getting. And you're part of the package, aren't you – a footballer and his WAG? Oh, hey, you don't mind being called a WAG, do you?'

Amy knew she didn't mind when Asha teased her about it. After all, she'd been Damien's girlfriend way before all this craziness started. But coming from Lauren, it made her bristle. She wasn't an accessory – she and Damien were equals. 'Well, actually –'

Lauren didn't leave a space for her reply. 'I know some of you lot hate that word, though I don't know why. It would be a dream come true, for me.' Lauren sighed. 'Hey, you seem miles nicer than the only other WAG I've met here. Maybe you can give me some pointers? I hoped this job would mean I'd meet tons of footballers and get invited to flash parties, but it turns out that most of it is done on the phone. Oh, apart from Mrs Snooty Control Freak in there who's like *always* here.'

Amy almost smiled in spite of her irritation, because Lauren was clearly describing Claudette.

'Between you and me, I sometimes wonder if it's more than, you know, *professional* between her and Spencer.' Lauren paused meaningfully.

Amy frowned. She'd seen Claudette with her husband Danny and they bickered like crazy – but it was in a happy, couply way. She'd felt madly jealous of them kissing at a film premiere last week, when Damien hadn't even turned up. Surely Claudette couldn't be cheating on Danny?

Lauren lowered her voice to a whisper. 'Anyway, it's probably just wishful thinking, cos I totally dream of having a chance with Danny Harris. Who *wouldn't*? But I don't think he'd be one to play away.' She laughed, adding, 'Unfortunately!'

Amy didn't find that very funny after what she'd been through when she suspected Damien of cheating on her. She wished Lauren would just stop talking now.

Instead, Lauren leant forward and asked, 'So, where can I go to meet footballers? Spencer and Miranda keep everything secret and locked away. My book listed some private members' bars that you sleb types hang out in, but I can't get in. I need connections, and you'll do!' She made super-irritating puppy eyes at Amy. 'You'll help me, won't you?'

The words were out of Amy's mouth before she could stop them. 'I don't think so,' she muttered. 'Though you definitely need *help*.'

Lauren's eyes widened in surprise and she made a short, insulted sound.

Just then the door opened and Claudette's unmistakeable drawl blared out, 'Ah, there you are, Amy. Come on in and meet Spencer. He has a fabulous proposal for you.'

Amy felt Lauren's glare on her back as she walked across the reception room to the office.

Claudette shut the door firmly and said, 'Spencer, this is little Amy, right on time. I told you she was reliable.'

Spencer was tall and striking but nothing like Amy had expected. He had kind eyes, for a start, and a crinkly smile that lined his otherwise smooth dark skin. Amy had imagined him as a mean shark-like creature, ruthlessly tearing people's lives apart with his make-or-break access to the media.

But instead, he shook her hand and asked her to take a seat before he said enthusiastically, 'So! Claudette tells me you want to work in television.'

Amy looked at Claudette, whose expression said 'Amy, you'd better go with it and do as you're told' and also 'Isn't Spencer a genius?' at the same time.

'Uh . . .' said Amy, not quite able to bring herself to say 'Yes'. She bit her lip and wished she was with Asha and Susi choosing scarves at the station, like she'd told Damien.

'Well, that's great, really great,' he said, sitting on a large leather chair behind a massive oak desk covered in papers and framed photos of a cute, gappy-toothed kid. 'It's a fabulous choice of career for a girl like you. You know, Miranda's been saying what a shame it is that you and Damien have turned down all those endorsement offers. Especially that new unisex fragrance campaign – it was so perfect for you! "Young Romance by Damien and Amy".' He sighed. 'I can't believe you weren't interested!'

Amy remembered Damien telling her something vague about getting offers and turning them down, but nothing as specific as a perfume named after them. She thought she should ask him about that some time. It sounded pretty cool.

'Anyway, it's good to hear about your ambitions.' Spencer steepled his fingers in front of his face as if he was about to say a prayer. 'Now, let me warn you that it's a pretty tough world to break into, although it certainly helps that your profile's increasing right now. But I'd still have said it was early days for you, if it wasn't for Claudette here. And also thanks to Frances Kemp, who's a senior producer and says that her niece speaks highly of you.'

Amy remembered Kylie's Auntie Fran from the party – she was a bossy-looking woman with stylishly cut silver hair and an impressive attitude, and she was producing the *Bandwagon* reality TV show. Amy wondered what exactly Spencer was getting at, but he didn't keep her guessing for long.

'Frances is planning some promotion of *Bandwagon* on daytime television. How much do you know about the show?'

'Er . . . not much,' said Amy, feeling Claudette's eyes on her. It was only a few days since Claudette had been furious with Amy for not telling her what she'd heard from Rosay about the programme, especially the part about Trina's unwelcome return from Brazil to star in it.

'Well, OK,' Spencer said. 'What you have is a competition between a girl band, The Miss Exes, and a solo act, Paige Young. The girls are filmed rehearsing and competing in different musical styles over the two weeks – well, they're doing cover versions from three pop music divas. There are three live heats, each with an audience vote, and the act that wins the most heats will choose the songs for the final. The public vote after the final, added to the votes from the heats, decides the overall winner.'

Amy nodded, wondering what this had to do with her.

Spencer continued, 'There will be various off-shoots from *Bandwagon*, both live and pre-recorded. And *The Morning Show* wants to feature a style summary before each live show. So basically that means running an interview every few days.

And since Claudette has had to turn the opportunity down –'
a strange look passed between Spencer and Claudette – 'and
Kylie has refused to be involved *again*, we've talked Frances
into giving you a stab at it. It's only a ten-minute slot, so not
too demanding.'

As he went into more details, including where she should
go, starting tomorrow, and what time and exactly how long
they needed her for, Amy could only stare in amazement at
him. Surely he couldn't be saying what she thought he was,
which was that he and Claudette – and Kylie's aunt – wanted
her to be a *style expert* on daytime television?

'Best of all,' Spencer added, 'it means you'll need to spend
a fair amount of time behind the scenes at recordings of
Bandwagon. Claudette tells me you have your own reasons for
wanting to keep an eye on the proceedings, and on the five
young ladies involved.'

'Especially Trina Santos,' Claudette added casually but
pointedly.

Amy's insides churned with dread, even though she'd
known all along that this must be what it was all about.

'Yes, of course, the infamous lead singer of The Miss Exes
is bound to create some interesting moments.' Spencer gave a
light laugh. 'I don't represent her, of course, or the other three,
though at Greene and Jessop we pride ourselves on having
most of the Royal Boroughs team and staff on the books.
Miranda's working on securing Courtney and her boyfriend,
and Marie Brown, the other singer, has approached me.
There's talk that the group's going to be as big as Girls Aloud.'
He nodded briefly at Claudette. 'Shame about all the scandal
breaking last week, but I really couldn't prevent it.'

Claudette said through gritted teeth, staring at Amy, 'Yes, that one gave *most* of us a shock.'

Spencer said pleasantly, 'You can't win 'em all!'

Amy looked at the ground. She refused to feel bad about not having told Claudette about Rosay's secrets. Although it looked like she'd have to now. This was making Amy's head hurt. Why couldn't it be simple like it was back home, where her friends were genuine and all looked out for each other?

Spencer smoothed a sheaf of papers on his desk. 'So, anyway, it all works out perfectly. Claudette tells me you'd like me to handle any gossip you hear on set that could affect the team.'

It suddenly struck Amy that Spencer didn't seem to know what was going on between Claudette and her – either that, or he was covering it up well.

Claudette looked coolly at Amy. 'That's right. You'll tell me everything you hear, won't you, Amy? I'll be unavailable during the day, but you can leave me a message if it's urgent, darling.'

'Why?' Amy asked. 'What will you be doing?'

Claudette looked away and said through gritted teeth, 'I'll be busy. But I'll call you every evening for a report.'

Spencer nodded as if this was a perfectly reasonable request, which stopped Amy from asking more questions. 'I'll be in touch with Claudette regularly, consulting on how to act on what you hear, as necessary,' he said. 'She's always been my main contact for overall Boroughs-related press matters.'

'Thank you, Spencer, you're marvellous,' Claudette simpered. Then she tuned her smile to 'even more insincere' and added, 'You too, Amy.'

Now Amy was wondering how she was actually going to do this – both the television thing and spying on the cast of *Bandwagon*, including her friend and her new flatmate. A flutter of panic joined the dread in her stomach.

'But . . . But I don't know anything about television.'

Spencer shrugged. 'Oh, you really shouldn't worry. You'll be interviewed by Julia Lightman, and she's a true professional. Frances said you'll mostly have to read the autocue – some of the interview will be scripted, though they might want your input for the script. But I can tell you know about style.' He smiled at her appreciatively. 'And honestly, there will be a team of staff to tell you what to do. Just think of yourself as a famous face, pushing up the *Bandwagon* ratings.'

Amy thought she heard Claudette scoff softly.

'But the main thing to remember is that you'll be gaining valuable TV experience. Claudette tells me that it's your dream to be a presenter.'

Claudette gazed haughtily at the ceiling. Amy's mouth felt dry.

'And there's payment involved too, of course. You might want to consider getting an agent to handle that side of things. Or I can do it, if you like . . .'

Amy sat up straighter. She wondered whether it was the kind of money that could cover her credit-card debt. 'How much payment?' she blurted out.

Spencer told her a figure that made her heart pound. She'd lost track of exactly how much she'd been spending, but surely an amount like that would be enough to cover it?

He added, 'If things really work out for you there's also a possibility of well-paid spin-off promotional work. Claudette, for example, would have used it as a launch pad for endorse-ment work in the skincare industry. She's always done well in that sphere. She'd get the work anyway, without this.' Spencer looked proudly at Claudette, who nodded in thanks. 'But obviously your interests are different. Claudette tells me you're into health and fitness, and when I mentioned that to Frances, she said there might be a chance of starring in a celebrity workout DVD that the channel wants to market as a Christ-mas gift. I know it's August, but it's already almost too late for that kind of thing. And there could be magazine tie-ins and chat-show appearances linked to this, too. It is a shame Claudette's had to miss this opportunity.'

That look passed between him and Claudette again. Amy narrowed her eyes warily and wondered what exactly was going on there. This had to be part of some grander scheme of Claudette's, because surely there was no other explanation for her taking a back seat?

'Oh, and by the way, Frances mentioned the *Bandwagon* launch party tonight. Can you make it?'

'Yes, you should *definitely* go to that,' Claudette agreed, making it obvious to Amy that she didn't really have a choice in the matter. 'I'd love to hear all about it!'

'Yup, it should be good. You'll need a special code number to get in. I'll get my assistant to text you the details.' Spencer smiled brightly and leant back in his chair. 'Congratulations, Amy, on the start of your career in television.'

4

Amy needn't have worried about keeping Claudette's threats a secret from Asha and Susi. It proved to be simple when Asha didn't let her get a word in edgeways.

'Susi said to text you and tell you not to meet us again, but I said, no, this time get her to come!' Asha was practically shouting, with a mixture of excitement and the difficulty of making herself heard above the din of the busy station concourse. 'In fact, I said we should wait until we were actually on the train and you were all, like, waving us off and crying and stuff. I thought I could leap off the train and go, "Surprise!"'

She acted out the jumping, nearly knocking over a tourist who was teetering about under the weight of a huge backpack. He regained his balance and scuttled away without giving Asha a second glance.

'But then my sensible sister here pointed out that we might "lose the open return portions of our tickets in the barriers" if we did that – those are her exact words, cos you know she talks like a total station guard –'

'What*ever*, Asha!' Susi rolled her eyes at her twin sister. 'Anyway, Amy wouldn't have cried.'

'Course she would! She loves us soooo much! Don't you, Amy?' Asha flung her arms around her friend.

Amy hugged Asha back, thinking that if she got any more surprises today her head might explode. 'So what are you saying?' she asked. 'You're not going back to Stanleydale?'

'That's right,' said Susi, smiling.

'Nope,' her sister added. 'We're staying here forever!'

'We're staying for two more weeks, as long as we've done OK in our GCSEs and don't get called home in shame. Results are out this Thursday, don't forget!'

'Oh, yeah,' Amy said. It seemed such a long time since she'd taken those exams, her head full of the excitement of her boyfriend being signed by a Premiership team.

Susi was still explaining things. 'You know how we couldn't leave yesterday? Because Uncle Dinesh's friend desperately needed help with this stock-take in his shop? Well he liked us so much that he offered us jobs –'

'And it pays loads more than we could earn in Stanleydale and Uncle Dinesh said we could stay with him and we pleaded with Mum and she said yes! And it's going to be dead glam!'

'Amy, don't listen to her.' Susi shook her head. 'Asha, seriously, you're the only person in the world who could think *office supplies* are glam.'

Asha sighed. 'When will you see the potential? We'll be in central London, where even the pigeons are super-cool! And it's not the stationery and office chairs I'm excited about, believe me. It's all those gorgeous young businessmen coming in to *test* the swivel chairs and *pose alluringly* with packs of paper that I'm interested in. All those, like, male office juniors or whatever, Susi! Wearing suits! They'll even be respectable enough for *you*!'

Susi brushed her comment away with a sweeping hand gesture. 'OK, let's get back to sanity.' She lowered her voice. 'So, Amy, how's it going with Damien?'

'Why are you whispering?' Asha asked loudly. 'No one's listening. You can say whatever you like in a city this size and everyone just ignores you.' She proved it by singing a bit at the top of her voice. Sure enough, no one gave her a second glance.

Susi sighed and raised her voice, but only a notch. 'Has he turned over a new leaf like he promised?'

Amy thought about the time she'd spent on the phone yesterday explaining to her fiercely protective friends about how her break up with Damien was all a misunderstanding. Persuading them had been so hard that she'd left out quite a few of the details, like Damien closely guarding Paige's secret, and Josh asking her out and making Damien act jealous. After what had happened, she really didn't want her friends to see Damien in any kind of bad light.

Now she added fresh reassurances with a long account of how brilliant he'd been since they'd got back together.

'OK, good,' said Susi. 'Well, he'd better be, or he'll have us to answer to, won't he, Ash?'

'Hey, you should come and see the shop!'

Susi sighed. 'OK, he'll have *me* to answer to, and possibly Asha too, once I shake her out of her stationery-induced dreamworld.'

'Come on, honest! I'm sure Uncle Sunil won't mind. Amy needs to know where it is so she can come in for a chat. And then we should check out the best lunch spots for flirting with fit business guys. It's right near these totally cool office blocks.'

'Asha, seriously, if Mum could hear you now she'd have us on that train in ten seconds. It's a serious job. And we're not supposed to call him Uncle Sunil, remember? He's not just a family friend now, he's Mr Mishra – the boss. And he makes our old boss look like a mouse. Amy won't be allowed to hang around chatting, not unless she buys several flatpack office tables –'

'Amy probably could buy herself a few as a present from Damien!' Asha gave a cheesy wink. 'Nothing says "I love you, forgive me for being a prat" like office furniture!'

Amy shifted uncomfortably. She'd taken Asha shopping in Topshop a couple of times since she'd arrived in London and she hadn't liked to admit she was using her own – or rather, her dad's – money. She'd enjoyed buying clothes for her friend the same way she'd got used to splashing out on herself. But Asha had never paid much attention when Amy came to pay, and for some reason she seemed to think Amy was spending money that Damien had given her before they'd split up. In fact, Asha had said, 'I'll tell Susi they were freebies you got in the post so she doesn't moan at you about using his money, OK?' and Amy had just laughed and added some accessories for Susi to their purchases. She was no longer the Stanleydale Amy who had to save for months to buy a new outfit.

'Um yeah,' Amy mumbled. Then she remembered she hadn't told them her own news – or, at least, an edited version of it. 'But I probably won't have time to hang around any shops. Because, listen – I've got a job too!'

She told them as much as she knew, leaving out the parts

about Claudette's bribery, but including the bit about the perfume and the possible exercise DVD.

'Wow, that's amazing,' Susi said, though she gave Amy a bit of a worried look.

Asha pouted. 'Oh, now you've made our shop job sound rubbish.'

'That's because it *is* rubbish, Ash,' Susi said. 'Seriously, well done, Amy. That's really exciting.'

There was a short silence while Asha visibly sulked, but it was interrupted by a girl who bounded up to Amy and waved a phone in her face.

'Oh my God! You're Amy Thornton! Can I get a photo with you? I think you're well cool – much better than Paige Young! What a bitch, running off with your boyfriend! No wonder Scott White cheated on her. Though I love his hair. He's Essex's gift to male fashion, he is. I even made my boyfriend get a Scott White do. Damien Taylor's all right too, don't get me wrong. But what Paige did was just cheap!'

Before anyone could correct her, the girl threw her arm around Amy, held the phone at arm's length and pressed a button that made a camera-like clicking noise. She smiled approvingly at the picture, muttering, 'My friends won't believe this!' Then she skipped away and disappeared into the crowds.

Asha recovered first. 'Yeah, OK. I can't imagine ever getting used to that. Good thing you've got us on hand to keep your feet on the ground, right, Ames?'

Amy nodded, relieved that Asha had snapped out of her mood.

'Right. Let's go somewhere and celebrate the fact that *all three of us* have fab new jobs. Amy, I bet you know all the best celebrity-studded cafes.'

Amy didn't really, but she thought hard. 'Well, I saw a place earlier called Coffee Coffee. I heard some famous people go there,' she said, feeling slightly guilty about not telling her friends exactly how she'd heard that.

'Great! OK, let's go there and hang around sipping wheat smoothies, or whatever the beautiful people do. Come on!'

Asha set her face in a determined smile and led the way, not looking back at Susi or Amy.

In the time it took to reach Coffee Coffee, find a table that Asha approved of, sit down, order and wait for their drinks, Amy got five texts. She read them cautiously under the table while Asha enthused about seeing a well-known Radio 1 DJ three tables away and how this cafe was close enough to Mishra's Office Supplies for her and Susi to visit at lunchtime if they were ever allowed to take breaks together.

The first message was from Claudette: 'Thx for this. Am counting on you baby. Will be in touch. P.S. Pls esp. watch Trina.'

The others were all from Damien, saying: 1) He loved her; 2) He missed her; 3) Kylie had been round and wanted to speak to her about something urgent; 4) He'd booked them a table in a posh place so could they do the chips some other time and what time would she be back?

She excused herself and went outside to ring him. It was a quick, awkward chat in which she told him she couldn't make it tonight and she'd explain later. He told her that Paige had spent all afternoon getting ready to go to a party, implying that all he'd done was sit around moping and missing Amy.

'She's leaving in a bit,' he added. 'Some of the lads will be there, you know, and Paige says I should go. But I wanted, you know, a night out with you.'

Amy hesitated. 'Paige is talking about the *Bandwagon* party, isn't she?'

'How do you know about it? Are you invited?' Damien sounded surprised, and there was something else in his voice that Amy couldn't quite make out. 'Oh, wait, I get it. *You're* going to that party? So that's the reason we can't go for dinner tonight?'

'I'll explain later, honestly.' It was too complicated and she had to decide exactly what she was going to tell him. 'Listen, Damien?'

'Yeah?'

'I'm really sorry about this. Thanks for booking that table and everything. We can –'

She realized the phone had gone silent. She checked, but the signal strength looked OK. She wrote Damien a text filled with apologies and kisses, and 'see you soon', sent it and went back to the twins.

Then she sat back and tried to relax, although she was secretly checking her phone at regular intervals, expecting the text with the party details to arrive any second. Susi must have noticed because she gave Amy a funny look as Asha chatted away, but she didn't say anything.

Nothing came through from Spencer, Claudette or Lauren.

Or from Damien.

5

Being alone in Paige's flat felt weird. Amy had to remind herself that it was her place now – and Damien's – at least for a while. She wondered why she wasn't feeling more excited about living with Damien. It was supposed to be perfect! But right now the flat definitely didn't feel like home. In fact, she'd probably been slightly more comfortable in the cottage at Caseydene, on those lonely nights that had led to breaking up with Damien.

And even after all the promises they'd made to each other since then, tonight was turning out to be a lot like one of those nights.

First Susi had dragged Asha back to their uncle's house after another couple of drinks at the cafe – with Asha protesting that it was still early and Susi stressing that they had to be up at dawn to commute to work the next day. Then Amy had headed home, checking her blank mobile all the way. She still hadn't heard a thing from Lauren, and she didn't have her number to chase up the party code she needed. She didn't know Spencer's number either, and there was no way she was calling Claudette if she could help it. She'd called Damien instead, but his phone went to voicemail.

And now here she was, and the flat was empty. It was also spotlessly tidy, with all the pug ornaments gone, and the rubbish cleared off the floor. So Kylie had truly moved out now.

But where was Damien?

She looked around to check whether he'd left her a note, like he used to at Caseydene, but there was no sign of anything. She tried to call him again, but she still got nowhere. Had he decided to go to the party with Paige? But wouldn't he have told her?

She knew she should be getting ready for the party herself, but as she was still waiting for that text, she thought she'd give her parents a quick ring first. She tried to keep her voice breezy as she told her dad that she might be on telly, and that he and Mum should look out for her and maybe record it for Nan. He seemed to be in a bad mood, though, grunting something about not knowing how the DVD recorder worked, and how she shouldn't let Damien's fame go to her head. Then he went on at her for ages about how football was a serious sport, and nothing to do with glamour, and she'd do well to remember that.

After that call Amy felt even worse. All thoughts of the party left her mind – she just wanted to speak to Damien. She tried to ring him three more times before she switched off her phone in annoyance. Let him try to get through to *her* and see how *he* liked it!

She curled up on the sofa and sighed, looking at the clothes she'd been wearing all day. It was probably the longest she'd worn any one outfit since she'd got to London and started changing multiple times a day to keep up with her stylish friends. Her clothes looked as tired as she felt.

The next thing she knew, the entry phone was ringing in her head and she realized she'd fallen sound asleep. She stood up slowly, yawning and stretching, then quickened her pace when she realized the ringing hadn't stopped. It had to be Damien – he must have forgotten his keys or something. She added that to her mental list of things to give him grief about, after 'not answering the phone'.

But as soon as she picked up the entry phone she heard a girl's voice blare, 'Amy, let me in right this second! You'd better have a good reason for not being at the party!'

There was only one girl who talked to her like that. 'Rosay?' she asked sleepily.

'Course, who else? Oh my God, don't tell me you were asleep already? Just let me in!'

Amy buzzed Rosay in and she thundered past, air-kissing Amy before making herself at home in the flat that she'd shared with Paige and Trina over a year ago. She went straight to the kitchen, put the kettle on and leant back against the counter.

'You know, I thought I'd never visit you here,' she told Amy as she selected two large mugs from the cupboard and started making tea. 'This flat has bad memories for me. I've even blanked out the stupid landline number – I thought of trying it when you didn't answer your mobile. Anyway, I don't intend to hang around Paige any more than I have to already. But right now the coast is clear. I know exactly where she is. And I had a feeling I'd find you here. Why weren't you at the party?'

'I was waiting for a text with the details. But –'

'But you turned your phone off, didn't you? Hmm, I know there's something going on and I'll get to the bottom of it in a minute. Come on.'

She handed a mug of tea to Amy, took the other one and marched out, glancing around as she settled on the sofa. 'God, it's spotless! Has she been on one of her cleaning jags again? They used to drive me crazy. Along with everything else Paige did.' She mock-shuddered. 'You know, I still don't get why you'd want to live with *her*! Don't forget I've got loads of money again, Amy – we could have had such a laugh at Caseydene!'

'Don't worry, we still can.' Amy sat down next to her friend. Lack of money hadn't exactly stopped Rosay having fun before. She found herself wishing this was Rosay's flat instead of Paige's. Then she reminded herself it was her own place too, even with all the framed photos of Paige's pop-star days dotted around the room, and the neat piles of fashion magazines on the coffee tables.

Rosay held up her mug as if she was about to propose a toast. 'Well, it's good to see you – I was missing you already!'

Amy clinked her mug with Rosay's. 'It's good to see you too,' she said, 'even in the middle of the night.'

Rosay pointed at the time display on the digibox. 'Lightweight! It's right early. The party's still in full swing! Which is why I'm here, checking up on you. Are you OK? What's going on?' She looked closer at Amy. 'You look all right, apart from the criminal way you're crumpling those clothes. Don't you believe in nightwear? You know they have some great designer lingerie at Orange County.'

Amy smiled. When it came to fashion criticism, Rosay just couldn't stop herself. 'I fell asleep in my clothes.'

Rosay gave her a 'duh' look. Then she smirked. 'And to think you're going to be a style expert. I heard some rumour about you following us around the *Bandwagon* set and presenting a programme about what we're wearing. Is it true?'

'Sort of. I'm going to be interviewed –'

'Wow, I knew it! I obviously taught you well, even if I forgot to talk about nightwear!'

Amy pretended to pout and Rosay laughed.

'So go on, what's wrong? It's Damien, isn't it? He was moping around acting like someone stole his football at the start of the party. What happened?'

'I don't know,' Amy said miserably. 'I didn't even know he was there.'

'Everyone was there, except you. Didn't he tell you he was going? Or was your phone off already? What was all *that* about?'

'He wasn't answering his phone. I got fed up trying him. That's why I switched mine off.' So it was official: he hadn't wanted to speak to her. Maybe they hadn't sorted out their problems after all. Or, more likely, she'd just ruined it all when she'd turned down the meal with him this evening. And then she hadn't even made it to the party. It was a total disaster.

'He probably meant to take your calls, but he was just too busy discussing the offside rule or whatever with a bunch of boring footballers. That's all most of the boys did tonight. At least, at first.' Rosay shifted a bit on the sofa.

Amy gripped her mug. 'What do you mean?'

Rosay sighed. 'Well, I'll tell you everything I saw, OK? That's what friends are for.' She took a deep breath. 'So, OK, picture the party. Most of the football players are huddled on one side of the room, talking shop. Then there's Kylie, wearing latex leggings and swanning around like she owns the place, which I suppose she does, what with it being her aunt's do. And some girls dancing in the middle, with Paige and Trina totally getting their claws out every two minutes. They're as annoying as each other!'

'Rosay! Trina's on your team in *Bandwagon*. Aren't you supposed to support her?' Amy's remark sounded half-hearted even to her – all she could really think about was Damien. Rosay sounded like she might have some bad news about him and she was dreading it already. Why couldn't things be easy, like they had been back home? She and Damien used to fight over stupid, simple things like which film to see at the multiplex. Then they'd make up within minutes and everything would be brilliant again. Now it was all secrets and jealousy and complications.

'You're right, and Trina's all right really. But as for Paige,' Rosay grumbled, 'some things never change.'

Amy shrugged. She knew there was no point in trying to stand up for Paige, not where Rosay was concerned.

'Anyway,' Rosay continued. 'So then there's some perma-tan girl who's trying too hard – never seen her before. First she's chatting away to Scott White, and then she crosses the room to the group of footballers and she's flirting like crazy with every one of them before she homes in on that ugly goalie. And, well, you know Steve – he doesn't even care that his girlfriend is in the room. He's like Scott White without the looks! So he's lapping up the attention when suddenly Courtney leaps off the dance floor and strides over to reclaim him.'

'You mean there was a fight?' Despite being desperate to hear the Damien part, Amy was finding herself getting drawn into Rosay's story.

'Hang on, I'm getting there.' Rosay took a long sip of her tea. 'OK, so Courtney's screaming like a banshee at the perma-tan girl and even Trina and Paige stop sniping at each other to go over and listen, and Trina puts in a word or two to back up Courtney. And that's when Scott struts over, causing a total stir as usual with his bad-boy hotness.' She paused. 'You know, I still can't believe he showed his face at the party after that "Scott White is a Creep" number we sang the other night! He's got some nerve. He totally thinks he's God's gift, just because he's completely gorgeous.'

Amy nodded in vague agreement, wishing Rosay would get to the point now.

'Yeah, um, anyway.' Rosay sounded flustered. 'So yeah, Scott hasn't been paying attention and he reads the situation all wrong and tells *Trina* she's out of order. So Trina has a go at him, and then suddenly Paige is screaming at both of them! And at this point Josh walks in late and heads straight for the argument, with his face all "team psychologist to the rescue".'

Rosay laughed but Amy didn't. She'd started to get butter-flies the second Rosay mentioned Josh.

'So Damien was watching all this?' she asked tentatively. She had a horrible feeling she knew where this was going.

'Oh yeah, I'm just getting to that. Amy, you never mentioned Damien had such a short fuse. I didn't think he was that sort of guy.'

Amy's heart sank.

'So, yeah, one minute Damien's standing there as bemused as the rest of us,' Rosay continued. 'I mean, I was wondering whether to get the bouncers myself, but it was all just talk and it was sort of entertaining, you know. And the next minute he's marching towards Josh looking like he wants to kill him. What's up with *that*?'

'I don't know,' Amy mumbled. She really didn't want to go into what could be behind it, and besides, she needed to hear the rest – fast. 'And then what happened?'

'Oh, not that much, really. Someone obviously did call security because suddenly these big bouncers are chucking the guys out and –'

'All the guys?'

'No, just Josh and Damien. I guess they were the only ones who looked like they were going to have a proper fight. Though Josh was going "Calm down" a lot –' Rosay did a terrible imitation of Josh's New Zealand accent – 'and I don't think anything actually happened because Damien was back in the room after a couple of minutes and the bouncers seemed OK with it. Josh probably gave him one of his counselling sessions or something.' She smirked. 'Anyway, it broke up the mass argument, that's for sure.'

'So that was it?' Amy asked quietly.

'Well, yeah. The perma-tan girl seemed to get all chatty with Paige for a bit but she left not long afterwards, probably because Courtney wouldn't stop shooting daggers at her. And Paige went back to sniping at Trina and eyeing up Scott when she thought no one was looking, plus she added a bit of glaring at *me* to the mix. So I decided I'd had enough of the party and got a cab here.' Rosay sighed. 'Though I did try to call first. I thought you might want a chat, what with the Damien thing, and you not being at the party.'

There was a short silence. Amy stared at her mug. 'It sounds like quite a party,' she said, stalling for time. She felt like telling Rosay all the Josh stuff, including the part about Claudette. But then she remembered Claudette's threats. Rosay had only just left all her troubles with bad publicity behind – it wouldn't be fair to land her right back in it. She'd have to be ultra-careful what she said.

'It was. It was very exclusive,' Rosay said. 'I don't know how the perma-tan wannabe managed to get in and start all that trouble in the first place, not unless she arrived with someone who was invited. We each had special access codes texted to us that we had to show at the door and everything. Look.' She pulled her phone out of her bag, glanced at it and then said, 'Oh, I forgot I had it on silent. Hold on, I'll just check this message.'

Amy put her head in her hands and went over everything Rosay had told her. Had Damien really meant to start a serious fight with Josh? She watched as Rosay pressed buttons on her phone, read her text and, with a wide smile on her face, started typing a reply.

And why hadn't Amy received the invitation text? If Amy had been at the party she could have talked to Damien and found out what was going on with him, and probably stopped him from behaving the way he had. She found her own phone and switched it on just to make sure, but nothing had come through. Spencer's assistant obviously hadn't sent the text.

Spencer's assistant . . . who had a bad fake tan and was desperate to meet footballers at all costs.

Lauren, Amy realized. Lauren hadn't passed the details to Amy, but had used them for herself. It was the only explanation.

She also seemed to have tried to get off with Courtney's

Steve, and started a fight that spread through the whole party, including Damien.

Amy couldn't decide who she was angrier with – Damien for his behaviour, or Lauren for causing all the trouble in the first place!

Rosay put her mug down, shoved the phone in her bag and stood up. 'God, Amy, I'm really sorry but I have to go. I said I'd meet someone after the party and it's sort of important.' She turned away. 'And I can't explain right now, but we can definitely chat another time. Really soon, I promise.'

'It's OK,' Amy reassured her. 'I've got to get things ready, anyway, for my first day at work tomorrow. I'll see you there, yeah?'

After Rosay left, she didn't even try to ring Damien again. She was still tired but this needed sorting out and there was only one thing for it. She'd wait in his room, and the minute he got in she'd make him explain everything.

This time it wasn't the entry phone that woke her up. It was someone gently touching her shoulder and whispering her name.

Amy groaned as she stirred. How many times could she be disturbed in one night?

Damien was sitting on the edge of the bed. He was wearing his Royal Boroughs tracksuit and his deep dark eyes were serious.

'Amy. I'm really sorry to wake you up.'

She sat up and yawned, noticing the sun streaming through the slats in the venetian blinds she hadn't closed properly the night before. She remembered that she'd meant to confront

Damien. But in daylight and half-asleep, she couldn't muster the same anger she'd felt last night.

'What's the time?' she managed to grumble. 'Have you only just got in?'

'No!' He gave a tiny smile that didn't reach his eyes. 'No, it's six-fifteen and I've got to leave for training, but I didn't want to go without talking to you first. I didn't want things to be . . . like before.' He made a face. 'I wasn't *that* late last night, honestly, but when I got back you were already completely crashed out! I didn't want to disturb you so I slept in your room. You know, I only stayed at the party because I thought you were coming.'

'I was supposed to be there. But . . . oh, it's a long story.' Amy wondered why her stomach felt full of knots. She used to know what to expect from being with Damien – and it was never this odd mixture of warmth, annoyance and mild panic that she'd been feeling since her arrival in London.

'Right. Well, listen . . . I'm sorry about last night. I think I . . . was a bit out of order.' Damien ran a hand through his hair. Amy thought he looked utterly gorgeous. And upset. She wanted to pull him into her arms and tell him not to worry – but first she wanted to hear what happened, in his words. And also possibly have a go at him.

'Did you get into a fight?'

He gave her a surprised look. 'No!' He sighed. 'OK, sort of. Another shouting match, like with Scott last week. Nothing else, honestly. Anyway, there were bouncers everywhere so . . .' He paused. 'How did you know?'

'Rosay came over.'

'Oh.' Damien frowned. Amy knew he didn't like Rosay.

'Yeah, she wanted to see if I was OK.' She gave him a look that said 'Unlike *you*'.

'Why didn't she just call you?'

'She tried, but I'd switched my phone off.' This time she didn't hold back. 'I got sick of not getting through to you,' she said. 'Why weren't you answering?'

Damien was quiet, bunching his hands into fists and staring at the ceiling.

'Damien?' Amy didn't think she'd ever seen him look so miserable. 'OK, what's going on? Is there something you're not telling me?'

He shook his head. 'I should ask *you* that question.' He still didn't look at her.

She took a deep breath. 'What do you mean?'

'OK. Well, for a start, I heard something last night about some job you've got. In television, or whatever. Something to do with the programme last night's party was for. Is that true?' He looked at her at last, his eyes full of confusion.

Amy nodded. 'They want me on daytime telly, talking about *Bandwagon*. But I only found out about it yesterday.' She thought quickly. She should be able to do this without lying. 'Claudette, er, asked me to do it. As a favour, because she was supposed to be doing it, but she can't make it. I was going to tell you . . .'

'But you didn't, did you? When you phoned me, I mean. When I was waiting for you to come home . . .'

He looked at the ceiling again and the silence seemed to go on forever.

Then he said quietly, 'Amy . . . is there something going on?' He screwed up his face miserably. 'Oh, I can't do this. I can't say it.'

Her annoyance flooded away and she reached for him, found his hand and held it tightly. 'What's wrong? Tell me.'

He sighed. 'I don't know. I thought we sorted things out but . . . Well, yesterday I really thought you might . . . you might have been with *him*.' His eyes darkened. 'With Josh, I mean. He denied it but . . . well, he would, wouldn't he?'

'Damien!' Amy couldn't believe what she was hearing. 'Why would you think that?'

He shrugged. 'You were acting all weird and you rushed off. It was like you wanted to, you know . . . *run away*. You were gone for ages, and you were only supposed to be seeing Asha and Susi off at the station. How long can it take, even if there's a delay? And then you cancelled our date like that, for some stupid television party thing. You didn't even try to invite me. Honestly, Amy, it . . . well, it felt like the worst. I turned my phone off because I didn't want to hear your . . . excuses, or whatever.' His face clouded with anger. 'When Josh walked into that party yesterday, I half expected you to be with him. And I have to admit, Ames, the thought of that . . . Well, it made me totally furious!'

Amy wanted to laugh and tell him he was being ridiculous – but then she remembered how she'd felt last week when she thought Damien was seeing Paige behind her back. She knew how consuming it had been – how the suspicion had grabbed her and not let go, to the point where she broke up with Damien without even hearing his side of things. Without trusting him.

She knew she should feel more sympathetic to her gorgeous, caring boyfriend, who had just been totally open with her even though she knew that talking about his feelings wasn't exactly his strong point.

Or at least, it hadn't been until lately, when Big Carl had forced him to talk regularly to Josh, in his role as the team psychologist.

That was totally ironic.

'So, listen . . .' He looked straight into her eyes, his face grim and serious. 'Will you tell me, because it's driving me crazy and I can't think straight. I don't want to lose you. Is there anything going on with you and Josh?'

'No, of course not,' Amy said.

And it occurred to her that it might be a perfect time to tell Damien about the Josh photo and Claudette's threats and maybe even her own money worries. Maybe it would take her panicky feelings away, and make everything normal and easy between them again, for good.

'I knew it. I did, honestly. I'm sorry. That party was so crazy, I got kind of . . . swept up in all the shouting,' Damien said.

Amy was about to blurt out the truth when he leant over and kissed her in that delicious way that made her forget everything for ages, until he leapt up and said, 'Right! I've got to go and face Big Carl! I hope he hasn't heard about last night.' He paused by the door.

'Yeah, me too. Damien –'

'Listen, why don't you come and meet me at the training ground today?' he said enthusiastically, and Amy knew her chance to tell him was over. He told her the time they'd probably finish. 'And we can definitely do something tonight. I miss you so much, Ames.' Then he glanced at the clock. 'Oh no, it's really late! I'd better run!'

But instead of running out of the door, he ran back to her and kissed her again. Then he left.

Amy sighed and picked her phone off the bedside table, finally switching it on. There was a message from an unknown number, reminding her of where she needed to be today and when. It was signed 'L' so it must be from Lauren, who'd actually bothered to pass on a message for a change. Amy fumed and typed: 'Thanks. BTW I know about last night and will speak to your boss'.

Then she thought about how heartbroken Lauren would be if she lost her job. The girl was clearly desperate, and possibly bonkers, and really pretty harmless if you didn't count how irritating she was. And Amy was feeling way more generous and relaxed now that she and Damien had sorted things out. Amy added 'if anything like that happens again' to the end of the message and hit 'send'.

She worked out she had about half an hour before she needed to start getting ready. She put her head back on the pillow, but she couldn't make her mind shut up. Why hadn't she told Damien everything just now? What would he say if that photo ever got out?

She'd just have to make sure it never did.

Paige started hoovering loudly and Amy gave up on sleep altogether.

6

After trying on about ten outfits, some of which still had tags on, Amy made a face at herself in the mirror. Her first actual interview was tomorrow, the morning before the live programme in the first music category, which was Britney. She'd been told there would be another interview on Friday, before Madonna night, then the following Wednesday for the Mariah Carey category, and lastly the live grand final a week on Friday.

But even though Amy wouldn't be in front of the camera today, she was supposed to be some kind of style expert behind the scenes on a television set, and she needed to look perfect. She wished she'd had time to buy something new especially for today.

Finally she pulled on a tunic dress with an asymmetrical neckline that Rosay had given her before she left Caseydene. She'd said the designer was up-and-coming, just like Amy, and that the colours were better suited to her. Amy had to admit it *was* cool and stylish without being too elaborate. She grabbed one of her Primark belts and some new peep-toe shoes from Nine West, and the look was complete.

She heard Paige rattling and crashing around in the living room.

Great – a second opinion.

But the minute she opened the door, Paige started moaning at her. She was eating a doughnut, carefully holding a plate underneath it to catch the sugar, and she was pacing around the room taking large bites in between rants.

'Oh, you're up. The place looked right scruffy this morning.' There was a sugar-filled pause. 'For a minute, I thought Kylie had moved back in! You left two dirty mugs on the coffee table last night.' She took another bite of the doughnut. 'And one of my magazines was open next to it. You read it and didn't put it back.'

Amy raised her eyebrows but decided not to say anything because Paige was looking pale and stressed. 'Oh . . . didn't I?' she said instead, wondering if she'd made a huge mistake when she agreed to live here.

Paige tutted primly and walked to the kitchen. 'No, you didn't.' She finished the doughnut and pointedly washed up the plate as she talked. 'I bet Damien didn't even tell you what I said about keeping this place tidy. I should have known he wouldn't. Honestly – men, they're all the same!'

Then Amy watched in horror as Paige's face crumpled and the plate dropped into the sink. It clattered but it didn't break.

Amy walked over and tentatively put her arm around her. 'Paige . . . are you OK?'

Paige was obviously struggling not to cry. She took a deep, shuddering breath, clutching the sides of the sink. 'You're going to ask me if I'm taking my insulin properly, aren't you? Or whether I've been drinking, like all the papers keep going on about!'

'No,' Amy reassured her, taking her arm away. 'No, honestly. I'm just asking if you're OK.'

'I'm fine! Of course I'm fine!' Paige's voice trembled. 'Why wouldn't I be? It's not like I didn't know Scotty would do this to me! Trina warned me about it when . . . well, you know. When he left her for me. Once a cheater, always a cheater, that's what she said. And she was right, of course.' Then she let out a sob. 'Well, I don't care about Scotty! He can go out with Rosay – so what? He's been with just about everyone else I know. What's it to me if my *ex-boyfriend* starts seeing one of my *ex-friends*?' She picked up the plate again and busied herself drying it and putting it away.

What? Amy watched her, startled. Scott wasn't going out with Rosay – was he? Surely she would have mentioned it last night! It had to be a misunderstanding. Amy remembered the series of scandals breaking last week, including the text messages from Scott to the mystery 'Miss X' in the papers. It had turned out that the whole dirt-dishing mission was part of a publicity stunt by The Miss Exes to promote the launch of *Bandwagon*. But, although one of The Miss Exes was Rosay, none of them was actually the girl in the incriminating pictures of Scott. Rosay had told her that.

Or had she?

'Miss X isn't necessarily any of us. But in a way it's *all* of us, you know, getting our revenge on all the cheating footballers – all the cheating *men* – of this world,' she'd said.

Now Amy thought about it, that wasn't exactly the same as saying outright that Rosay wasn't the dark-haired girl pictured with Scott. But surely she couldn't have been? Rosay didn't think much of Scott.

Although she really had it in for Paige. It was possible that she'd try to get papped with Scott just to get at Paige. Maybe that's what Paige was talking about.

Paige shut the cupboard door and sniffed again, and Amy realized this wasn't the time to sit around analysing gossip. What Paige needed was a shoulder to cry on.

'Hey, it's all right.' Amy tried to soothe her. She plucked a tissue from the box sitting tidily on the kitchen counter and held it out.

'No, it's not! It's not!' Paige sobbed. 'I want him back!' She took Amy's tissue and blew her nose for ages. 'Sorry. You probably think I'm crazy – you have a gorgeous and amazing boyfriend who would never mess around the way Scotty does.'

Amy bit her lip, thinking about the way she'd been convinced that Damien was cheating on her with Paige. Even now, she wasn't too sure how she felt about Paige calling Damien 'gorgeous and amazing' like that.

'God, Scott's practically as famous for his love life as he is for football. He had an offer from a publisher for a book about it, you know. Yeah well, I've got a good title for them – *Scott White's Guide to Scoring On and Off the Pitch*!' Her attempt at a laugh came out as an odd sniffing sound. 'But I don't think I even care! I still love him, Amy, whatever he does!'

Paige dabbed at her eyes. Amy tried desperately to think of something to say to cheer her up.

'I'm not sure about Scott and Rosay, you know,' Paige said. She looked at Amy, her damp eyes full of hope. 'Some girl mentioned it last night, plus I saw the way he looked at her . . . but I didn't actually witness anything else, if you see what I mean.' She took a deep breath. '*You* know, though, don't you,

Amy? You must do – you've been living with Rosay. Will you tell me? Now we're flatmates and everything . . . Am I right? Are they together? Please tell me. Honestly, I'd rather know.'

'Oh. Er, yeah. I mean, er, no, I don't think Rosay's seeing Scott,' Amy mumbled. She had doubts in her mind now.

'Really?' Paige straightened up, scrunching the tissue in one hand and straightening her wispy blonde hair with the other. 'Oh, thanks, Amy. You're a real friend.'

Amy nodded, unsure of what to say.

Paige threw the tissue in the bin. 'Hey, we'd better get going, hadn't we? I'm really glad you're going to be working on the set, or whatever.' She laughed, seeming like a completely different person. 'You can have fun watching me totally out-sing and out-dance the talentless Trina!'

Amy had only been on the television set for an hour, but her head already felt ready to explode.

The pre-recorded parts of *Bandwagon* were supposed to involve real footage of the girls preparing for the live mini-concerts and the grand final, but so far it seemed to be entirely staged.

Amy had watched about twenty-five takes of the same section of a group singing lesson. It was led by a singing coach called Jorge, a man with a tiny beard, a soft, calm voice and seemingly endless patience. The four Miss Exes and Paige were standing at the other side of the piano from him, displaying varying amounts of confidence as they sang lines from an old Britney hit.

Trina Santos easily had the most confidence – she kept tossing back her multi-coloured hair and oozing supermodel attitude, sneering like this was all beneath her. Next was the petite, blonde Paige Young, who was standing tall despite her size. Paige had moved as far from Trina as she could get away without falling out of shot. She looked pale and gaunt, like she hadn't quite recovered from this morning's outburst. But whenever Trina tried to put her down, which was every five minutes, she was always ready with a comeback.

On the other side of Trina was Rosay Sands, her newly extended and blonde hair cascading over her deeply tanned shoulders as she frowned in concentration. The other two girls, Courtney West and Marie Brown, were hanging back slightly. Marie in particular looked like she wished the ground would swallow her up. Amy didn't know much about those two, except that Courtney was the goalie's girlfriend who had got into a fight with Lauren. The cast of *Bandwagon* were all supposed to be girlfriends or ex-girlfriends of footballers, but Amy didn't have any idea who Marie was connected to. It was probably someone from another club – a token gesture by Kylie's Auntie Fran to make it look like she didn't exclusively favour her niece's boyfriend's team.

Amy looked behind the girls at the set. The pretend living room they were all standing in was clearly supposed to be in the singing coach's house. Someone had even put real photos and books on the shelves behind the girls' heads, and the place looked homely in a spotless way, as if Paige had just tidied it.

But if you looked beyond the boundaries of the laminate flooring, there were acres of masking tape leading to the grey grime of the studio floor. Wires and cameras were everywhere, and a mess of people milling about with headsets and clipboards were barking orders at each other in the dingy warehouse-like open space.

Amy was lurking behind a huge unused camera, wondering what exactly she was supposed to be doing. She'd been introduced to a few people when she first arrived, but their names and roles were all a blur now. She'd watched what looked like hundreds of people making preparations, including a few who fussed around Paige and The Miss Exes with make-up brushes and powder. Amy had spent a while making a mental note of what each of the girls was wearing – they were grand, ballroom-style gowns made by selected designers especially for the programme, and they were absolutely gorgeous. But just as she finished, a boy had handed her a pink sheet of paper that listed the clothes anyway. 'You Amy Thornton? This is from wardrobe,' he'd mumbled.

'One more time, girls and Jorge!' called a woman with cropped blonde hair who was standing outside the pretend living room. Amy thought she must be the director or studio manager, or whatever the bosses here were called, as she seemed to be issuing the most orders. Occasionally she seemed to be told things through her headset, and then she'd bark even more. 'Trina, we need you to turn to your left a bit. Get closer to Paige!'

Trina tossed back her multi-coloured mane again and gave Paige a withering look. 'No, thanks. I'm all right here.'

Paige shrugged as if to say that was fine with her, too.

The woman sighed. 'OK, move your head a little nearer, then. Camera two's going for the close-up.'

'I can't,' Trina sneered. 'Paige's ego is already taking up all the available room.'

'Well, could you just tilt your chin?'

'Which one of her chins?' Paige said innocently. 'You'll have to be more specific.'

Trina narrowed her eyes. 'I'm not surprised you're seeing double –'

'It's treble, at least.'

'– your eyes are so puffy! I'd say use teabags, but you don't drink tea, do you? Unless it's *Irish* tea.'

Paige laughed. 'I think you mean Irish *coffee*.'

'Yeah, and you'd know. Anyway, I suppose you have to drink lots what with all those doughnuts you're always eating.'

'At least I don't look like a doughnut.'

'God, Paige, how old are you? Three? No wonder the papers are shocked about the way you drink. Talk about *underage*.'

Rosay rolled her eyes at them. 'Can't we just get on with this?'

Paige and Trina both glared at Rosay.

Amy noticed the short-haired woman grin at a nearby man in scruffy jeans. Then she tapped her headset.

'OK, we'll take it again, but this time the producer would like us to capture that rivalry on film. Say it like you mean it, girls!'

Amy didn't think they'd have any trouble with that. In fact, three takes later, the production team decided the insults had gone too far for a family show, and they would film The Miss Exes and Paige separately. The girl-band members were sent to their dressing rooms.

Amy stretched. Her feet were aching in the Nine West wedges she'd selected to go with her work clothes. She wasn't used to standing around like this for so long – her old life-guarding job involved a lot more sitting, and her swimsuit and flip-flops were a lot more comfortable. She wondered how Asha and Susi were getting on in their new job. Maybe she'd give them a quick ring – after all, there hadn't been any ward-robe changes yet, and no one really seemed to need her here.

She wandered off towards the dressing rooms and leant against the wall in a quiet corridor, trying Asha first, as she was less likely than Susi to get stressed out by a phone call in work hours.

Asha answered the phone in a bored voice. 'Hello, glitter-ing star.'

Amy laughed uncertainly. 'Hi, Ash. How's the glam new job?'

'Oh, ha ha. Good one. Hold on, Susi's right here.'

'Oh. OK.' Amy guessed she was in the middle of something.

'Amy! How's it going?'

'I was just going to ask you the same thing. It's actually pretty boring.'

'Well, snap. See, Ash, I told you! Amy's as bored as we are.'

Amy heard Asha in the background say something like 'huh'.

'Oh, I thought it sounded like you were busy. Is Asha OK?' Amy asked Susi. 'She was almost a bit . . . well, *off* with me just now.'

'Oh, she'll get over it. She read something online about your role on *Bandwagon*, and how you're Britain's new voice of style or something. Apparently, three magazines are fight-ing about having you as a columnist.'

'Really? I don't know anything about that. You know those sites are packed full of lies,' she reminded Susi.

'Yeah. Well apparently, *Just Gossip* are in talks your publi-cist about it. Asha's gone a bit green, that's all. It's nothing a good shouting-at by her sensible seven-minutes-older sister won't fix. I'll get on to it as soon as I get off the phone, I promise.'

'Oh, right,' Amy said, ignoring the sinking feeling in her stomach. 'Well, you guys should come and visit the set one day if you can. I'm sure I could get you in. And tell Asha this isn't glamorous, I swear. I've just been standing around so far.'

'Snap again, except we've been sitting. I don't know why Uncle Sunil – I mean, Mr Mishra – went on about being desperately short-staffed and needing us both here. We've only had one customer all morning. Apparently certain days get madly busy, but Mr Mishra says if it's quiet me and Ash can go to lunch together, so hopefully we'll get to go to that cool Coffee Coffee place again! And we're allowed to make phone calls and use the computer and stuff. Asha's found some excellent gossip sites. I can tell you all kinds of ridiculous lies about your new friends, if you like.'

'Go on, then. I've got time.' Amy sat down on a plastic chair in the corridor. She really didn't feel like going back to the studio yet.

Susi said, 'Yeah, me too. Hang on. I'll find you the descriptions of the Top Twenty Super-Hot WAGs, as voted by readers of *Men's Stuff*. It's pretty entertaining, in a horrifically sexist way, especially when you consider that most of the women are more successful than their partners. I mean, everyone knows pop star Paige Young and glamour model Trina Santos. But who's ever heard of any footballers, except the big famous ones?'

Amy laughed. 'Most football fans have, Susi. That's probably at least half the nation.'

'Yeah, well, not me. So listen. At Number Twenty it's Marie Brown.'

'Oh, really? From *Bandwagon*? I was wondering about her – who does she go out with?'

'It calls her "Mrs Pete Carlton",' Susi quoted.

Amy wracked her brains. 'Oh, yeah. I think Damien used to talk about him.'

'Exactly. *Used to*. See what I mean about footballers? There's way too many to keep track of. Anyway, then it's got this picture of Marie in some leopard-print leotard thing, and a description of her. "Red-haired Marie might seem shy and retiring, but we've heard she's a total tiger when you light her fire!"' Susi read it out in a silly voice, then added, 'Yeah, in your dreams, *Men's Stuff* writers!'

Amy smiled. She was really glad she'd called, despite the weird way Asha was acting. Susi was cheering her up.

As Susi worked her way up the chart, adding sarcastic comments to every description she read, Amy's mind wandered on to the other part of the job she'd taken on: having to report daily to Claudette. She wondered what exactly she was going to say. Would Claudette be annoyed with her about missing last night's party, when she'd made it clear that Amy should be there? Mind you, Amy could get Lauren into trouble if she reported what had happened, which would serve her right, even though Amy had offered to give her another chance.

On balance, though, Amy decided it was more important to keep herself out of Claudette's bad books than to get Lauren into them. And Amy knew about the party's main event from Rosay's commentary. Claudette wouldn't have any reason to suspect she hadn't actually been there.

'New entry at Number Eleven . . .' A change in Susi's voice made Amy listen more carefully. She sounded excited. 'Amy Thornton.'

'You're kidding!'

'I am not. You're the *Men's Stuff* Number Eleven Super-Hot WAG. And everything it says about you is lovely, Amy. You're on the rise.'

Amy felt like screaming, though she wasn't sure whether it would be a scream of delight or of horror. 'You sound like a magazine yourself now, Susi!'

'No, that's what it says,' Susi explained. 'It says you're on the rise. Apparently you're only sixteen but you already have beauty, brains and ambition, plus you look great in a swim-suit.'

'Is there a picture?'

'Course there's a picture. That's what *Men's Stuff* is all about. Although your dad would freak out if he saw this. It's that one of you at Water World, when being stalked by photographers was still a rare thing for you.' Susi's voice went nostalgic. 'Wow, was it really only last month? You looked so *innocent* then, before you moved in with your boyfriend and became *Mrs Damien Taylor*,' she teased.

'Shut up!'

'Sorry. I'm just standing in for Asha until she gets over her strop.'

Amy laughed. It was true – Asha had been the one totally teasing her about the way spending summer with Damien would make Amy qualify as a 'woman of the world'. It was beyond embarrassing.

Amy listened out for Asha's voice in the background but

there was silence. 'So who's above me, then? Why aren't I Number One?' she joked, changing the subject.

Susi tapped at the computer. 'There are a couple of your Boroughs lot, actually, in among the other big name stars. Trina Santos is at Number Nine with her "curvy dusky beauty", Kylie Kemp is "the ultimate blonde airhead, but with a body like hers, who cares" at Number Eight, and Paige Young is "pretty, fit and pretty fit" at Number Four. Who *writes* this stuff? Someone should try defining *him* just by what he looks like.'

Amy thought about how much Trina would hate knowing that Paige was higher than her in the chart.

'But you'll never guess which of your mates has beaten you all.'

'I know. It's Claudette,' Amy said, trying to keep her voice neutral. Claudette was stunning, but she also had a Spencer, who seemed to entirely dedicate his PR skills to her. She always got every bit of positive publicity going and never, ever ended up on the Fashion Police pages. Claudette had to be at Number One.

'No, someone else,' said Susi. 'That's a point – how weird that Claudette's not even on the list. Anyway, it's someone you know better than her. It's Rosay Sands!'

'Really? Rosay? Wow!' Amy was shocked and pleased at the same time. Spencer obviously didn't know anyone at *Men's Stuff* who he could bribe.

'Yeah, she's at Number Two, looking nothing like I remember her from last week. I mean, she seems to be in her underwear, for a start. But also her hair's a different colour and length and she looks like she's been in Barbados for a month.'

'Oh yeah, she's got a new look,' Amy explained.

'Well, listen to what it says: "The daughter of celebrity photo agent Matt Sands and Boroughs' First Lady Barbie di Rossi, Rosay's got the right combination of savvy and beauty to take on wild-boy Scott White. And she can tame us anytime."'

'That's so cheesy,' Amy giggled.

'I know!'

'I don't understand why everyone's talking about Rosay and Scott White all of a sudden,' Amy added. 'I really didn't think there was anything going on between those two.' It was weird how this kept coming up today.

'Yeah, well, I don't think Rosay gets a say in this. I told you it was horribly sexist. Besides, it ties in with this blog Asha found, the one called *My Secret Scandalous WAG Blog!*'

'You've been reading blogs like that?'

'Yeah.' Susi laughed. 'Loads of them. It's livened up our morning. Anyway, this site claims to have a quote from Scott himself, all about Rosay. Hang on, I'll find it for you.'

Amy waited, frowning and wondering how everyone seemed to know this gossip except her.

'Here we go. It was told to "a secret source close to the footballer, at an exclusive party", if you can believe that. Apparently Scott says, "Rosay is amazing. She might not realize it yet, but I know we're really meant for each other."'

'Wow,' Amy breathed. Paige wouldn't be happy. In fact, from what she knew, *Rosay* wouldn't be happy. 'I don't think Rosay even likes him.'

'Typical,' said Susi. 'Caveman or what? He might as well hit her over the head with his club and drag her back to that stupidly big house he lives in with those five cars you told me he owns. It's official. Scott White really is a creep.'

The rest of Amy's time in the studio was pretty uneventful, unless you counted listening to the constant bickering between the members of the band. Even the timid Marie ended up joining in, during the shooting of a disastrous choreography scene where Courtney kept hitting everyone in the face by swinging her arms the wrong way and out of time. Eventually Marie turned round and snapped at Courtney with a viciousness that Amy wouldn't have thought possible from what she'd seen of her so far.

But all of that looked like idle chatter when compared to the out-and-out bitch-fest that occurred whenever Paige and Trina stood anywhere near each other. Amy noticed it was definitely always Trina who started the comments, but Paige gave as good as she got.

When the studio session was over, the girls dispersed, with cameras still trailing Trina and Paige hoping to capture some 'real' backstage footage that would make good television.

Then Amy was called in to meet the team who had been assigned to oversee her interview the next day. After a quick buffet lunch of weird sandwiches sprinkled with cress, the staff carefully explained the show to Amy in detail: where she'd sit, how to read the autocue, where to look and what to expect at various stages of the proceedings. They asked for her opinions on the dresses the girls had worn today, and they made notes, telling her it would all get made into a script by a member of the staff. Lastly, she was introduced to Julia Lightman, who seemed as nice and mum-like as she always did on television. She put Amy at her ease right away.

In fact, Julia Lightman was making Amy miss her own mum. She decided to give her a ring really soon, even though she'd been planning on avoiding her parents for a while after the last couple of times she'd spoken to them. But really it was her dad who seemed to have a problem with her, with the way he'd totally disapproved of her moving out of Caseydene, and last night's reaction when Amy told him about the television job.

Yes, the way things were going with her dad only increased Amy's dread of the moment she had to break it to him about his credit card. She decided she'd try and speak only to her mum, at least until she'd earned the money to cover the bill. That had to count for something. Also, maybe her dad would soften when he'd actually seen her being interviewed a few times. Amy's mum sometimes teased her dad about having a bit of a crush on Julia Lightman.

By the time Amy was ready to leave for the day, she was exhausted. Still, she was lucky her job was pretty interesting. She felt a pang of guilt as she thought about Asha feeling miserable in the shop job. She'd have to play this down when she told her about it later. That's if Asha ever decided to talk to her again. She couldn't believe one of her oldest, dearest friends was acting like this. It wasn't like her to get jealous in a serious way.

Amy walked away from *The Morning Show*'s offices and back towards the lift. She was starting to know her way around the building, and it felt pretty cool to walk around the place where so many famous TV programmes were made. The lift doors opened and Amy spotted at least three familiar faces from the telly, including a celebrity chef her mum liked. Amy smiled to herself and tried to pretend there was nothing unusual about being in a lift with him. But now she really was dying to ring her mum.

As soon as she left the building she pulled out her phone. She glanced at the time first – if she left now, she could probably get to the Royal Boroughs training ground in time to meet Damien like they'd planned.

Amy hailed a taxi and settled in the back. She used the ten minutes they were stuck in heavy traffic to chat to her mum, telling h r an exaggerated story about being in the lift with the chef and how he had flour in his hair. It was great to hear her mum laugh – she hadn't long been in remission from that horrible cancer scare, and she still was nowhere near being herself again.

Sure enough, after a couple of minutes Amy's mum said, 'I need a little lie down now, Amy love. Shall I put your dad on?'

'Oh, no, it's OK. I'm . . . oh, I've arrived! I have to go.' She hurriedly said goodbye and hung up. This time it wasn't even a lie. Amy paid the driver and smoothed her clothes in the reflection of the shiny black doors before the taxi drove away. She'd just started walking towards the entrance to the train-ing ground when she spotted a familiar face coming in the opposite direction.

It was Josh. And he didn't look particularly pleased to see her.

7

Amy decided her best bet was to act totally normal. Or as normal as possible, considering that the last time she'd seen Josh was when he'd asked her out at the start-of-football-season party, and she hadn't said yes or no – she'd just avoided the question and run off. Then, according to Claudette, he'd seen her kissing Damien a few minutes later and left the party because of that.

She also couldn't forget that Damien had nearly had a fight with him last night. And that she was being blackmailed about a picture taken of her and him together. Although nothing had ever actually happened between them, they'd spent a large amount of time together over the past couple of weeks. Amy had chatted to him about life and school and her mum and all sorts of things. They knew a lot about each other. She'd almost say they were close friends – until the party. Now she just felt awkward as he walked up to her.

'Er, hi, Josh.'

'Hi, Amy,' he said, not smiling.

Despite everything, she couldn't deny that he looked fantastic right now. His biceps bulged from under a tight white

T-shirt and his eyes smouldered as he said, 'So . . . you're here to see Damien, right?'

'Um, yeah.'

There was a long pause.

'So . . .' Amy started.

'No, I'll go first.' Josh jumped in, which was just as well as Amy had no idea what she was going to say. 'I don't want things to be . . . awkward between us.'

'Um, OK,' said Amy, thinking it was kind of too late for that.

'OK.' Josh took a deep breath. 'I probably shouldn't even mention it, but maybe if I do it will clear the air.'

Amy remembered teasing him for sounding like a counsellor, or something out of a self-help book, half the time. His parents were both psychologists and it was in his blood. She should have known he wouldn't be able to avoid the issue, like any normal guy would. She'd be much happier talking about football rather than this.

'So . . .' Josh continued, 'I'm sorry about . . . what I said the other night. I didn't realize you and Damien were trying to work things out, despite everything.'

Amy felt her eyes narrow as she remembered the things Josh had told Damien as part of his 'settling in' counselling sessions. His advice hadn't helped Amy and Damien's relationship at all. But Amy didn't think he'd said those things deliberately to break them up. He couldn't have – he was too nice. She'd had the occasional moment of doubt about it, though.

Josh was still talking, gazing at her earnestly. 'I didn't mean to tread on any toes when I, er, asked you . . . I mean, well, I'm just really sorry.'

The way he was looking at her gave Amy butterflies in her stomach, which was annoying. 'No, that's OK.'

Josh shook his head. 'No, it's not. It's even caused some problems at work – I should have known it would, really. I didn't think it through. All I could think about at the time was, well . . . you.'

Amy looked away.

There was a pause, and then Josh's voice brightened. 'Anyway, I'm wondering about finding another placement, to be honest. I'm not sure if it's working out for me here – and it's not just . . . this. Working for my parents' friends is a bit stifling, you know? Plus there's this weird glamorous side – the other day, Carlo's PR guy even approached me with some promotional opportunities.' He sighed. 'And Carlo's cut back my hours, so I have lots more free time, but . . . you know, sometimes I feel like I'm cheating. My mates from the course are working hard at proper down-to-earth jobs, like fitness training and working in leisure centres. Maybe I could even get something back home in New Zealand.' He looked into the distance. 'I think my tutors would understand. They did say before that they weren't sure about this as a placement, but Carlo insisted and he's very influential. What do you think?'

Amy's heart leapt. If Josh left, would that mean Claudette's threats became meaningless? She'd still have to explain the photo to Damien, of course, which would be terrible. But all the stuff about Carlo being forced to resign and Damien's career being ruined – would that all stop?

'Oh, well maybe you should . . .' she began, then she couldn't believe she'd even thought of encouraging him to do something for her own selfish reasons. 'You should really think

72

about it a lot, and make sure you do what's best for you,' Amy finished. She sighed quietly to herself.

Josh nodded. 'You're right. Thanks, Amy. I don't really want to leave. I've made some good friends, and that includes . . . you.' He looked around nervously. 'Hey, I heard you moved out of Carlo's house. I suppose that means you won't be at the pool any more? I mean, because I still use the courts and I really miss talking to you . . .'

There was another incredibly cringeworthy pause, during which Amy wondered if it was actually possible to die of awkwardness.

'Oh, no, I have to work now, so I can't.'

'Oh, are you party planning for Barbie again? At Caseydene?'

'No, I'm . . . I'm doing a television thing.'

'Really? Television?' He raised his eyebrows at her. 'I thought you wanted to be a physiotherapist. Or something in sports.'

'Well, yeah, I do,' Amy muttered. 'This is a holiday job. You know my friends Asha and Susi, well they're working at this place called Mishra's Office Supplies and I thought I should do something too. It's just for the break and then I'm going back to do A levels . . .' Amy realized she was babbling and managed to stop herself.

'All right, well, just anytime, if you want a chat –' Josh stopped in his tracks as a rumble of voices got closer to them.

It was a group of footballers coming out of the training ground, looking showered and fresh, and laughing and joking among themselves.

Amy immediately checked to see whether Damien was

among them, and she was fairly sure Josh was doing the same. But he wasn't there. She could only spot Danny Harris, Steve the goalie and a couple of the others.

She inched away from Josh as Danny and his team-mates approached.

'Hi, Danny,' she said, her voice coming out higher-pitched than normal. She wondered why she felt so guilty. How much did Claudette tell her husband? Did Danny know about the photo of her and Josh? She hadn't even considered that before – that other people might know. Then she reminded herself that there was nothing to know, and if everything went to plan no one would ever think differently.

'Hi, Amy, how are things?' Danny asked with that easy-going manner he always had. He certainly wasn't casting glances at her and Josh or acting remotely suspicious. 'You meeting Damien? He's going to be a bit late – Big Carl wanted to talk to him again. I'm not sure if you can get in – want me to pop back and tell him you're here?'

'Oh no, it's . . . it's OK,' Amy said. 'I'll wait.'

'OK. Well, I'd better go, now I can make it to Monty's for a change!' Danny laughed. 'I'm a free man – got to make the most of the partying!'

The other team-mates called out jibes about Claudette having Danny under her thumb.

Danny laughed it off. 'They're right, of course, but who cares?' He gave Amy a conspiratorial wink and moved closer to say quietly, 'Can't wait for her to get back from her mum's. Truth is, I miss her like crazy.'

Amy smiled at him, marvelling at how close he and Claudette always seemed, and also feeling slightly shocked at the thought that Claudette was off doing something as normal as visiting her mum.

'Come on, mate, stop chatting up the birds! It's your round!' Steve grumbled.

Danny laughed again. 'You coming, Josh?' he asked. 'Break the habit of a lifetime and socialize with us British louts?' He smiled at Amy. 'Damien's been talking about bringing you along later too. Lucky you, eh?' He laughed.

Amy smiled, hiding her surprise. Damien had never taken her out with the boys before, even though she'd suggested it a few times.

'OK, yeah,' Josh said. He looked at Amy, 'See you there, Amy?'

If it was a question, she didn't answer it. She just said good-bye to Josh and the others.

'Let's go, lads!' Steve called. They all piled into a minivan with tinted windows that was waiting halfway down the street.

Amy was left in silence, wondering why seeing Josh had left her feeling so shaken up.

She checked her phone. There was a message from Damien, which must have come through while she was talking just now. It said, 'r u meeting me? Will be about an hour late. Sorry Ames. xxx'.

She texted back to say she'd meet him in an hour. Then she hailed a passing cab, thinking about how natural it felt to do that now.

She knew exactly what she wanted to do with the time.

Amy started at one end and worked her way gradually along the boutiques closest to Stadium Gardens. The first time she entered her dad's PIN she felt that familiar stab of guilt, but it was soon replaced by the amazing feel of the shopping bags in her hand. She relaxed into her task, adding more and more fabulous new purchases. After all, tomorrow she would be in the spotlight; she'd be on television and the whole of Britain could be watching. Well, maybe not the whole country, at eleven o'clock on a Wednesday morning, but who knew? She was still going to be talking about style, and she had to look the part. Plus, the money she was earning for it would pay for all this, she assured herself.

Even though she was doing some kind of speed-shopping, the time still went amazingly fast. She reached Orange County, an exclusive boutique Rosay had introduced her to, and decided it had better be her last stop before meeting Damien. She explained to the personal shopper that she was in a hurry. The skinny woman asked her some questions and then instructed her to make her way straight to the changing rooms and chill out on the sofa while she selected a few items for her.

Amy accepted the offer gratefully, sinking into the sofa and trying not to think about all the shopping bags at her feet. What would Damien say when he saw them?

Just then she heard a familiar snuffling noise at her ankles and she felt something tugging at her sequinned bag. She looked down in surprise. Sure enough, there was a highly groomed and chubby dog looking up at her with his huge, imploring eyes. It was Poshie Pug, Kylie Kemp's dog.

'Poshie! What are you doing here? Are you allowed in here? Where's your mummy?' Then she couldn't believe she'd actually said those words to a dog. She stood up and looked around, laughing to herself. One of the changing cubicles had its sparkly orange curtain drawn.

And sure enough, with a swish of glitter, the curtain opened and Kylie Kemp appeared in front of her. She was wearing a gold and black dress, which clung to her every curve and looked utterly amazing.

'Amy!' Kylie squealed, her huge blue eyes widening with surprise. 'I don't believe it! This is just so incredible – if there's anyone in the world I want to see right now, it's you! Wow, this just proves it! It's, like, meant to *be*! I'm so happy!' She rushed towards Amy and air-kissed her three times.

'Er, hi, Kylie,' Amy said, trying not to stagger backwards away from Kylie's enthusiasm. 'It's nice to see you too. You look fantastic.'

Kylie did a twirl. 'You think? See, that really means a lot to me, because I know you're *The Morning Show*'s newest style expert.'

Amy looked at her carefully for signs that she was teasing, but she didn't find any in Kylie's blankly cheerful expression. 'Oh, er, thanks. But, you know, it was mostly thanks to Claudette and your aunt that I . . .'

'Oh, rubbish, don't put yourself down. Auntie Fran knows what's good for business, and you're so hot right now! Everyone's talking about you, Amy! I saw you in *Just Gossip* last week and it said, "Amy's style is organic and glamorous at the same time!" I have no idea what that means, but it has to be extra good, right? Like organic veg – it's extra good for you, isn't it!' She laughed.

Amy found herself joining in. People might have told her that Kylie was stupid, but really 'organic and glamorous' didn't mean all that much to Amy, either.

'So I really mean it, I'm over the moon that you're here.

I was looking for you yesterday – did Damien tell you?'

'Oh, yeah, he did.' Amy remembered the text.

'I want to talk to you in private, so this is much better than Spooky Towers. Don't you find,' she lowered her voice to a whisper, 'the walls have *ears* there?'

'Er . . .'

'Only joking!' Kylie sang at normal volume. 'It's not *really* haunted, don't worry, I don't want you losing any beauty sleep. Not that you need it! But I meant the way the zombies try to listen in . . . But anyway, this isn't about zombies. Or ghosts.'

'No?' Amy said, starting to feel exhausted and wondering where the assistant had got to.

Kylie plonked herself on to the sofa in a whirl of sparkles. Poshie jumped on to her lap and started pulling at the sequins, causing Kylie to squeal, 'Bad dog! I haven't bought it yet!' But then she tickled his ears anyway. 'Amy, sit down, I want to ask you something big and serious.'

Amy sat down, feeling apprehensive. 'Is it about Paige?' she asked. She wondered whether she should tell Kylie about this morning's outburst. Kylie always showed a lot of concern for her friend.

'Oh, no, it isn't.' Her blue eyes clouded with worry. 'Why, is she doing it again?'

'Doing what again?'

'Never mind, I swore I wouldn't tell. And she promised she'd stop, so I'm sure she did. Anyway, I know you and Damien are looking after her for me.' She nodded earnestly. 'No, this is about me. But it's a huge, massive secret. You can keep a secret, can't you, Amy?'

'Er, yes,' Amy replied, remembering the time when that would have been the easiest thing to promise.

'Good. I knew it! I said to myself, if anyone can keep a secret, it's Amy! Plus really, the way things are going with everyone's relationships right now, you're about the only person I can tell anyway. Paige bursts into floods of tears every time I mention Johann these days – it's not healthy, is it? I'm really not looking forward to breaking the news to her.'

Amy's head was spinning now. She let Poshie lick her hand, which calmed her down a bit. 'Sorry, Kylie, what are you talking about?'

'Oh! I haven't told you yet, have I? OK, it's like this. I'm planning something special for after our boys' big match.'

'Our boys are playing a big match?' Amy wondered why Damien hadn't mentioned it.

'Well, OK, it's just a match, but it's against last year's league winners, so it's a big deal. Though this year we're going to win the double, of course! Cos we're the best!'

'When is it?' Amy asked, feeling stupid for not knowing.

'Saturday. Don't you know? Of course you do! You're teasing me, aren't you?' Kylie laughed. 'I always fall for it! Anyway, so I'm having a big garden party afterwards – or rather, Johann is – but, well, can you help me out with it? Because I know you're brilliant at party stuff – I saw what the start-of-season party was like, and I heard that was all you.' She stroked her dog's head. 'And sorry about Poshie trying to ruin it.' She cooed at him. 'Naughty doggie.'

'No, that's OK,' Amy said, her head spinning again. 'And my friends helped with that party; it wasn't all me. But are you asking me to help you plan your do at Johann's? Because there isn't much time . . .' She wondered whether Asha and Susi would be able to help again.

'Oh, listen to you! You sound like a total professional! Speaking of professionals, it looks like they're ready for you!' Kylie pointed as the personal shopper came in with clothes that exactly fitted Amy's requests. Amy noticed the assistant look disapprovingly at Poshie, and she wondered how much Kylie must spend in here to get away with bringing her dog with her.

'We were in the middle of talking about something private,' Kylie told the personal shopper. 'No offence at all, but if you could leave us a minute, that would be really great!'

'Sorry, we won't be long,' Amy added, feeling guilty about what Kylie had said.

The assistant hung the clothes up on the rail, looked at Amy and Kylie and, with one more disgusted look at Poshie, she left the changing rooms.

'So what was I saying?' Kylie breezed. 'Oh yes, I don't need you to plan my party! It's all sorted! The weather's been lovely so we're going to be in the garden and I've hired a marquee and caterers and all the best of everything. The only thing that needs a bit of attention is the big surprise moment! That's where you come in. Amy, I need to ask you a favour. I just need someone to do something for me on the night. Because . . . Omigod! I can't believe I haven't told you the most important thing! OK. Wait for it . . .'

Amy waited while Kylie looked ready to explode with excitement.

'Me and Johann are going to announce our engagement!'

'Wow!' said Amy.

'I know! Wow is right! It's going to be the biggest news of the year, and the biggest wedding of next year! Or maybe the year after if we can't get it all sorted in time, because I want the works, you know. It's going to top Claudette and Danny's tacky Bahamas do, easily. No disrespect to them. We're going to talk to *Hello!* about giving them the exclusive, and I'm getting the top designers to bid for the privilege of making my dress.'

She held out her left hand and looked at it thoughtfully.

'I bet you're wondering why I'm not wearing my engagement ring yet. Well, it's mostly because of the surprise, of course, but also partly because I didn't like the one Johann chose so I'm picking out a new one.' Kylie paused dreamily, then added, 'Me and Johann are getting married! Isn't it wonderful?' She beamed.

'Wow, yeah. Congratulations,' Amy said, smiling. Kylie's enthusiasm was infectious. She was genuinely happy for her too, and it was nice to have something like this to feel good about in this strange new life she was leading.

Kylie put Poshie down and did another twirl in her dress, talking excitedly about Saturday and what she'd like Amy to do. Then she turned back to Amy. 'So will you help me out?'

'Yeah, sure, I'll try.'

'Oh, I know you can do it. He'll listen to you. Also I know you can keep a secret – you're like me, always careful what you say. I'd never tell anyone's secrets, not even the really juicy, tempting ones.' She looked thoughtful. 'Like that thing about the researcher from *Bandwagon* – that Welsh one. He's going to lose his job if he's not careful, you know – I'm so sure he's not allowed to go around snogging the cast. Well, one of the cast, anyway. Lucky it was only me that saw them, and I'd never breathe a word. From what I saw, it looked like true love, and I'm not one to get in the way of that, even if Auntie Fran would kill me if she knew!'

Amy wondered if Kylie ever listened to herself when she spoke. She also knew that Claudette would be delighted if she could find out who Kylie was talking about. It seemed like exactly the kind of gossip Claudette was after.

'So yes, speaking of true love, please don't even hint to Paige about me getting engaged, will you? She should hear it from me. I promise I'll tell her before the party.'

'She'll be really happy for you,' Amy said without much conviction.

'No, she won't. Not right now. But I'll deal with it, OK?'

'OK.'

'Thanks a lot, Amy. I'll tell you what, though. It's going to be a night to remember!'

8

Amy was only half an hour late for Damien, though she would have been much later if she'd popped home to the flat first to drop off her shopping bags like she wanted to.

When the taxi stopped, she paid the driver quickly and ran out towards her forlorn-looking boyfriend, who was sitting on a brick wall by the entrance.

'Sorry I'm late,' she said, giving him a kiss while holding the shopping bags behind her back. 'I was . . . chatting to Kylie Kemp and I lost track of time.'

Then she felt instantly bad about almost lying to him, and she added, 'And I got some clothes. Things I need for my first interview tomorrow, you know?' She moved her arms so that he could see the shopping bags. 'More freebies.' The lie slipped out before she could stop it.

But he barely glanced at the bags. 'Oh, don't worry. I've only just got here myself. Big Carl wanted words, you know. About twenty million of them.' He didn't smile. 'It's good you saw Kylie, though. She was looking for you yesterday.'

'Yeah, you said. She had some news and . . .' She remembered she wasn't supposed to tell anyone about Kylie and Johann. But maybe that didn't include Damien? She knew

Damien worshipped Johann and practically wanted to *be* him. On the other hand, it wasn't exactly an important secret, and Damien looked like he had bigger things on his mind. He was kicking his trainers against the wall and staring into space.

'Damien, are you OK?'

'Yeah, sorry.' His eyes locked with hers, finally, and she felt that rush of electricity that she always did around him. Maybe she found Josh attractive, but it was nothing compared to the way Damien made her feel. He could take her breath away just by looking at her. And as for when he kissed her, which he was doing now . . .

The kiss was over too quickly, though, and Damien still looked miserable afterwards. 'Anyway, it's brilliant that you're here,' he said. 'I can't wait to have that night out we keep talking about.'

'OK, if we go home I can have a shower and change –'

'No, let's just go straight out. I'm taking you to Monty's, and the others all left ages ago. You said before that you wanted to go on a lads' night out?'

Amy looked at the clothes she'd been wearing all day. And Damien wasn't exactly dressed up either. 'But what's it like there? Are they even going to let us in looking like this? The paps will go crazy.'

'Let them.' He pouted defiantly. 'Why don't you just not worry about that for once – like old times?'

Amy smiled at the memory of not being followed around or having to look perfect all the time. She shook the shopping bags in her hand, now she wasn't worried about Damien seeing them any more. 'At least I should drop these off at home.' And then she could change really quickly. Damien might not care but she was supposed to be a fashion expert in a matter of hours.

'You can leave them here. Or take them with us and change there. I don't care, Ames. I just want to go out right now.' He stared at the ground.

She reached for his hand. 'Are you sure you're OK?'

'Yeah. It's just been a tough day, that's all.' He jumped down from the wall, still holding her hand.

'Right. Well, tell me all about it when we get there, OK?' she suggested as he led her to the edge of the pavement and started looking for a taxi.

Damien stayed in the same strange mood all the way through the taxi journey. Amy held his hand and hoped he'd snap out of it. Every now and then he'd catch her giving him worried looks and he'd squeeze her hand or give her a tiny smile, but he just wasn't being himself.

Amy filled the silence by chattering on about her day, trying to make him laugh with stories about the *Bandwagon* set and things that Paige and Trina had said to each other.

'What is Trina's problem?' Damien asked angrily when Amy told him about one of the more far-fetched put-downs.

Amy felt a mixture of relief that he was actually listening to her – she hadn't been too sure of it before – and annoyance that he was immediately leaping to Paige's defence.

'Well, maybe Trina isn't completely over the way Scott cheated on her with Paige.'

'It was years ago!'

'A year. Not that long.'

'I thought you said Trina was a changed person? She was full of human kindness and worked with orphans?'

'Yeah,' Amy admitted. 'Claudette told me that. Said she was a born-again confession-maker, or something.'

'Well, then, she could have a bit more respect for Paige as well.' Damien frowned. 'Poor girl. Everyone's out to get her. I know she's still all secretive about her diabetes, but the papers are full of stuff about her drinking, and Scott's useless – he joins in with all the jokes about Paige when he *knows* it's rubbish! And I've tried to shut them up, but I have to watch it – I don't want those rumours about me and Paige starting up again.' He tightened his grip on Amy's hand.

'Oh. Well, don't worry about the Trina thing. Paige knows exactly how to get back at her, I swear. You should have heard them today.'

Damien shrugged. 'If you say so. You know I don't care about all this gossip stuff anyway, Ames.'

'I know. If it's not about football, you don't want to know,' she tried to tease him, but he just wouldn't smile. 'So what's the football gossip, then? Are you all gearing up to the big match on Saturday?'

'Uh, yeah,' Damien said.

'I can't believe I didn't know you were about to play such an important match! I can't wait. It's going to be so brilliant watching you play at last.'

Damien looked out of the window. 'Ames, you know . . . I might not get played,' he said dully.

'You will, you're their newest star! I heard the way Big Carl was going on about you last week! I'm so proud of you, Day.

I must remember to tell Dad – well, as if he won't already know! He'll *have* to figure out how his DVD recorder works now.'

She shuffled her shopping bags and laughed loudly to cover up the guilty feelings that flooded in as soon as she'd mentioned her dad. Luckily, before she could think about it any more, the taxi drew up outside an ordinary-looking building with a thick oak door. A tiny red sign said 'Montgomery's'. The only thing that gave away its status as one of London's top private members' bars was a velvet rope suspended between two metal bars outside, guarded by a man in a burgundy uniform and peaked cap. A short queue of people stood by the rope, all dressed in super-elegant clothes even though it was early evening and the sun was only just starting to set.

'Are you sure they'll let me in here?' Amy asked.

'Don't worry, you'll be fine with me,' Damien replied confidently.

As soon as they got out of the taxi, still holding hands, a photographer called out their names. There was a ripple of voices and then cameras seemed to appear out of nowhere, snapping away.

Amy gritted her teeth and gripped her shopping bags as Damien led her straight to the front of the queue. She felt everyone's eyes on her as the doorman lifted the rope and said, 'Good evening, Mr Taylor.'

'He knows your name!' Amy whispered, and then she instantly felt stupid. Apart from the fact that Damien was pretty famous now, he also probably came here loads. It was so weird that he had this whole other life, one she didn't know much about.

Inside Monty's it could have been any time of the day or night. The lighting was dim and there were groups of stylish-looking people sitting around tables and on sofas, as well as a thick crowd of bodies at the bar.

'Wow, Damien, this is fantastic,' Amy said as she took in the elaborately decorated ceiling and the antique-look foyer. It contrasted with the sleek glass and silver of the bar area. A few people walked in behind them, completely ignoring the amazing decor. Amy supposed they were all used to it.

Damien didn't seem to notice any of it either. 'Do you want a drink?' he asked, his face still set in that grim expression. 'Anything you want. They'll serve me and they won't notice what you do; it's not really a problem.'

Amy spotted a teenage It Girl in the distance, the daughter of a famous singer and a film star. The girl was wearing a skimpy, shimmery dress and holding a champagne flute in each hand, and she was gyrating alone on the dance floor as she tilted her head and knocked back each drink in turn.

'Um, maybe just an orange juice,' Amy said. She was starting to feel nervous and out of her depth. Not to mention seriously under-dressed.

'OK. The cloakroom's over there. Want me to check your stuff in with mine?' Damien said.

Amy couldn't get over how at ease Damien was here. The Damien she went out with in Stanleydale would have taken one sniff of the glitzy, rich-kid atmosphere of this place and made some joke about finding the local pub instead. She felt even younger than normal right now.

'No, I'll, er, change and meet you in there,' she said, seeing a sign for the ladies on the other side of the cloakroom.

'OK. The Boroughs lot are usually in the far corner, on the platform behind the rope.' Damien pointed. 'Or do you want me to wait for you?'

'No, no, it's OK. I'll find you.' Amy wanted to take her time. She wasn't sure what she was going to wear, or whether she'd bought anything that was right for a place like this, let alone anything that her shoes would go with. She wondered why she hadn't put her foot down – Nine West wedges and all – about going home first. But Damien was in such a strange mood. She'd get the truth out of him later.

She was heading for the ladies when her phone rang.

The caller display said 'Claudette'. Amy couldn't believe she'd forgotten about having to recount the day's gossip.

At least her timing was good – if she'd phoned any earlier Amy would have had to make some excuse to Damien. She looked around for somewhere private to take the call. The foyer was too echoey and people were walking past all the time.

Just beyond the cloakroom and the toilets, she found a maze of corridors, each leading in a different direction and meeting in a grand wooden staircase. Away from the modern-looking bar, the building could easily have passed for a school or council office – it had oak-panelled walls and a vaguely musty smell, plus there were plaques on the wall listing the engraved names of 'Honourable Members' and dates from a hundred years ago. She chose one of the quiet corridors and leant against the wall, fairly sure she couldn't be overheard.

She took a deep breath and accepted the call, probably a split second before it rang off. 'Hi, Claudette.'

'Hi, darling,' came the familiar voice. 'I hope you didn't forget about me?'

'Course not,' Amy lied. She stepped forwards, checking for people, but the whole area was still deserted.

'Good. I knew I could count on you. So tell me all about how it's going. A lot must have happened, what with last night's party and the filming today. I'm listening.'

Amy gave Claudette a rough description of the party fight as she'd heard it from Rosay, focusing mainly on Courtney shouting at some strange girl who'd been all over Steve. Sticking to her earlier decision, she didn't let on that she thought the girl was Lauren from Spencer's office. She also left out the Damien and Josh part, not wanting to add to Claudette's satisfaction in holding that photo over her. Her heart pounded as she spoke and she hoped her voice sounded normal. But Claudette seemed happy with the account.

'Interesting. Looks like we need to keep an eye on Steve's behaviour. I'll mention it to Spencer, though I think Steve's actually a client of Miranda's now. And what about today? Were Trina and Paige at each other's throats?' Claudette laughed lightly. 'Can you tell me exactly what Trina was saying?'

Amy reported bits and pieces of the bickering, and tried not to think about how weird and horrible this all felt.

'So you haven't got anything else for me?' Claudette pushed her. 'Nothing else you've heard that you think I should know?'

The news about Kylie flitted briefly into Amy's head, but she was pretty sure Claudette wouldn't want to hear that. It was happy stuff, and Claudette wanted the damaging gossip

– she'd made that clear. But remembering her conversation with Kylie, combined with the pressure to tell Claudette something, made Amy suddenly blurt, 'There is *one* thing.'

'Oh yes?' Claudette's trademark drawl didn't give away any excitement. 'What did you hear?'

'Well, one of the *Bandwagon* contestants – I'm not sure who, but I doubt it's Paige – is having a . . . I don't know, an affair or something, with one of the researchers on the programme. A Welsh boy.'

Claudette laughed. 'Really? How cute. Are you sure? How do you know that?'

Amy gripped her phone nervously. 'I, er, heard about it. From someone who saw them.'

'That's good stuff! Very good, Amy! It seems you've got the hang of this business after all.'

Her praise made Amy smile for a second, until she remembered what she was doing.

Claudette continued excitedly, 'If it's Trina Santos, maybe we can have her booted off the programme and all the way back to Brazil! I'm sure what she's doing is against the *Bandwagon* rules. It would make things unfair for the other contestants – *Bandwagon* is a competition, after all.'

Amy's heart sank. 'But you can't do that, can you? I mean, you're just going to talk to Spencer about keeping it out of the papers, aren't you? Isn't that how it works?'

She heard an odd sound in the background at Claudette's end of the call – a high-pitched cry in the distance.

Claudette's voice grew hurried and distracted. 'Yes, yes, of course. Well, that's nice work, Amy. I knew I could rely on you. More tomorrow, OK?'

Claudette ended the call abruptly and left Amy holding the phone in the empty corridor, feeling like she was miles away from the music and chatter of the bar area, and from Damien.

She took a deep breath and headed back towards the staircase, glancing up the other empty corridors as she passed. But, halfway up the next corridor, she saw something that made her look twice.

It was Scott White with his arms around someone.

She didn't mean to stare, but she couldn't help it.

Scott was with Paige.

Amy rushed away. She was fairly sure they didn't see her – they were talking and they seemed way too involved in each other.

So it looked like Paige and Scott were back together after all. Paige would be happy. And so much for the gossip sites and their quotes about Scott and Rosay. Amy should have known that stuff was rubbish.

She hoped Paige knew what she was doing, though, because a lot of the gossip about Scott did seem to be true. And Damien knew for a fact that he'd been seeing other girls.

Amy decided to change quickly and find her boyfriend. He must be wondering what was taking her so long. But as she neared the cloakrooms, she saw Damien standing by the main door.

She walked over and kissed him lightly, saying, 'Sorry, I couldn't find the right thing to wear.' Then she wondered why she hadn't just said she'd got a phone call, or something closer to the truth. Why had the bigger lie tripped off her tongue so easily like that? She looked at his face but he didn't even seem to be listening.

'Why are you here and not in there?' she asked him. 'Is something wrong?'

'Ssh, Ames,' Damien replied, nodding to his left. He mouthed, *Cameras.*

She looked where he'd indicated and, sure enough, there was a group of people holding technical equipment. They weren't filming, though – they were standing about looking bored.

'It's your lot,' Damien said quietly. 'From *Bandwagon*. They were filming Paige but they've lost her.'

'I've seen her. She's with –'

'I know. I saw them too but I didn't let on. I think the cameras are driving her mad, and anyway, some things are private, even if I think she's wrong to . . . Well, never mind.' He glanced at the film crew and his voice got even quieter. She had to lean close to hear him. 'You know, Ames, I really wanted to take you on one of my boys' nights, but it turns out I'm not really in the mood for a place like this. Can we go somewhere else, just the two of us? Do you mind? We can go home first, if you want.'

'Oh, OK,' she said. 'Yeah, that sounds good.' In fact, Amy thought, it sounded perfect.

He put his arm around her and they walked out, ignoring the bright flashing lights of the paparazzi.

9

The next day, under a different set of lights, Amy felt like she'd walked into a trap.

For a start, the studio lights weren't just bright – they were blinding. No wonder the make-up person and the stylist had gone mad over her, putting her usual beauty routine and barely-there look to shame. You needed a lot of make-up to stand up to this kind of glare.

Julia Lightman was also caked in make-up, but, worse than that, she was asking Amy a lot of questions. And they weren't the questions Amy had been expecting, the ones with the scripted answers ready to scroll over the huge camera-like screen that was pointing at her.

Amy fiddled with the belt on the print micro-dress she was wearing over skinny jeans for her first interview. They weren't her choice of clothes – a stylist had dressed her earlier, telling her she could keep the clothes. She was slightly upset because she'd arrived in an outfit that Kylie had helped her choose in Orange County yesterday – clothes that were simple yet elegant. But the micro-dress she'd been changed into was ballooning out around her middle, the jeans were digging into her waist and she felt ridiculously self-conscious.

She shifted on *The Morning Show*'s sofa and wondered how many ultra-famous people had sat in this very spot, talking to Julia Lightman. There's no way any of them could have been as nervous as she was now.

She took several deep breaths.

'So how are you finding life in London, Amy?'

She forced herself to smile. Before the cameras rolled, they'd told her that smiling was important. 'Oh, I . . . It's great. I'm enjoying it a lot.'

'And you're visiting your footballer boyfriend, of course, the talented young Damien Taylor. I heard you stayed in the luxurious home of Royal Boroughs manager Carlo di Rossi. What did you like about that?'

'Well, yeah, it was great.' Amy widened her smile and hoped that would make up for the lack of words. She tried to ignore all the people watching her, doing their jobs with high-tech equipment that was all trained on her. 'I enjoyed it a lot.'

If Julia Lightman was getting annoyed with her, she didn't show any sign of it. 'That's lovely, Amy. So tell me, because the viewers at home are dying to know. What's it like living the life of a footballer's girlfriend? Is it really all about shopping and glamour? Tell us all about it!'

Amy's grin froze at the word 'shopping'. What if her dad was watching? She didn't want to talk about shopping! Or glamour, for that matter. Her dad wouldn't approve of that, either.

Julia Lightman filled the silence like the professional she was. 'I mean, do you go to lots of parties? Do you mix with the other footballers' wives and girlfriends? Is it as glamorous as we all dream it would be?' Julia laughed and pulled an envious face, as if her life as one of Britain's most famous TV presenters wasn't equally, or probably even more, filled with glamour.

'Er, yeah, sometimes,' Amy said, smiling. Her insides churned. 'I'm enjoying it.' She suddenly felt like crying. 'It's great.'

'Great, Amy,' Julia Lightman echoed. 'It's nice to get this insight into your life. Well, of course, we've brought you here to talk about the fabulous new reality TV show, *Bandwagon*. And in particular, about the clothes worn by the contestants. So, right now they're working on their Britney numbers. Can you tell us something about what you've seen Paige Young and The Miss Exes wearing?'

Amy breathed an invisible sigh of relief as her answers started to scroll on the screen. She concentrated hard on reading out her answers in all the right places, and she even remembered to smile, although she noticed out of the corner of her eye that they were cutting frequently to shots of the girls in their various outfits. The cameras seemed to be on her much less.

The first part of her interview had felt like an eternity, but now the time started to flash by. Before she knew it, the cameras were off and Julia Lightman was congratulating her.

'You were fabulous, Amy. Well done, you're a natural.'

'Oh, er, thanks, but . . .' Amy tried to reply, but Julia was already sweeping away in her stylish full-length jacket, laughing and joking with some members of the crew.

Amy spent the rest of the day on an adrenaline high, not quite believing that she had to do it all again on Friday, and twice next week.

* * *

The following two days passed in a daze of *Bandwagon* sets, shopping and spa sessions in the late afternoon, and evenings with Damien, each more fabulous than the last. On Tuesday after Monty's, they'd ended up going home and changing, and then Damien had taken Amy to a cosy Italian restaurant. Damien had finally snapped out of his strange mood, and he and Amy had chatted and laughed and had a brilliant time. Even being interrupted several times by girls asking for autographs (mostly Damien's, but also Amy's) and men asking about Big Carl's tactics for the season couldn't ruin it. It had almost felt like one of their dates in Stanleydale, but on a grander scale.

On Wednesday they'd had a night in. Damien had ordered a takeaway and they'd snuggled in front of the telly to watch the live *Bandwagon* broadcast. The food was like no takeaway Amy had ever had before – Damien had dialled the number of a 'dinner service' that delivered from one of London's most exclusive restaurants. A man in a black uniform had brought it, and the food was elaborately presented on platters with lids. Amy and Damien kept catching each other's eyes and giggling as they tried to work out what everything was, and afterwards Damien said, 'OK, you win. Tomorrow we go out for chips.'

And they had, although they went to what felt like the poshest chip place in the world. It was in a part of London that Damien said he wouldn't mind living in, as it was close to the training ground. So after the chips they'd wandered around looking in estate agents' windows, gasping at the prices and feeling very grown up, until a drunken girl had started shouting, 'Damien Taylor, will you be mine?'

They had made a getaway in a taxi and gone home, where Amy insisted on watching all the episodes of *Bandwagon* on 'Watch Again' to prepare for her interview. Damien had sat through half a programme and then fallen asleep on her shoulder looking completely adorable.

Amy hadn't been able to stop herself laughing as she'd watched Wednesday's live *Bandwagon*. It was like a very early round of *X Factor*, except it featured clothes that looked like something out of an obscure entry in *The Eurovision Song Contest*. The Miss Exes put in a terrible performance, with Trina horribly out of tune and Marie and Courtney dancing completely out of time. Amy noticed Rosay gritting her teeth in the middle and desperately trying to do her part. She looked the best, too, in a gorgeous vintage mini skirt and shimmery Dolce and Gabbana top. Paige would have looked as good in her tiny black strapless Versace dress, except that she seemed stumbling and awkward and she forgot a couple of her lines. Despite this, or maybe because of the sympathy vote, Paige was the winner of the first audience vote, which had raised loads of money for the children's charity that *Bandwagon* was supporting.

When Amy finished watching the programme, she found an after-show analysis that featured angry calls from viewers who thought Paige might have been drunk. This was followed by a couple of calls from people saying they felt sorry for Paige and she'd been through a lot with her cheating scumbag boyfriend and it was normal at her age to enjoy partying.

Amy's evenings with Damien were only ruined by Claudette's calls, which she kept sneaking off to answer. Damien seemed too preoccupied to notice, and Amy managed to keep Claudette happy with bits and pieces of news about Trina and Rosay's rows. Amy hadn't yet come up with anything more major and nothing bad seemed to have come of her reporting the thing Kylie had told her anyway, which was an odd relief.

Then on Friday, after an interview with Julia Lightman, which had gone much more smoothly than Wednesday's, Amy was proved wrong.

When Julia congratulated her and swept off again, Amy was on a total adrenaline high and she needed to talk to someone – and preferably not her dad, whose calls she'd ignored all day on Thursday. She thought she might ring Susi, although she'd been avoiding her too, because Asha was still being weird and it was sort of upsetting her. But today she didn't care. She needed to talk to a friendly voice, urgently. Amy found the door to the dressing room she'd been assigned earlier, pushed the handle down and barged in.

There was a scuffle and a couple sprang apart in front of her. Amy stared at a familiar-looking purple velvet ball gown – in fact, she'd been talking about it to Julia Lightman just now, saying that the look wasn't right for the Madonna category but it somehow flattered Marie's pale colouring. But now the velvet looked decidedly more crushed than Amy remembered, and the bright redness of Marie's face clashed with it. Standing next to Marie was a boy in wide-legged designer jeans and a black polo neck top.

'Shut the door!' the boy shouted.

'Oh, God. Sorry,' Amy blurted. 'Wrong room. I'll just –'

'No, you've got the right room, Amy,' came a commanding voice behind her.

They all looked round. It was Kylie's Auntie Fran, or more

99

importantly, it was the producer of *Bandwagon*, standing with her hands on her hips and looking like she meant business.

She spoke sternly. 'We've been looking everywhere for Will. It seems you've found him, Amy.' She turned to the boy in the jeans. 'William, hiding in here won't help your case. I told you to collect your things and be off the premises, and that's exactly what you should be doing right now. There's no time for romantic goodbyes.' She gave a tight smile. 'We'll sort out your pay and be in touch – you can think of it as a reward for confessing to this earlier, when we asked about the rumours. But if you speak to the press about this – or if you're back in touch with Marie before the end of the contest – then I promise you there will be hell to pay. We have a great legal department and we *will* sue you for breach of contract.'

Everyone stared at Frances, who really didn't look like someone's kindly aunt right now. She reminded Amy of her head teacher at school, only a million times stricter.

Marie's voice shook when she said, 'If he goes, I go.' She stuck her chin out.

Frances stared hard at Marie for several seconds. Then she said coolly, 'I won't be threatened, young lady. So. Fine, you're off the show too.'

'What?' Marie gasped.

'Yes, you can go. We have enough talent in the other three Miss Exes.'

'But . . . what am I going to tell Pete? He was counting on the money from this. I told you at the interview how much we need this!'

Will gave Marie a look of pure confusion.

'I'm sorry. It's really not my problem.' Frances's smile was clipped.

When they'd watched *Bandwagon* together, Amy had asked Damien about Pete Carlton. Apparently, he wasn't a Boroughs player but played for another London team, and everyone had raved about him until he'd torn a knee cartilage. He'd had surgery and physiotherapy but the injury had recurred and, although he'd recovered again, Damien said his manager had lost confidence in him. 'It's like my worst nightmare,' Damien had told Amy. 'At this rate, he'll never get off the subs bench. If he doesn't get transferred soon, that could be it for him.'

Marie's voice quivered. 'I don't care. I'll sell my story. I'll make more money that way.'

'If you want to do that to Pete, that's your lookout.' Frances was completely unruffled. 'It could affect the lives of your family and friends, not to mention Will's.' She looked at her ex-employee almost sympathetically. 'But, ultimately, it will be a flash in the pan. The money won't be anything compared to what you could have earned as a member of The Miss Exes, especially once *you've* paid the lawyers for breach of contract too. That band is going to be huge, if I get my way.' She raised her eyebrows. 'And you might have noticed that I tend to do that.'

There were tears rolling down Marie's cheeks now. 'OK, I'll stay. Forget it. I'll never see Will again, if that's what you want. It was just a bit of fun, anyway. No offence, Will.'

Will looked shocked and wounded.

Amy wished she could disappear. She edged towards the door.

Frances shook her head. 'I'm sorry, I've made up my mind. You're a wild card, and you've broken the rules of the game. If this does get leaked to the press and either of you are still on the show, we'll have accusations that The Miss Exes have had favourable treatment over Paige's solo act, and people will say the show is a fix. I can't have that – I want the game to be fair. We also want the maximum number of audience votes at the grand final.' She smoothed down her silver hair. 'That money goes to charity, remember? Everybody wins. Except you, I'm afraid.' She smiled then, almost kindly, but her words didn't match her expression. 'If you're not *both* off the premises in half an hour, I'll call security.'

Marie swore at Frances. Will swore at Marie and stormed out of the room. Amy didn't know where to look.

The silver-haired woman left the room muttering into a headset that was clipped to her ear. 'Yes. It's sorted.' She started walking down the corridor, but because Amy was near the door she could still hear as Frances added, 'Honestly, thank goodness for Spencer Greene tipping us off before the scandal got out of hand. I don't know where he gets his information but . . .' Frances's voice faded as she turned the corner.

Amy bit her lip. Before she could think it through, she blurted, 'Oh no, I'm really sorry.'

Marie had taken a compact out of her clutch bag and was dabbing at her eyes. She sniffed as she looked up at Amy. 'Thanks, sweetie. But it's not your fault. She already knew – God knows how.' She sighed. 'We were so careful, even though it was hard with those cameras following me around!' Then she frowned. 'I think Kylie Kemp might have seen us together the other day. Will says I imagined it, but I swear I saw the backs of those ridiculously high heels she wears when we were in the . . . Never mind.' She snapped her compact shut.

'Anyway, I bet Kylie went telling tales to her aunt!' She clenched her fists. 'Well, I'll get her! And I just happen to know of the perfect opportunity to do it!'

Marie definitely didn't seem like the quiet, shy girl Amy had thought she was. It seemed Susi's online magazine was right about her after all, with that comment about her turning into a tiger. But Kylie was so sweet and trusting! She didn't deserve this.

'No, don't!' Amy said.

Marie put the compact in her bag, shook her red hair and stared at Amy expectantly.

Amy didn't have a clue what to say next. 'I mean, even if Kylie saw you, she wouldn't have said anything. Not to anyone that mattered.' She hesitated. 'Or anyone she *thought* mattered, anyway.'

'What are you talking about?'

'I'm talking about . . .' Amy was starting to wish she hadn't said anything in the first place. How would she get out of this?

'I mean . . . me. Kylie did see you, and she told me and I . . . told the wrong person. I'm sorry.' Amy held her breath.

'Don't be ridiculous!' Marie narrowed her eyes at Amy. 'It's nice of you, trying to take the blame for your friends, but thanks for confirming I was right about Kylie. She has it coming to her and, believe me, she's going to get it. Now excuse me.' Marie pushed past Amy. 'I have to be out of the building in half an hour and I'll need to find a way to explain this to my boyfriend so that I can make sure he still *is* my boyfriend. All thanks to Kylie Stupid Kemp.'

She walked away with a look of utter determination on her face.

10

Amy was exhausted. The day was turning out to be *way* more eventful than she'd have liked.

She decided she'd better warn Kylie about this mess sooner rather than later, so when the day's shooting was over she took a deep breath and called her from the dressing room. Kylie was in the middle of a major beauty session, but she seemed happy to hear from Amy, even when Amy began her faltering explanation of what had happened, leaving out Claudette's involvement.

Kylie gasped at first, exclaiming, 'But I don't get it! We're both so good at keeping secrets!' Then she laughed it all off, saying, 'Anyway, it sounds like it wasn't true love at all. So it doesn't really matter, does it? In fact, I think I've done them all a favour.' Kylie certainly didn't seem remotely worried about Marie's threat, and by the time Amy hung up she felt a bit better about everything. If only admitting to *all* her mistakes could be this easy.

As she left the television studios, Amy sent Damien a message to say she wouldn't meet him at the ground today but she'd see him later at home. She was leaving quite early today, which was a relief. She didn't get much time to relax these days. When she was on *The Morning Show*, Amy had to get up at dawn and the only thing that made this bearable was leaving with Damien – his car would drop her at the television studios on the way to the training ground.

She realized she shouldn't really complain. It was a dream come true to have a job like this one. Asha and Susi were definitely still trapped and bored at work right now.

Amy ignored the group of loitering paparazzi who stirred into action as she walked across the studio car park. She let the cameras flash around her as she weaved through the photographers and into a taxi.

As soon as the taxi pulled away, Amy got her phone out. Trying not to think about the way Asha was acting, she pressed the button to return one of her missed calls from Susi.

'So have you got them yet?' Susi said instead of 'hello', her voice brimming with excitement.

'Got what?'

Susi gasped. 'I can't believe you just asked me that! What day is it?'

Amy looked out of the window. The taxi was stuck in a wide line of traffic. 'Er, Friday.'

'Ye-es. Friday. The day after Thursday. A whole day for post to be forwarded.' There was a stunned pause, and then Susi added, 'I don't believe it! You really have forgotten!'

'Forgotten what?' Amy wracked her brains. 'Susi, tell me!'

'No, I'll make you suffer. You'll probably find out when you get home, if your dad's done what my mum did and forwarded the envelope. And I bet he has, knowing your dad.'

'Envelope?' The taxi lurched away, in time with Amy's memory jolting. 'Oh my God! GCSE results! They came out yesterday, didn't they?'

'Yay! You've got it!' Susi laughed. 'Although you clearly haven't. You've lost the plot and A-List Amy has taken over. Are you sure you're coming back to Stanleydale for A levels? Or are you going to be full-time celebrity or whatever instead? Me and Asha saw *The Morning Show* highlights on the website, Wednesday and today. You were fantastic.'

Amy laughed with her friend. 'Oh, so online they edited out the bits where I said the same thing three times, then?'

'Rubbish, you were great. So where are you now? Hiding away at the studio again? And if so, what's that traffic noise?'

'No, I finished work early today.' It felt strange calling it 'work', when it was nothing like what Susi and Asha were doing. After the Marie drama, she'd spent a couple of hours watching the four remaining members of the *Bandwagon* cast practise a dance routine with a skinny Portuguese choreographer. Trina had been showing off by chatting him up in his own language, but he'd made it fairly obvious, even before Paige pointed it out, that he found Trina irritating. Tensions were running high with rumours spreading fast about why Marie had been kicked off the show. Frances had made an official-sounding speech about Marie having requested to leave 'for personal reasons', not that anyone had believed her.

Tonight's live show was in the Madonna section, and Amy had struggled not to laugh at some of the outfits the Wardrobe department were coming out with. They'd gone through retro looks and clearly picked the least flattering. She never thought she'd get to see Trina Santos in cowboy boots or Courtney in a pointy-breasted basque, but they sort of suited them, as she'd told Julia Lightman earlier.

She'd also spent time trying to memorize Trina and Paige's insults to each other to tell Claudette later, even though after what had happened with Marie, Amy really never wanted to speak to Claudette again. But how was she going to get out of it?

Maybe she could just tell her. She'd explain to Claudette that she couldn't do this any more, and she'd face the consequences. Damien's football career would survive – he was so talented, how could he fail? He had a match tomorrow and the whole country would see what a great footballer he was. Everything would be OK. It had to be. She couldn't go on like this.

Susi was telling Amy how bored she was in the shop, and how the highlight of her day so far had been going to Coffee Coffee with Asha at lunchtime and trying to spot celebrities to gossip about.

'How is Asha?' Amy asked, although the question she really wanted to ask was, 'Is she talking to me again?'

'Oh, fine. She's fine,' Susi said vaguely. 'She's just . . . er, popped out right now.'

Amy's eyes prickled. She didn't feel like pretending any more. 'Susi, Asha's going to get over this . . . whatever it is . . . isn't she? I miss her!' She blinked hard and stared out of the taxi window into the traffic.

'Oh, Amy! Of course she is! Don't worry, Asha loves you to pieces. She's just a total pain who's gone temporarily insane and refuses to listen to her wiser older sister.' Then Susi lowered her voice to a near-whisper, so Amy knew that Asha must be there after all. 'She's still acting a bit jealous, to be honest. It's sort of getting worse. She saw pictures of you at some private members' bar that *GossMonger.com* says you went to on Tuesday night, and you were with one of those actors she madly worships. He was standing right behind you!'

'Was he?' Amy had been too busy lately to check the papers and websites for photos of herself. She also didn't really feel like reading gossip at the moment.

Susi said at normal volume, 'I *told* her you probably didn't even notice!' Then she lowered her voice again. 'I don't know what's got into her. I keep trying to explain that you didn't choose this life –'

Amy heard a door slam in the background. 'Was that Asha?'

Susi gave a small gasp. 'Have you got some kind of Bond-style spy-cam mobile phone that only Damien's wild riches can buy? How did you guess she was here? I thought I hid it really well.' She sighed. 'Anyway, she's gone now.'

'Because of me?'

Susi laughed. 'Hey, maybe Asha's right about you after all! Self-centred much, Amy? It's not all about you, you know!'

Amy's heart sank. 'I'm sorry, Susi, I didn't mean it like that, I . . .'

'Shut up, I'm teasing you. God! It's exhausting having to fill in for Asha when I talk to you, as well as be myself. I'm not very good at it.' She laughed again. 'Anyway, don't worry. Asha didn't leave because of you. She left because she has a date, and I'm covering for her with Mr Mishra, who actually doesn't seem to care that much anyway. He's turning out to be the most relaxed boss in the world – all that talk in front of Uncle

Dinesh was some kind of act!' She lowered her voice. 'I'm actually starting to think he's only employing us because he fancies Mum. Wait till you hear what he said about her!'

Susi put on a silly voice and Amy wanted to laugh but something was stopping her. She felt deep pangs of longing – she so badly wanted to be with her best friends.

When Susi finished her Mr Mishra impression, Amy mumbled, 'So did you say Asha has a date?'

'Yeah, that's right.'

Amy's stomach ached. Asha used to tell her everything. 'I can't believe I didn't know.'

'Well, you couldn't have, even if she wasn't acting like a brat. He only asked her out a few hours ago. He came in the shop this morning and you should have seen her, falling over herself to serve him.' Susi giggled. 'And then he asked her out and she's been on cloud nine ever since! Only now she's floated off with him. They've just gone to the sandwich place across the road.'

'Oh, wow! That's crazy. Will she be OK?'

'Yeah, course! Don't worry, I can practically see them from here, and we have each other on speed-dial,' Susi said. 'In fact, I might ring and check up on her in a minute, ha ha.'

Amy sighed. 'I've got to see you and Asha – I miss you like mad and you're only up the road. We never get together in London!'

'I know, it's a shame,' Susi agreed. 'You know what Uncle Dinesh is like – he expects us home well early on work nights, and we can't risk him moaning to Mum and sending us home. That's why Asha's gone on such a weird early date. Mum will never get to hear about it, of course. Though she's been ringing us all day today – it nearly killed her not opening those GCSE-result envelopes and we left before the post this morning so we don't know what we've got yet.'

Amy was thinking quickly. 'Hey, you'll be allowed out on Saturday night, won't you? Damien's got a big match and there's a party afterwards at Kylie's. I'm so sure she wouldn't mind me inviting you. And Asha would love it!' She jiggled on the taxi seat in excitement and the driver glanced in the rear-view mirror with a bored expression.

'That sounds great, Amy!' Susi said.

'I know. It's perfect! In fact, if it works out then why doesn't Asha bring her new guy, too? She can impress him with the flash surroundings of Johann Haag's luxury garden.' Amy had never actually been there, but Damien had described Johann's place to her and it sounded amazing and grand.

'I don't know about that,' Susi said.

Amy sighed. 'Oh. Do you think she wouldn't come because of me?'

'No,' Susi said quickly. 'No, I mean, he's not going to be all that impressed. In fact, he's probably already been invited anyway.'

'What do you mean?' Amy gulped, wondering what Susi could mean. 'Hang on – she's not . . . ? Is Asha going out with a footballer?' A footballer who shopped for stationery at Mishra's Office Supplies and asked out the gorgeous assistants? That sounded totally weird.

'Not exactly. I wasn't going to say until I knew how it went, but it won't hurt to say now. It's that sports psychology guy from Damien's team. You know, the one she thrashed at tennis the other week.'

'You mean Josh?' Amy tried to keep her voice neutral. 'Asha's going out with Josh?'

'Yeah, Josh. That's it. Apparently he found out where Asha was working and tracked down the shop especially to ask her out. He told her all that – he doesn't hold back, does he? You know, I never thought I'd say this, but I kind of agree with Asha on this one. Isn't it just the most romantic thing you ever heard?' Susi sighed.

Amy thought back to her conversation with Josh outside Stadium Gardens – had she mentioned where the twins were working then? He certainly didn't seem interested when she told him, but she wasn't exactly thinking straight at the time.

'Anyway, Amy, call me the second you get your results, OK? And me and Ash will do the same. God, she'd better not be late back!'

'But, Susi . . .' Amy said as the phoned clicked off in her ear.

By the time the taxi drew up on Elm Street, Amy was longing for a bit of a rest and some time to think about everything that had happened. She hadn't told Susi and Asha much about Josh – at first because there wasn't really anything to tell, and later because there were other things to talk about. Damien, mostly – she'd spent ages over the past weekend convincing her concerned friends that she was right to get back with him. And she'd left out the fact that Josh had asked her out, not wanting to talk about Damien's jealousy.

Still, Amy wondered whether she should try to tell Asha what had happened – or rather, what hadn't happened –

between her and Josh, just in case that photo ever got out. It would look so much worse if Asha hadn't been warned. She remembered now how Asha had gone on about how fit she thought he was.

But if Asha wasn't even talking to her, Amy couldn't be sure that telling her something like that wouldn't make things even worse between them.

She sighed. It looked like she was back to square one with Claudette – now was not the time to put a stop to those phone calls and risk that photo getting out. There would probably never be a good time.

The resident paparazzi were oddly absent and she savoured the quiet, camera-free walk into the block of mansion flats. She didn't even mind that one of the so-called zombies was coming out of the main door as she went in, and he stared at her for what seemed like ages after she said a polite hello. All she wanted was to get in and make a cup of tea and sort everything out in her head.

But when she opened the door, the first thing she saw was the envelope, redirected in her dad's familiar scrawl. Amy couldn't believe she'd been more worried about all the stuff with Claudette than about getting her exam results. Before she came to London she could never imagine forgetting about them. But she'd done well in the mocks so she hoped there wasn't anything to worry about.

Amy slid her finger into the flap at the back and tore across the top, suddenly missing her parents like crazy and feeling totally alone. She wished she could call her dad and talk to him without feeling completely guilty about the money she'd spent. She was worried that even the money she was earning on *Bandwagon* wasn't going to be enough to cover the bill. How much had she spent now?

Pushing those thoughts out of her head, her stomach churned again as she pulled the paper out of the envelope.

Well, maybe she'd tell him now. She'd phone him with her grades and he'd be happy and her mum would say something lovely to her about what a difficult year they'd all had, and wasn't Amy great for doing so well in her exams despite it all. And then Amy would admit that she'd been using her dad's card and she was sorry – but it didn't matter because she was earning money to pay back the debt. She could pass exams, and she could work her way out of tricky situations. There would be no reason for her parents not to be proud of her.

As long as she could keep things going with Claudette and the photo of her and Josh didn't get out, of course. But surely after she'd finished backstage on the show and went back to Stanleydale, Claudette would have to agree to an end to it all.

Amy sighed and shut her eyes as she unfolded the paper.

She stared at it.

She checked the name at the top, but it was definitely hers.

She sank back on the sofa and blurred her eyes at the piece of paper, but the results didn't change.

They were bad.

She had Bs in Citizenship and Maths. Then there were a couple of Cs, and the others were lower.

They weren't completely terrible. But they weren't what she needed for the science AS levels she'd enrolled on. In fact, she wasn't completely sure that they were enough to get into the school sixth form at all. She hadn't really listened too closely when the teachers had talked about that kind of thing, because she really didn't think it would apply to her. Her heart thumped in her chest. She'd never had a problem with school. True, she'd got into trouble for skipping a day, back when Damien had his important football trials. And she'd been a bit distracted by all the fuss when he'd got transferred, right in the middle of exam season. But Damien hadn't even *taken* his A levels, and no one seemed to care about that.

And Amy's mother had been ill last year! It hadn't affected her mocks and her mum had mostly recovered by the time the exams started, but still . . . She couldn't accept that these were her results! Maybe she should write to the examiners and tell them all this, and they'd take pity on her and raise her grades.

Then she couldn't believe she'd even thought of that sort of excuse. Her new life was really getting to her. Besides, her dad would be devastated if he thought she was blaming her mother's illness for her bad results. He'd gone out of his way to make sure everything ran smoothly at home when Mum was in hospital and he'd done everything he could for Amy, including getting her counselling, which he didn't exactly believe in.

There was no way she could tell her dad about this.

Amy looked at her phone. Damien was due home soon. She tried to imagine what he'd say. Maybe he'd blame himself for distracting her. It might put him off for his big game tomorrow.

Amy pressed some buttons on her phone and replied to one of her dad's many recent texts: 'Call me, Amy. Are you OK? Dad'.

'I'm fine! Really sorry I'm always so busy!' she wrote.

'Having a brilliant time! Thinking of you and Mum! Lots and lots of love. Your Amy. xxx'

She sent it and stared at the results slip again.

A few minutes later, a call came through from her dad. She let it go to voicemail, each ring screaming louder in her ears. She waited a while before listening to the message: 'Amy, it's your dad! I forwarded an important-looking envelope yesterday. Let us know when you get it! I think you know what it is. Your mum can't wait to hear from you. Honestly, love, please try to find time to give us a call – we want to hear your voice!'

She sent another text. 'Got your message but can't talk right now! Sorry! At the studio. Your envelope hasn't arrived – maybe tomorrow? Lots of love from your Amy. xxx'

She felt guiltier than ever as she sent it. It was easier to lie in a text than in a phone call, but that didn't make it right.

On the other hand, she was just buying herself time to figure things out, and once she did, she could present her mum and dad with a plan. It was harmless, and it would make things easier for everyone.

A message came through from Susi: 'Asha's home! Has another date with J on Tuesday. Woo hoo! Can't do Saturday because we have family celebrations. For us!!! Yes, we opened them!!!!! Double WOO HOOO! As and A-stars all round! How are yours???? R u home? Call us!!!!! NOW! Celebrate with us!'

Amy sighed. Susi didn't really mean 'us', with Asha not talking to her. She wouldn't be celebrating with them, even if she had anything to celebrate. She texted back a message similar to the one she'd sent her dad, about how her envelope might be lost in the post, and she tried desperately not to feel bad about it.

She went to her room and tucked the results slip into a drawer. Then she installed herself on the sofa, found the 'Watch Again' listings on the cable and watched *Bandwagon* until Damien came home.

When he did, he was in a similar mood to hers. He moaned for ages about some of the other players and about Big Carl, and he certainly didn't remember anything about GCSE results being out this week. She couldn't blame him when she'd forgotten it herself.

They cooked pasta together – perfect pre-match food, as Amy pointed out – and she made more sympathetic noises as Damien talked. There were a couple of moments when she felt like telling him, but then she thought she'd better not add to his worry about his Premiership debut. He was obviously feeling nervous. She'd tell him after the match.

They settled with their pasta in front of the television to watch the live broadcast of that evening's *Bandwagon*, followed by the announcement of the result after the news. While the news was on and Damien was making them a drink, Amy went to her room and gave Claudette a quick ring. She'd never done it that way round before, but it seemed to work – there was a lot of noise in the background and Claudette was too distracted to ask many questions. She said Amy could have the weekend off but she'd expect a full report after Tuesday's filming.

'I heard about Marie,' Claudette added, 'and I can only say, shame it wasn't Trina. Still, what can you do?'

Amy heard the noises in the background get louder again.

'Got to go, darling. Have a lovely weekend and don't forget I want to know all about Kylie's party too!'

She hung up, leaving Amy wondering how much Claudette knew about Kylie's party. Claudette seemed to know *everything*!

Amy joined Damien back on the sofa, where they watched the Miss Exes win the Madonna heat by a tiny amount. Damien sighed and worried aloud about how Paige would take it, which Amy found slightly annoying, though she had to admit that, from what she'd seen on set lately, she was a bit worried about Paige too. She had definitely lost the carefree, easy-going streak she used to have before all the Scott stuff happened.

Amy looked at Damien, who was lost in thought and looking miserable again. Right now, the flat at 13 Elm Street was filled with a bunch of right grumps. What they needed was a great football match followed by a big, exciting party to cheer them up.

11

The box at Stadium Gardens was oddly quiet considering it was the first match of the season and a battle of football giants.

The icy hush might have been due to the absence of Claudette, who seemed to make the wives and girlfriends stick together in their own weird way. Or it might have been because the seating area was effectively split. Paige was sitting with Kylie and as far as possible from Rosay, Trina, Courtney and the others. Amy was next to Rosay but desperately trying to shoot friendly glances at Paige whenever possible, just to show she wasn't taking sides.

At regular intervals, Trina would say some variation of: 'Why is *she* here? She has nothing to do with this team now that Scott has dumped her!'

Paige would reply loudly along the lines of: 'I'm here because I've always supported Royal Boroughs and I came with my friend Kylie, and I dumped *him*! Why are *you* here, Trina? Oh, I remember. It's because you're a fake wannabe and you think it's good for your image!'

Then there would be a pause while Trina thought of a comeback, and this would go on until something interesting happened on the pitch. A lull would follow, but the insults started flying again as soon as the football action died down.

It was tough having friends who hated each other.

It got even tougher every time the crowd got into full swing. The Wirral United fans had travelled a long way and arrived ready to out-chant the Royal Boroughs regulars by several decibels. Every time Scott White got anywhere near the ball, the Wirral fans sang a dirge-like, top-volume rendition of 'Scott White Is a Creep', and Amy noticed Paige visibly bristle while Trina laughed. Once she even threatened to join in, calling out, 'It's our song, everyone!'

Amy sighed and Rosay looked uncomfortable.

A couple of minutes before half-time, the Boroughs conceded a goal and Courtney gritted her teeth and complained quietly to her sister, who'd come with her to the game in matching clothes and Gina heels: 'I told him. I told him to get an early night, and Big Carl told him, and he didn't get in till after nine thirty! I swear, if he gets dropped I'm dropping *him* so hard it's gonna hurt!'

Amy could see Big Carl pacing around at the side of the pitch, putting a hand through his gelled and immobile pepper-grey hair and shouting at the top of his voice. But, try as she might, she couldn't see Damien. He hadn't played yet, and every time there was a substitution, she craned her neck to get a better look in case he came on. But she couldn't even see him on the bench. Wasn't this supposed to be his big debut? He'd been training so hard and been so dedicated – surely Big Carl would play him? Amy didn't understand it.

Damien didn't play in the second half either, and there were no more goals, just lots of shouting, chanting, singing and jeering.

After the match, Amy couldn't wait to get out of the stadium. Damien sent her a short text to say he'd be late, and she knew from the charity match she'd gone to before that there wouldn't be much chance of seeing him before the party. She went home with Paige and spent hours getting ready, wondering what she would say to him later. He was bound to be upset about not being played. She should definitely keep her GCSE results news to herself a bit longer.

When it was time to leave, Amy knocked at Paige's bedroom door. They hadn't actually arranged to go to Kylie's together, but Amy assumed they would. She and Paige had an odd sort of friendship – Paige acted friendly enough, and she'd smile at Amy on set, but at home she'd moan non-stop about tidiness and clam up if Amy tried to ask her about her day or her plans for the evening. In fact, Amy thought Paige probably got on better with Damien than she did with her, and she had to remind herself not to worry about that.

There was no answer from Paige's room. Amy stood outside wondering whether to knock again.

'Come in,' Paige's voice came softly, just as Amy was about to give up and walk away.

She opened the door and poked her head round it. 'Hi, Paige, I wondered if you were ready to leave for – oh.' Amy stopped in surprise. Paige was tucked up in bed, looking like she'd just woken up. There were huge dark rings under her eyes and she looked as pale as the pure white covers she was pulling to her chin.

Amy kept her hand on the door handle. 'Oh, I'm sorry. Are you OK?'

'I'm fine,' Paige said, yawning. 'No problem. Are you off to Kylie's?'

Amy nodded, still hesitating in the doorway. 'Aren't you coming?'

'No. She told me about . . . you know. The engagement announcement. I know she told you too. She broke it to me gently but . . . Well, I think I need a night in, anyway.'

'Oh. OK,' Amy said, wanting to ask Paige whether this meant she was still heartbroken about Scott. Had she misunderstood what she saw the other day? Or maybe there was something else going on. Maybe Paige was ill again – something to do with her diabetes.

'Are you sure you're feeling OK?' Amy said, feeling pathetic and wishing there was a better way of finding out.

'Yeah, I'm really fine. I'm happy for her.' Paige looked thoroughly miserable. 'I'm just . . . tired, you know. It's been a tough week. Have a good time, Amy.'

Paige closed her eyes and Amy shut the door behind her quietly, thinking about Paige's reputation as a party girl. She almost wished she could tip off the papers about what was really going on, maybe by telling Claudette – would that stop everyone falsely accusing Paige? But she knew Paige wouldn't thank her if she did that. For the first time, Amy realized that Paige really didn't mind the rumours – she almost hid behind them, as if she thought they were more acceptable than the truth. It was really messed up that Paige seemed to think having diabetes was worse for her image than a suspected alcohol problem.

Amy felt weird about turning up at the party by herself. As her taxi arrived, she saw rows of posh cars and limos draw up by the grand entrance. Couples emerged in twos, oozing matching glamour as they strode towards the entrance, making Johann's mansion look like some kind of Noah's ark for designer-clad beautiful people.

Amy pulled at the classic silver Monroe-style Vivienne Westwood dress she'd chosen for tonight and reminded herself she looked as great as them and had every right to be there. She'd even picked this dress on purpose because it was a genuine 'gift' from a boutique she'd been to with Rosay, and she knew she wouldn't feel guilty wearing it. Taking a deep breath she headed for the entrance.

The security guards seemed to recognize her and nodded as she arrived, standing aside to let her through. As soon as she was inside the grand-looking hallway, she spotted Danny Harris, also on his own. He waved and walked over.

'No Damien?' he asked after he'd said hello. 'Oh, let me guess – Big Carl's still lecturing him.'

Amy smiled. 'I think so. But he said I should come here and he'd meet me later.'

'I'm on my own too,' Danny said. 'I wanted to go and see Claudette this weekend but there was the game today, and then she insisted she didn't want me in Essex afterwards. She always gets so funny about me spending time with her family. I know her mum's laid up with a broken leg right now and Claudette's busy running around for her and sorting out her brother, but I could have helped too. I'm not that bad, am I, Amy?' He gave her a charming smile that wasn't remotely flirty, and she thought what a nice man he was. 'You'd let me hang round with *your* mum and little brother, wouldn't you?'

Amy thought again about what an unlikely picture Danny was painting, of the ruthless Claudette suddenly acting like Cinderella, slaving away helping out her family rather than stressing about breaking a nail at the spa.

'My mum would love you, but I'm not so sure about my little brother,' she told Danny.

'But I'm great with kids!' Danny did a mock-pout. 'I've already told Claudette I want us to produce a whole football team of our own when we grow out of our youthful partying stage!' He laughed. 'And Claudette's little brother loves me. Between you and me, I think that's why she doesn't like me to go there much – I steal the limelight from her! So why do you think your brother wouldn't like me? Wouldn't he even want a signed photo of me? If he doesn't support the Boroughs, he could get a good price for it on eBay or in the playground, you know.'

'He wouldn't even be interested in that,' Amy said seriously, watching Danny's face fall even further.

'Really?'

'Really. But only because he doesn't exist. I don't have a brother!'

Danny groaned. 'Oh, I get it! You're taking the mickey!'

'Sorry.' She laughed.

'I can see why Claudy likes you. You have the same sense of humour. Come on, let's find the rest of the gang – I think they're all in the garden already.'

Amy followed him, wondering whether it was true that Claudette liked her, and whether she'd ever seen any evidence of Claudette having a sense of humour.

They joined a small group of footballers standing just outside the marquee, and she scanned the guests, relieved to see there was no sign of Josh.

Danny tried to include her in the loud post-match analysis that was underway, but Amy was distracted, taking in her grand surroundings. The garden was landscaped and huge, and the lawn they were standing on shone a deep green in the floodlights. It was obviously tended carefully, as Amy noted when she stood on something she thought was a bottle top and looked down. It was a sprinkler, embedded in the soil, and there were lots of similar ones nearby. The whole place looked like one of the stately homes her mum occasionally liked to go to – the kind that had tearooms that sold homemade cakes. Of course, tonight was far more glamorous, and more about champagne and canapés. Amy helped herself to some food from a passing tray. Within seconds, there was a familiar snuffling at her feet and she looked down and smiled at Kylie's dog.

'Hey, Poshie,' she said. 'I like your blue bow – very stylish. You'd better not be after the canapés again.'

Poshie snuffled a response and Amy laughed, reaching down to tickle his fur. 'I bet you love living here – all this space to run around.'

'He does! He's much happier than he was at Spooky Towers!' Kylie said enthusiastically, appearing at her side. 'Hi, Amy, I'm so glad you're here.' She lowered her voice. 'You'll never believe this but I'm a nervous wreck about later! Where's Paige?'

'She, er . . . couldn't come. She was really tired.'

'Oh.' Kylie's smile dropped, but she recovered it quickly.

'Never mind. I know she'll be happy for me eventually. Things are just really hard for her right now.'

'But isn't she back with Scott now? Only I thought . . .' Amy trailed off when she saw the expression on Kylie's face. Oh no – had she said the wrong thing?

Kylie took her arm and dragged her away from the group. Then she said, 'Sorry. Didn't want to talk in front of them, or Johann will tell me off about not inviting Scott again. Anyway, about Paige being back with Scott – I should hope not! If I hear she's even spoken to him, I'm having serious words with her. He's bad news. Why, do you know something?'

'No, no,' Amy said quickly, wondering why she was lying. It was starting to become a habit – only it felt better when she called it 'keeping secrets'. 'So, tell me more about when and how you want me to do this thing. I'm so excited for you and Johann!'

'Me too!' Kylie squealed. She told Amy some details of exactly what she wanted to happen. 'And Damien can help you.' She glanced at the group of footballers. 'Where *is* Damien?'

'Still at football.'

Kylie frowned. 'You sure? Johann got back hours ago.'

'He texted me to say Big Carl was giving him another lecture.'

Amy expected Kylie to laugh, but her frown deepened instead. 'Well, anyway,' she said, 'I hope he'll be here soon. He knows how important tonight is, doesn't he?' She looked at Amy. 'What? You didn't tell him?'

'Er, no. You said it was a secret.'

Kylie laughed. 'Yes, but obviously not from Damien! I

mean, if I tell you, I've told him, right? That's how couples work! Johann and I know everything about each other.' She looked at Amy. 'Oh, I get it! You've gone overboard on the secret thing because of that stuff with Marie, right? Well, don't worry about her – as if she could get to me anyway! I have nothing to hide, apart from you-know-what and we're announcing that really soon! Speaking of which, I agreed to work the room a bit with Johann before the big announcement so we'd better get a move on! See you later, Amy. And thanks so much for helping with this.'

Kylie tottered away with Poshie at her Christian Louboutin exotic python heels, her sapphire pencil dress hugging her curves and making her waist look even tinier than usual. She joined her tall blond fiancé-to-be, holding his hand and laughing. As Amy stood wondering what to do next, someone snaked an arm around her and she looked up.

Damien! He pulled her close and kissed her. Even though he hadn't played in the match, he must have trained today because he had that wonderfully fresh post-football smell about him.

'Hi, Ames.' He grinned at her, looking utterly gorgeous in his best Armani trousers and the shirt she'd chosen for him on one of her shopping sprees.

'You're here!' she squealed, not caring what she sounded like. She was so happy to see him. 'What happened to you today? Weren't you supposed to be playing?'

A shadow crossed his face.

'Never mind, there's plenty more games!' she said quickly. She hadn't meant to upset him. 'I'll watch out for you at the next one.'

'Uh. Yeah, OK,' Damien said. 'So where is everyone? Is Paige here?'

Amy managed not to give him a funny look. They'd been through this and she knew that Paige and Damien were just friends. 'No, she's at the flat. She fancied an early night. But listen, Kylie's given us an important job to do tonight. The thing is . . . she's told me an important secret.'

Damien nodded casually. 'Is it to do with her and Johann's engagement?'

'You knew?' Amy asked in surprise.

'Yeah, Johann told me a while ago. He said it was secret until tonight, so I didn't like to mention it.' He folded his arms.

'I can't believe you knew!' Amy felt like having a go at him for not telling her, but then she realized how ridiculous that would sound when she already knew and she hadn't told him, either.

'So what does Kylie want us to do?' Damien asked.

He listened quietly with his arms still folded as Amy explained it. In fact, he seemed a bit moody again tonight, like the way he'd been at Monty's. Amy found herself making up for it by injecting extra enthusiasm into what she was telling him, talking up her utter excitement at the fact that Kylie and Johann were getting engaged. 'Isn't it just so amazing!' she said. 'They're going to have the most fabulous wedding. She's so lucky!'

He nodded absent-mindedly, seeming lost in his thoughts, but she knew he'd listened because when the time came, he gave her a hug and said, 'Right, let's do our bit for the couple of the year!'

At the allotted time, the staff got busy rounding everyone up and into the marquee, telling the guests that there would be a short speech. Amy waited with Damien beside the tent for their cue, stifling giggles as they wrestled to keep the surprise quiet.

'Hey, everyone, thanks for coming to our party!' Kylie was saying into the microphone, blushing prettily and swinging her hair. 'Johann and I have got something to say to everyone, but we wanted someone extra-special to help us make the announcement. So . . .'

Amy nudged Damien, who was helping her hold Poshie. 'It's time.'

'But I swear he's straining to run off in the opposite direction,' Damien grumbled. 'He's going to go the wrong way.'

'Someone extra-special . . .' Kylie repeated on stage.

'Kylie's waiting for us! What are we going to do?'

'I don't know,' Damien said seriously. Then he caught Amy's eye and laughed. 'Oh my God, what are we doing here, trying to get a dog to take an engagement ring to our friends? This is mad!'

'I know!' Amy suddenly saw the funny side. 'Let's just let him go. He's bound to head for Kylie! He always does. She's his mummy, or whatever. He's got like a homing instinct!'

Her words were barely intelligible through her laughter, and Damien was cracking up too as he said, 'OK, if you say so!'

'Someone extra-special to make the announcement.' Kylie said again on stage, with a note of increasing desperation. 'So . . .'

The crowd were hushed, waiting.

Amy offered Poshie the ring box, as Kylie had instructed. Poshie loved jewellery, and he snaffled the box lightly in his jaws just before she and Damien let go of him.

Poshie yelped and ran into the marquee towards Kylie.

'See?' Amy said.

'Phew,' breathed Damien, squeezing her hand.

'Poshie! Have you got it?' Kylie asked. 'Yay! Ladies and gentlemen, what my lovely pug here is trying to tell you is that . . .'

Amy and Damien both whispered encouragement from the sidelines as Poshie dropped the ring box at Kylie's feet. But then the little dog rushed out of the marquee, barking loudly as he ran off.

'Poshie, get back here!' Kylie's voice matched the pitch of Poshie's yelps. 'Thanks for bringing the ring, but you were supposed to be on stage for the announcement of our engagement!'

A murmur rose up from the crowd as Poshie launched himself at a dark figure in the distance. The figure started jumping up and down and screaming for help, but the people in the marquee were distracted by a sudden spluttering noise.

All at once, every sprinkler in Johann's garden spurted into action, including the ones located within the tent area. The water came at full force, squirting and twirling. It hit the canvas inside the marquee and poured down vinyl windows and all over the designer-clad guests, who yelped Poshie-like and tried to escape, only to find themselves equally drenched outside the tent as the sprinklers continued to pelt water all over Johann's broad lawn.

The black-clad figure in the distance moved closer, with

Poshie still attached at the ankle. The screams sounded female and hysterical. 'Get off me! Get off me, mutt! Kylie, can you hear me? I hope you're sorry now! This is for what you did to me and Will! And Pete!'

Kylie stood on the stage with liquid streaks of make-up trailing down her cheeks. Her gorgeous dress clung to her even more tightly than before.

'Marie, is that you?' she asked. Her smile froze for a second on her watery face.

Then she looked at Johann, who was totally drenched, and her guests, who were hopping around in the wetness.

She boomed out, 'Hey everyone, in case you missed it, Johann and I are engaged! As you can see, Poshie brought us the ring, and someone else made sure the announcement went with a total *splash*! So . . . I hope you all wish us well!'

Kylie laughed and kissed Johann as a puddle of water that had collected in a canvas fold reached critical mass and cascaded over their heads. A small, squelchy round of applause rose from the people who hadn't run away screaming.

Outside, Damien held Amy as the sprinklers whirled round.

'So, *now* how do you think we did?' he asked, his eyes full of laughter.

'Um, OK, considering,' Amy said. She felt a bit responsible for the Marie thing, though Kylie really didn't seem bothered. 'Should we try to switch them off or something?'

'Yeah, in a minute,' Damien said, swallowing hard. He pushed a lock of wet hair out of Amy's eyes and cupped her face, gazing at her in the floodlights. He said, 'Wow, you're gorgeous.'

She smiled and made a show of eyeing him up. 'You're not so bad yourself. Soaked Armani suits you.' She stroked his chest where his shirt was sticking to his damp skin.

He shut his eyes before leaning in and kissing her for ages.

Then he held her tightly and said in her ear, 'Amy, I love you.'

'I love you too, Damien,' Amy murmured. She thought about all the crazy things that had happened since she'd come to London and how it was all worth it for moments like these. This was why she'd come – to be with Damien. She couldn't believe she actually needed to remind herself of that, now that the summer had turned into an unexpected whirlwind of gossip and shopping and media attention.

She moved to kiss him again but he pulled back slightly, taking both her hands and looking deep into her eyes.

Then he said, through the whirling water, 'No, what I mean is . . . Amy, I love you. Will you marry me?'

12

Amy stared at Damien. The water spurted around them, making a phut-phut-phut noise. She wanted to laugh, but he didn't look like he was joking.

'Day,' she said, staring at several muddy people nearby who were starting to look like they were at Glastonbury. 'Please don't take this the wrong way but . . . are you serious?'

His face clouded again in its all-too familiar way. 'Yes. Why not? It's not like I planned this or anything – I mean, I haven't got any dogs to bring you a ring.' He gave a tiny smile. 'In fact, I haven't even got you a ring, because I only decided to ask you right this minute. But the truth is, I want to be with you. Always, you know? So . . . What do you think?'

The floodlights illuminated his dark eyes. He certainly looked serious. Amy's stomach was filled with an odd mixture of melting warmth, stirring butterflies and sheer panic.

'OK, well . . . If you're serious . . .'

She waited for a moment in case he started laughing or called out 'April Fool!', but he didn't.

'Well, I want to be with you always too. I really love you, Damien, you know I do. But . . .' Amy took a deep breath. 'I'm only sixteen, and you're only eighteen.'

Damien shrugged. 'So what? Kylie and Johann are only a couple of years older than us.'

'Isn't Johann in his mid-twenties? I suppose Kylie's eighteen,' Amy said. 'But don't you need permission from your parents if you're younger than that?' She tried to imagine telling her dad that she'd done badly in her GCSEs, run up a huge credit-card bill and was about to elope.

'But you're seventeen next month. We can have a long engagement. Besides, your mum and dad seem to like me, Amy. And my mum adores you. You know they'd all be happy for us.'

'I don't know, Damien . . .' Amy couldn't believe she was having this conversation. Her life had felt increasingly like a dream lately, but this seemed far-fetched even for that. What could she say that wouldn't hurt him? Apart from 'yes' – and she couldn't say that!

Damien ran a hand through his wet hair. 'You know, life's different for me now, Ames. Things aren't like they were in Stanleydale. I'm living kind of like Johann now, like a grown-up – I'm even buying my own place soon if . . . if I can. I just don't know if I want to do any of it . . . you know, without you. It feels weird.' He let go of her hands and fiddled with the heart pendant he'd given her, the one she always wore. 'And I know you want to go back home and do your A levels and go to uni and all that . . .'

Amy tried not to think about her results slip, stuffed into the drawer at the flat.

'. . . and you've got this whole TV job thing now, and it's all great, but . . . well, I don't want to lose you,' Damien finished.

Amy realized it was the second time this week he'd said that to her. Was this still something to do with the Josh thing? Her heart sank. 'What makes you think I'd *let* you lose me?' she said softly. 'We don't need to get married for that. We can just stay together, like we are now.'

'I know. You're right,' he said. He looked at the wet ground. 'OK. Never mind. I won't say any more about it. Maybe you can think about it, or something. Or not.'

He kissed her again, and they didn't notice the sprinklers being turned off, or Kylie and Johann dancing wildly, or the guests fleeing to their limos complaining that they'd sue for water damage to designer clothing. They didn't even see Marie being escorted off the premises by security, or hear Poshie snuffling in the mud at their feet.

Amy spent the rest of the night in a daze. Even being home and dry didn't seem to alter the cocktail of emotions coursing through her, and the odd tension between her and Damien.

On the one hand, they were completely wrapped up in each other, and it was brilliant. On the other, Damien seemed to have an edge of desperation about him, like he thought Amy was about to disappear and he needed to make the most of her. And it made Amy feel weird – like he expected too much of her, or something. She used to think they could make a long-distance relationship work, no problem. But now, when Amy thought about going back to Stanleydale, she was worried, and not just because of her exam results. What if Damien couldn't cope with seeing her less often? What if he wanted all of her . . . or nothing? Maybe that's what this proposal was all about. Maybe he wanted to be like the other footballers, who saw their wives and girlfriends whenever they wanted to.

She tried to ignore her worries and stick to the facts: they loved each other, they were together right now, and she had another week in London. But their happy, relaxed relationship seemed to have vanished, replaced by this edgy, nervous uncertainty.

The odd atmosphere carried on into the next day, when Damien came into her room and woke her up stupidly early. 'Come on,' he said. 'It's Sunday and no one's going to spring any last-minute training on me this time. I'm spending every single minute of my two days off with you.'

'How can you be sure?' Amy asked groggily. Damien's days off always started out full of promises and ended up with Big Carl calling him in for one reason or another.

'Because we're going away. It's a brilliant plan! I should have thought of it before. They can't expect me to go in if I'm abroad!'

'Abroad? But, Damien . . .'

'What? Why shouldn't we go? We can get last-minute tickets on the Eurostar and be in Paris by lunchtime. You've got a passport with you, haven't you?'

Amy nodded. It was one of the things her dad made her bring 'in case of emergency'. Like the credit card that she'd been using every day.

'Well, then. All you have to do is pack one of Rosay's funny-looking bags and we're off!'

Amy couldn't help thinking there was something majorly wrong with Damien. For the previous two weeks he'd been determined to do every little thing Big Carl instructed him to do, to the point where they'd ended up arguing about buying ice cream because it wasn't allowed on his diet. And now he was talking about taking off, when he knew full well his manager expected him to be around for extra training or for those sports psychology sessions.

'Damien, are you OK?' She tried to sound concerned but still casual, hoping it would help him open up. 'I mean, really, is there something going on?'

He hesitated, but then he said, 'No, course not! They're supposed to be days *off*, Ames, that's all. And I've barely seen you and . . . well, why shouldn't I spend them all with you, without interruptions?'

She couldn't argue with that, so she sighed and started getting ready. Her phone must have rung while she was in the shower because when she was drying herself in the bathroom she overheard Damien's voice, and as she moved closer to the door to listen she could tell he was talking to her dad.

'No, John, she hasn't mentioned it so it can't have arrived yesterday,' he was saying. Then, after a pause: 'I know, it's really not the same here. I've never even seen the postman, and we certainly don't know his name or anything! You're right, it really is a big city. Yes, I'm sure she'll tell you the minute it gets here . . . Yes, it's going OK. No, we don't know yet who's being played next week . . . Yes, you're right about the defence . . .'

Amy waited until Damien had finished talking football with her dad and hung up. Then she came out and pretended to be surprised when Damien told her he'd called.

'Did you tell him we were going away?' she asked, though she was fairly sure he hadn't, from what she'd heard.

'No, he didn't exactly let me get a word in,' Damien replied.

'He mostly went on about those GCSE results you haven't received yet.' He put his arm around her. 'I can't believe I forgot about those – I'm really sorry, Ames. You must tell me the second you get them. Though I just know you've done brilliantly!' He gave her a kiss. 'Why don't you give your dad a ring back and tell him about France?'

'No, I'll just text him to say hello,' Amy said quickly. 'You know what he's like about going abroad – he'll panic and give me long lectures about pickpockets. I'll tell him all about it when we get back, then he won't ruin his weekend with worry.'

She packed the smallest of Rosay's cases, selecting her clothes ultra-carefully because she'd never been to France but she'd heard everyone was dead chic there. Just as Damien had promised, within a few hours they were sitting in a first-class dining carriage that was all white tablecloths, proper silver cutlery and cloth napkins, eating fancy food and being offered wine by uniformed waiters as the train rolled through the Channel Tunnel.

She could get used to this part of the lifestyle: the respect Damien had been shown when he bought the expensive train tickets on his gold card; the admiring stares they got as they wandered to the luxury lounge to wait for the train; the way they'd been approached, more politely than at any restaurant in London, by people asking Damien football questions and – this was a first – asking Amy questions about who she thought would win *Bandwagon*. (She hedged with her answer and made it sound like she supported both sides, even though Damien chipped in annoyingly and said that Paige was the best.)

If she thought the train was grand, nothing could prepare

her for the hotel. They hadn't even booked anything, but Damien looked in a guidebook he'd bought before they got on the train and instructed a taxi to take them straight to the most expensive hotel listed in the book. It was amazing. It was at the top of a wide leafy boulevard and it dripped gold and ornate furnishings. They had a suite on the twenty-fifth floor that was bigger than Paige's flat in London, and they sat around watching the widescreen TV burble in French, not quite sure what to do with themselves.

Amy decided they should go sightseeing and Damien declared they should do it in style, so he asked the concierge to hire them a luxury car with a driver for the rest of the day and the next day. They took a boat trip on the Seine and strolled along the Champs-Elysées and saw all the touristy things the driver could think of. While Amy was distracted using Damien's mobile to take pictures of the cathedral at Notre Dame to show her mum – she'd left her own mobile switched off at the hotel on purpose to avoid any calls from Claudette, and also in case her dad rang again – Damien asked the driver for shopping recommendations. Then he surprised Amy by taking her to the classiest Louis Vuitton store she'd ever seen. He told her he'd buy her anything she wanted, and even though she did protest a little bit, she was soon in her element. She came out with a gorgeous summery dress that she left in the car when they climbed to the top of the Eiffel Tower and kissed as the sun set over Paris.

They didn't talk any more about the proposal, or whatever was bothering Damien, or any of Amy's problems, but it didn't matter because they were together and totally in love, and it was amazing.

13

The warm glow from Amy's Paris break with Damien didn't last long. First of all, there were the messages from her dad and Susi, which she got when she switched her phone on as the train rolled out of the Channel Tunnel and into the Kent countryside.

She replied to her dad to say she'd just been on a brilliant last-minute weekend trip, though she was back now and not to worry about her, and she forwarded the photos of Paris from Damien's phone with a note that he should show her mum.

Then she had a long text chat with Susi, all about how Asha had bought a bargain yellow pashmina to throw over her work clothes so she could rush off to tomorrow's afternoon date with Josh, which was to some kind of fashion show. Amy stifled the sadness she felt about Asha still not talking to her and told Susi all about Paris and how fantastic Damien was, but she didn't mention the proposal or any of her other worries. They were flooding back now: her GCSE results, Claudette's threats, the credit-card debt. She felt like turning round and getting on the next train back to Paris, but she didn't let on to Damien. Instead, she held him extra-tightly and she wished he didn't have to rush out to work at dawn the next day.

Amy had a short Tuesday at work watching the run-up to

the Mariah Carey round. The cast were sent home early as there seemed to be some kind of problem with wardrobe, and Amy stayed behind to see if she could help, until a stressed-out floor manager sent her away too. She didn't mind; her head was so full of worries that she was finding it hard to concentrate. She thought she'd use the time at home to relax a bit before making notes for tomorrow's interview.

But when Amy opened the door to the flat, she had a feeling that there were more urgent things to think about. Paige was sitting on the sofa stuffing an entire cupcake into her mouth, with a plastic container full of more cakes and a pile of empty paper cases beside her.

When she saw Amy, she pushed the cakes away. Her mouth was still full, though, when she said, 'Oh, hi. You're home early.' Her eyes flitted guiltily over the evidence beside her. 'So . . . I didn't get a chance to ask you today at the studio. How was Paris? And, er, would you like a cake?'

Amy tried not to stare at the crumbs on Paige's chin. 'Oh, Paris was great.' She remembered how crushed Paige had been about Kylie and Johann and she thought she'd better not say much more than that. 'And no, thanks. About the cake, I mean.'

'OK, I'll put them away!' Paige picked up the cake container and took it to the kitchen, scattering crumbs and cake cases across the floor as she walked.

Amy watched her. There was something about the way she was behaving that didn't seem right. She didn't look herself – her face seemed extra shadowy and grey. Amy wondered whether she should say anything. She wished Damien was here. He'd know what to do.

She stood in the kitchen doorway and shifted nervously. 'Paige?'

'Yeah?' said Paige, plucking an expensive-looking bottle of designer water from a row of identical bottles on the kitchen counter.

'Have you been eating cakes?'

Paige gave her a strange look. 'Yeah. So what?'

Amy squirmed. She thought she should probably leave it now. But something about her expression as she took a long drink from the bottle made Amy brace herself and carry on.

'All I mean is . . . Are you allowed to eat so much . . . sugar, you know, all in one go?'

Paige raised her eyebrows at Amy and put the empty bottle down. 'Amy, what are you talking about?' she asked good-naturedly. 'Not being funny, but what do you know about diabetes?'

'Not much,' Amy admitted. 'But I just thought sugar was –'

'Exactly.' She shrugged pleasantly, picked up the next bottle in the row and twisted the lid off. 'So let me explain. I *am* allowed to eat.' She laughed. 'Besides, I need the extra energy to beat Trina's annoying group.' She started warbling a line from an old Mariah song, shaking her hair back in a Trina-like way.

Amy smiled and nearly let it go. But the trouble was, Paige didn't *look* fine. She took a deep breath and tried again. 'Are you sure there's nothing wrong?'

Paige swallowed hard. 'Why would anything be wrong?' The bottle cap fell on the floor and rolled towards Amy's feet. Paige ignored it and took another swig.

Amy picked up the bottle cap and a couple of fallen cake cases. 'Well, you're normally so tidy,' she said, hoping Paige would take it the right way.

Paige sighed. 'I know. But right now, it's hard to care.'

'Paige . . .'

'What, Amy?' Paige twisted the bottle in her hand. She'd lost her usual easy-going tone. 'Go on, say it, whatever it is you want to say. You're worried about me? You think I'm not OK? Well, you're wrong! I've never been better!'

Amy took a step back. She was obviously handling this all wrong. 'Look, never mind. I'm glad everything's fine. I'm going to my room.' She started to walk away.

But Paige didn't even seem to have heard her.

'Yeah, and what makes you think your life's so perfect, anyway, Amy?' she asked.

Amy stopped in her tracks. 'I . . . I don't,' she mumbled.

'Well, maybe it is right now, but it won't last!' Paige continued. 'It never does. Last year I had what you have, you know. Or more! I had a song in the charts and the hottest boyfriend in the country.' She took another gulp of water. 'Well, you know the rest. I'm scrabbling about trying to relaunch my singing career, which means putting up with that humiliating reality show and Trina on my case every two minutes. And as for me and Scott . . .' She slammed the bottle down on the counter. 'But don't worry, because I'm totally in control.'

Amy turned back towards the kitchen. It definitely didn't sound like Paige and Scott were back together at all. She said, 'I'm really sorry, I didn't mean to upset you.'

Paige shut her eyes and took a very deep breath. After a couple of seconds, she said quietly, 'No, *I'm* sorry. Really. I didn't mean to be so . . . mean. Things have just been really mad lately, you know. Not just the papers banging on about Scott cheating on me, and the TV thing, and Trina's constant stupid comments, and all the extra stress with Marie being fired and Kylie's aunt on the warpath.'

Amy looked away, feeling instantly guilty.

'But also, well . . .' Paige paused for a few seconds, lost in thought. 'Can I tell you a secret?'

Amy groaned inwardly. She wasn't sure how much of this she could take. 'Um. Er, yes.' Maybe she should start saying no when people asked her that. It would make life a lot easier, and anyway, she barely trusted herself right now.

Paige sighed. 'OK. Well, I sort of had a moment with Scott. Last Tuesday, at Monty's. Though I had to get him away from the camera crew to talk to him properly, and no one saw us.'

Amy decided not to tell Paige that she and Damien had seen them.

Paige stared at the bottle in her hand. 'Kylie would kill me if she knew. She made me swear to stay away from him. And she's probably right, too. Because I said everything I could think of to get back together with him. I must have sounded *desperate*! And he gave me a hug and stuff, and he was nice to me, but he . . . well, he wasn't interested. He said he didn't want to play games any more. Well, *I* wasn't the one doing that in the first place.'

Her face twisted as if she was determined not to cry. She looked at Amy.

'Listen, you made me feel loads better the other day, but do you know for sure about Scott and Rosay? Because why would he be like this if he didn't have someone else – and if it wasn't serious? I've known for ages that he was seeing other girls, even when we were together. All that stuff in the papers wasn't exactly a surprise. But this time he's acting different, and I want to know why. If I know, then I can deal with it.' She frowned. 'Will you help me?'

'Me?' Amy muttered.

'I couldn't bring myself to ask Scotty at Monty's, not that he'd have told me the truth anyway. And there's no way I can talk to Rosay.' Paige walked back and busied herself tidying the kitchen, avoiding Amy's gaze. 'But you can. So would you? Will you ask her?'

Amy tried to smile, though this really sounded like bad news for everyone concerned. 'OK,' she said reluctantly.

'Great.' Paige gave her a sideways look. 'Can you do it right now?'

'What, you mean, phone her?' Amy wondered when she could stop getting involved in other people's complicated lives, especially since her own wasn't exactly a walk in the park right now. Her mind raced, tuning out Paige's reply as she found herself wishing she was somewhere else, like out shopping, or back in Paris where it felt like all of her worries had disappeared.

'So you'll come?' Paige asked.

'Oh.' Amy looked at her. 'Where?'

'Hold on, were you even listening?'

Amy shook her head apologetically. 'Sorry, Paige . . . What did you say?'

'I was inviting you to come with me to a fashion show. Lemon Aid.'

Amy tried hard to snap out of her daydream. 'Lemonade? Like the drink?'

Paige laughed. 'Now you're making me fancy lemonade! I'm so thirsty! It's a good thing I've only got healthy drinks here.' She pointed to the fancy bottled water. 'No, it's two words: Lemon *Aid*. It's like a fashion showcase, and you get to buy the clothes at auction afterwards.'

'An auction?' Amy asked.

'Yeah, for charity. It's held every summer and the di Rossi family always get loads of tickets to give out. Scott got me a ticket before . . . before. I was going to go with Kylie but she can't make it and I've got a spare ticket. You have to come – loads of the Boroughs girls are going. And Rosay never misses it.' She paused, smiling weakly at Amy. 'Please? I can lend you a yellow dress if you don't have one.'

'I don't think I have,' Amy mumbled, wondering how could she possibly fit into any of petite Paige's clothes when Amy was way bigger. Or rather, she had a 'fit athlete's body', as Asha kept reminding her. Amy and Asha had always loved swimming.

It suddenly occurred to Amy that Asha might be at this Lemon Aid thing on her date with Josh. It could be the same afternoon fashion show that Susi had mentioned, and she did say Asha had bought a yellow pashmina. Maybe Josh had been given some of the di Rossi tickets too.

'Well, you have to wear yellow,' Paige explained. 'It's like a rule. Lemon Aid, you see – it's sort of a gimmick, I suppose, but it's fun. The "Lemon" stands for something beginning with "London" and "Educational", but no one can remember the rest any more. The designers are all recent fashion college graduates. Honestly, you'll love it – you can buy lots of incredible clothes at bargain prices.' Paige smiled excitedly.

'One-offs, you know. Designers who will be the next big thing.'

'OK, I'll come,' Amy said impulsively, 'if you can find me a dress I can borrow.' She suddenly felt desperate to see Asha and have a chance to sort things out with her. She missed her so much, and it would be easier to speak to her face-to-face. Plus the whole event sounded pretty cool. And if the price she had to pay was talking to Rosay for Paige – well, Rosay was her friend, after all. It wasn't so bad, really.

Paige led Amy to her room, which was incredibly tidy. Amy hadn't looked around properly the other day, but today she took in the large canopy bed with a spotless white cover on it, a corner desk that held a flat-screen computer monitor, and the mirrored wardrobes running the length of two walls. She watched as a row of Paige reflections pushed tidy rails of clothes aside and extracted a zesty yellow tunic dress that was long, flowing and absolutely lovely.

'Here,' said Paige, handing it to Amy. 'It's Missoni, and it's quite a loose-fit style. Should suit you.'

Amy smiled to herself. Rosay would have said 'should *fit* you'. Paige was so much kinder – and yet, Amy felt more at ease with Rosay than she did with Paige. It was weird.

Paige rustled through her wardrobe a bit more and pulled out a tiny tailored dress in a brighter yellow. Its diamond-encrusted collar caught the light as Paige shook the dress. Then she grabbed an incredible golden silk gown with her other hand. It had a simple line and a look of Hollywood glamour, accentuated by a small belt at its waist.

Paige held both up in front of her. 'What do you think, Amy? The Fendi, or the Bill Blass?'

'Oh my God,' Amy breathed. 'They're both completely gorgeous.'

'OK, I'll try them on and you can tell me honestly,' Paige said, smiling. 'Wow, I'm so glad I still have a female flatmate! I thought I'd never manage without Kylie. You know, I knew she was dying to move in with Johann long before she told me. I was too distracted by *Bandwagon* to guess about the engagement, but I was still the first person she told about it, of course! Me and Kylie are so close – we know all of each other's secrets. But I'm getting the same feeling from you, Amy!'

Amy hoped Paige wasn't looking at her too closely in case her expression gave away that she'd heard about Kylie's engagement before Paige did.

But Paige carried on chatting. 'Look, I'll try mine on first, and then you can try yours. If you don't like it, there's more where that came from.'

She disappeared behind the open cupboard door and, seconds later, she swished out, wearing the Bill Blass gown. It looked like it was made of pure gold and it even gave her pale face some colour. It was amazing.

'What do you think?'

'It's gorgeous, Paige,' said Amy truthfully.

'Really? Hold on, I'll try the other one.'

She reappeared in the slightly funkier but equally flattering diamond and yellow dress.

Oddly, though, instead of being impressed at how great Paige looked, something was starting to niggle at Amy. She remembered when she was new to London and she'd seen Paige tucking something guiltily into her pocket in a cafe, and then the Saturday at Barbie's party when Kylie had pulled up Paige's top a tiny bit to check she had . . .

'Paige, where's your insulin pump?'

'Oh.' Paige wouldn't meet Amy's eye. 'I can't have it on with dresses like these. It would spoil the line.'

Amy nearly accepted that as an answer. It made sense.

But then she thought about all the times she'd been observing Paige lately, making a careful note of everything Paige was wearing so that she could talk about it to Joanna Lightman. The strapless, sequinned Britney-style dress? Another line that couldn't be ruined. The black cocktail dress she'd worn to Monty's on Tuesday? The sexy, clinging Madonna outfit? Snap, and snap.

The Mariah Carey backless dress? That too. The Marc Jacobs Moonburst sundress she'd worn to rehearsals today? Same again.

Every single thing Amy had seen Paige wearing lately was an outfit that wouldn't accommodate an insulin pump.

Amy spoke quickly before she could think about it too much and change her mind.

'Paige,' she said. 'You *are* still taking your insulin, aren't you?'

Paige hesitated for a long time, spinning in front of the mirror and looking pretty and . . . and exhausted. 'You're not, are you?' Amy demanded. 'You're not taking it. This is what Kylie was warning me and Damien about, isn't it?' It all came back to Amy quickly. 'When she told me she'd spoken to you and you'd promised.' She looked at her flatmate, who was rooted silently to the spot, reflected over and over again along the side of the room.

Then Paige seemed to come back to life. 'OK. I can explain. You see, things have changed.' She looked pleased with herself. 'I don't actually need the pump any more.'

'Don't you?' Amy asked, confused. Hadn't Paige herself said that there was no cure for diabetes? 'Do you use something else instead?' She thought about the few things she'd heard about diabetes in her life. She knew a girl in the year below at school had to have injections for it. Maybe Paige had started doing that too – injecting insulin instead of using the pump.

Paige said enthusiastically, 'No! I don't need it any more! I kept getting the amounts all wrong, anyway, taking it at the wrong times, or taking too much and making myself ill. It was such a *pain*. But I've got it wrong that many times that I've worked it out – if I'm careful about it, I can just use it occasionally with no major problems.' She beamed. 'See, I use it when it suits me, when I really need it. I know what I'm doing.' She swayed unsteadily for a second, frowning. 'But don't tell Kylie about it, OK, Amy? She makes a terrible fuss about this kind of thing, and I promise you it's safe. I trust you, remember. You're as good a friend as Kylie is.'

Amy thought about it again. Paige looked like a million dollars now, but there was still something not quite right about her.

'Paige, have you asked a doctor about this?'

'Believe me, I know more about my own body than any doctor could!' She made a face. 'And it's great to be back in control, you know, for the first time since I was diagnosed with this thing. It means a lot to me. You won't tell anyone, will you, Amy? Please?'

Amy made a non-committal noise. She wasn't sure she *could* keep this a secret. But Paige interpreted the sound as agreement.

'Thanks. So aren't you trying the dress on? I'm sure it's perfect. But quick, we'd better get going! I can't stand being late.'

By the time the girls left, they were the picture of yellow-toned glamour, Amy like a beam of sunshine in the perfectly flattering Missoni, and Paige like molten gold in the classic Bill Blass.

When they arrived at the plush central London hotel that was hosting Lemon Aid, the only thing that spoiled the stunning effect of their look was the worried expression on Amy's face as she wondered whether her flatmate was telling her the truth.

14

Amy had never been to anything like this before, but that didn't stop her being certain that she was at one of the best fashion shows in the world.

Beanpole-like girls in amazing outfits oozed huge amounts of attitude as they pouted and stalked down the catwalk to the thumping beat of a familiar remixed dance track. Amy recognized it as the music from the final reel of *Sex and the City*, which she must have watched a hundred times on DVD with Asha and Susi.

And now she was here, living the life of a much younger Carrie Bradshaw, while clothes as awesome as anything out of a Hollywood film were modelled in front of her.

And best of all, she was allowed to buy them. She could bid on these creations in silk, chiffon, cotton and fabrics she couldn't even identify, these bursts of colour and texture and originality. And with a swipe of her credit card, she could take them home at the end of the afternoon and they would be hers to own forever.

Amy was sitting in the front row – the VIP seats, Paige had told her – and so was Asha, a few seats up, next to Josh. Amy's hunch had been correct. She'd already tried to get Asha's attention a few thousand times, but Asha had been too wrapped up in her date to even notice Amy. Either that, or she was deliberately avoiding her, but Amy preferred not to think that.

Unfortunately, though, she kept catching Josh's eye when she looked over. And every time she did, he held her gaze seriously as if he was trying to tell her something.

Or maybe as if he fancied her and couldn't take his eyes off her.

And that was too awful to think about. Apart from anything else, he was now going out with her best friend!

Amy shifted uncomfortably in her seat and tried to focus on the incredibly sheer backless prom dress being modelled in front of her. She had to be imagining the Josh thing. She decided not to look over again.

Eventually, the final model strode away and everyone clapped for ages as a small man with a lopsided hairstyle made his way to the stage. He stood at the front and announced that there would be a champagne and canapé break before the auction commenced, and his ex-student designers would be mingling at the bar to answer questions.

Paige stood up and stretched. 'OK, this is the best part! To the bar!'

Amy followed her, thinking that it was no wonder Paige had a reputation for being a drinker.

The bar area was thick with fantastically dressed people. The men mostly wore lemon-coloured shirts under ordinary-looking suit jackets, but the women were clad in every imaginable shade of yellow. Gold-jacketed waiting staff circulated with trays of brightly coloured drinks. Paige stopped one and picked up a flute of bubbling champagne, and Amy asked for a soft drink and was handed a sunshine-coloured cocktail with a slice of pineapple and a yellow umbrella on the top. She sipped it and admired Paige's drink.

'It looks like it's got gold flakes in it,' she said.

'That's because it has!' Paige swirled the liquid in her glass and the flecks rose and fell prettily. It was like a classy version of a snow globe. 'It has twenty-four carat gold in it.'

'Is that safe? I mean, if you get real gold in your stomach?' asked Amy, hoping she wasn't sounding her age. If Claudette was here, she'd be calling her 'baby' right about now. But Amy had never seen anything like it.

Paige laughed. 'You know what they say: you are what you eat!' She took a long drink. 'Or drink, I suppose.'

Then the smile froze on her face and she grabbed Amy's arm. 'I just saw her. In the far corner. I can't look. Is she with him?' She stared at the ground.

Amy glanced over and spotted Rosay in a stunningly vibrant cocktail dress, laughing with a tall man in a suit. She looked closer. It was Josh, with Asha standing next to him, wrapping her pashmina tightly around herself as she talked animatedly, probably telling some joke and making everyone laugh, knowing Asha. Amy felt a pang and wished she were standing there with them instead of here, reassuring her slightly obsessive flatmate.

'No, she's not with Scott,' she told Paige.

'Oh God, of course not,' Paige said, rolling her eyes. 'How could that have been him? He's still at training!' She sighed. 'You know, I keep thinking I see him everywhere. It doesn't help that half the men in the country have copied his hairstyle, and his face keeps staring up at me from billboards and papers. Then I saw his name scribbled on the back of some school-girl's tote bag yesterday on my way to the studio. It just makes me miss him more.' She groaned. 'Maybe I'm going mad.'

'Or maybe you're just tired,' Amy suggested gently. 'And stressed.'

Paige ignored that and gave Amy an imploring look. 'But maybe Rosay *would* have come with him, if she could have. Will you ask her now? You can get her away from those other people and find out for me, can't you?' She drank the rest of her gold-flecked champagne. 'I'll chat to some designers or something, or go back in and sit down. I *am* feeling sort of tired, to be honest. Come and find me when you know the answer!'

Amy braced herself. All three of the people in the corner she was heading for were her friends. In fact, one of them had known her all her life. She and Asha had thrown Play-Doh at each other at nursery, scared off the nasty boys who'd been teasing Susi at primary school and moaned about teachers and homework at secondary school. They'd spent most Saturdays together searching for fashion bargains in Leeds, and analysed every detail of Amy's first date with Damien two years ago, when he was just the football-mad boy next door.

There was no reason for Amy to feel remotely scared.

'Um. Hi, everyone,' she said. She looked at Rosay, who was the least intimidating of the three of them right now.

Asha immediately stopped laughing, but she said, 'Hi, Amy.' She hugged her pashmina around herself.

Rosay beamed at her. 'Phew, at last I get another chance to talk to you without those crazy *Bandwagon* people milling about! I really miss you at Caseydene! The place isn't the same without you. Is it, Josh?'

Josh cleared his throat. 'No.' His eyes swept over Amy's dress and lingered slightly too long.

Asha narrowed her eyes, staring at Josh.

Rosay laughed and went on talking, seemingly oblivious to the tension that was crackling around her. 'You two were always at the pool together, weren't you? No wonder you hang around with footballers all the time – you're both sports mad! You're as bad as each other!'

Amy wished Rosay would stop talking, but since no one else was saying anything, she could sort of see why Rosay kept filling the silence.

'Though I reckon it was all an act! Mum says she walked past a couple of times and she saw you just sitting there chatting and sharing chocolate bars.'

'They were *health* bars,' Josh said, as if it would help.

Asha rearranged her pashmina. 'Oh, Amy never mentioned that you two knew each other so well,' she said casually to Josh.

Josh lifted his eyes and exchanged a look with Amy that felt like a series of sparks. It made Amy's stomach twist and plummet and it was deeply confusing.

Why hadn't she just looked away? She was sure she had guilt written all over her face, even though she truly had nothing to feel guilty about. But it didn't feel like it, especially not now that Asha was shooting daggers at her.

And then Asha fixed her eyes on Josh instead. Amy knew that look well, and it was *not* good news. It was mostly reserved for boys who were out of line, and Asha *never* held back.

'Look, Josh, thanks for bringing me to this weird thing with the crazy drinks and the funky clothes,' she began, unravelling her pashmina and revealing her work outfit of black trousers and a white blouse. 'But quite honestly, you've made it pretty clear it's not *me* you want to go out with. You've mostly only talked about one girl on both of our dates.' She glared at Amy. 'At first I thought it was because Amy was someone we had in common, you know, and that's obviously how you knew where I worked and how you found me to ask me out. But now I can see it's a lot more than that. And no offence, but I'm *not* prepared to be anyone's second choice!'

Rosay, finally stunned into silence, stared at Asha, Amy and Josh in turn. Her smile fell and the grand skirt of her dress swayed as she shifted from foot to foot.

'You? You're all right,' Asha said to Rosay. 'You're pretty out-there, and you can't half be bossy, and I know you think my clothes are crap, but at least I know where I am with you. But as for *you*,' Asha spat in Amy's direction, her voice rising in anger. 'You've changed! And you're welcome to your glamorous magazine lifestyle, but I want nothing to do with it! Or with you!' She threw her pashmina at Amy. Amy caught it and held it, unsure of what to do next.

The bar seemed suddenly hushed as people strained to hear what was going on in the corner.

'Asha, don't be like this,' Amy said softly, trying to hand the pashmina back. Asha had thrown a few tantrums over years they'd been friends, but it had never been so personal before.

But her friend – or *ex*-friend – didn't want to listen to her. Or even to look at her. And she certainly didn't want the pashmina.

Asha continued at the same volume, though it seemed louder because the bar was so quiet now. 'It's all very well letting your boyfriend pay for all your designer gear and foreign holidays while you mess around on some television set and pretend it's work. But don't come crying to *me* again when Damien shows an interest in some other girl, not when it's obvious you've been doing exactly the same thing – with *him*!' She pointed to Josh. 'Oh, forget it! I'm leaving.'

She stormed out, muttering, 'Excuse me,' as she pushed her way through a crowd of staring people.

The conversation in the room gradually started up again as people got back to their gold-flecked champagne.

Amy's eyes stung and she couldn't look at Rosay or Josh.

Rosay drummed her manicured fingernails on her glass. 'So, OK. Am I the only one with a brain here? Aren't you going to go after her?'

'She won't want to talk to me,' Amy said, biting her lip.

'Not you!' Rosay exclaimed. 'You didn't ask her to come here on a date, did you? I mean him!'

'Oh,' said Josh nervously. 'OK, yeah. I'll go.'

'You'd better. And apologize. A lot!' Rosay called after him as he left. 'Honestly. Men!' she said to Amy. 'Don't worry. They'll sort it out, and if they don't, she'll meet someone better. And she'll get over her jealousy of you, which is what it clearly is, and you'll make up. It'll be OK, you'll see.'

Amy did a miserable half-smile back. 'I don't know. I've never seen her like that before.'

She twisted the fabric of the pashmina in her hand. What Asha had said to her was terrible, but Amy was worried about what had gone on between her and Josh, too. That look had felt like a bolt of electricity. How could it have happened, when she had a boyfriend? A boyfriend who'd just proposed to her. What was wrong with her?

Rosay seemed to read her mind. 'Mind you, you should have seen the way you looked at Josh. Honestly, Amy, way to treat a friend.' She sighed. 'Though I probably didn't help, going on about your cosy chats. So, um, sorry about that.'

'That's OK,' said Amy doubtfully.

'Josh really fancies you, doesn't he?' Rosay asked, though it didn't really sound like a question. 'I can't believe I never noticed before. You know what? I reckon he went out with Asha to make you jealous. He knew you'd hear about it.' She shook her head. 'And I really hope she gives him hell about it!'

Another hush fell over the room as the man with the lopsided hairstyle announced that people should take their seats for the auction. As everyone started trooping back, Amy told Rosay she'd see her later. She headed off to find Paige for the auction, suddenly remembering that she hadn't asked Rosay about Scott.

Well, she'd explain to Paige that she'd do it another time. Right now, she felt like forgetting everything that had just happened, and buying some clothes seemed like the best way to do it.

15

It turned out that Amy didn't have to explain anything, because Paige wasn't there. Ten minutes into the auction, when Paige still hadn't appeared, Amy started to worry. She wondered whether to go and look for her, or maybe phone her.

She glanced back and saw Rosay sitting a couple of rows back with an empty aisle seat beside her. Amy waited for a lull in the proceedings and hurried towards the empty seat.

'Hey,' she said quietly as she sat down. She hesitated before saying the next thing because she knew Rosay hated Amy's flatmate, but she really needed to ask it. 'You haven't seen Paige, have you?'

To her surprise, Rosay looked a bit shifty.

'You *have* seen her?'

'Er, yeah. A little while ago. After you said goodbye to me, I went to the foyer and found a quiet corner to phone . . . To make a phone call. And I didn't notice at first, but Paige was right near, chatting to one of the designers.'

'Well, what happened? Did you have a fight or something?'

Rosay immediately went on the defensive. 'Listen to you!' she hissed. 'You're assuming we're *all* fighting, all because one of your oldest friends just threw a pashmina in your face!'

'Well, you looked all guilty when I asked about Paige! I'm worried about her.' Amy tried to keep her voice down.

Rosay scoffed. 'I don't know why. She can look after herself, or look for help at the bottom of the glass.'

Amy reminded herself that not many people knew the real reason that Damien had rushed Paige to hospital the week before. 'So what happened?'

'Nothing much. She . . . er, overheard something I said on the phone and she called me some not very ladylike things.' Rosay set her lips in a prim line, as if she'd never use the words herself. 'Then she said she was going to Kylie's, and she stomped out. I saw her flagging down a black cab, so you really shouldn't worry. Kylie will sort her out.' Rosay looked thoughtful. 'The only strange thing is that she's never called me names like that before, even when she was fairly sure I'd sliced all her clothes to shreds. Guess she doesn't love her clothes as much as . . .' Rosay paused and smoothed down the fabric of her dress. 'As much as I thought.'

'Ladies!' the auctioneer called. 'Do I hear a bid over there for this metallic silver sideless dress?'

'Yes!' Rosay called. 'She's bidding £500.' She pointed at Amy.

'Fabulous!' called the man in delight. 'Any advance on that, ladies and gentlemen?'

'Rosay,' Amy whispered. 'What did you do that for? I can't afford it!'

'I know you'd look great in a sideless dress,' Rosay smirked. 'And it's for charity. And anyway, you deserve it for upsetting your best friend and flirting with the guy my step-dad has tried to fix me up with since he arrived from New Zealand.'

'You never told me that!'

Rosay shrugged. 'What do you think all those invitations to lunch and free use of the Caseydene tennis court are about? Carlo's desperate to make sure I don't end up with a footballer, and Josh is a family friend. He thinks it's perfect.'

Amy smiled. 'I never thought of that.'

'Yeah, well, it isn't going to happen, is it? Especially not with someone my step-dad approves of!' Rosay shuddered. 'I'd much rather go out with someone he'd hit the roof about. That's how it should be.' She smiled.

A voice boomed out. 'Sold to the lady in the yellow!'

There was a smattering of laughter.

'Kidding, kidding, folks!' the auctioneer said. 'Sold to the lady we, of course, all recognize as the lovely Amy Thornton.'

Amy blushed as everyone stared at her.

She waited until people had turned their attention back to the stage before she spoke to Rosay again.

'So are you seeing someone? Someone your step-dad wouldn't approve of?'

Rosay hit her lightly on the arm. 'I hope you plan on wearing that sideless dress on set tomorrow. See if you can get it past the stylists. You might even shock the unshockable Julia Lightman!'

It was pretty obvious that Rosay was avoiding the question. Amy took a deep breath and finally asked her directly. 'Rosay, are you going out with Scott White?'

'Ms Thornton, is that a bid I hear for this patchwork shirt? Shall we say £300?'

Amy looked up and saw a sea of faces looking at her again. 'Um, yes, OK,' she stammered, though the shirt was pretty ugly. She just wanted an answer from Rosay. As the auction continued she whispered, 'Well?'

Rosay shrugged casually, but her eyes shone. 'Mm. Kind of. I'll tell you later.'

'Wow,' Amy muttered. 'Kind of' was not 'no'. So it *was* true. Rosay was secretly seeing Scott White. And even though it wasn't exactly a well-kept secret – people had been suggesting it to her for days, after all – Amy was shocked. Scott had broken Trina's heart. Then he'd broken Paige's heart. Every day there seemed to be a different woman's kiss-and-tell story about Scott in the papers. And Rosay knew all this. She'd joined in with the 'Scott White Is a Creep' song at the start-of-season party, which was now so popular that they'd heard the Wirral United fans chanting it when they played the Royal Boroughs.

Yes, Scott was absolutely famous for being a love rat, and Rosay hated cheating footballers. She'd made that very clear to Amy, almost from the moment they'd first met.

So why would Rosay want to go out with Scott?

'Don't look so shocked.' Rosay nudged her. 'It's not what you think.'

'Sold to *The Morning Show*'s newest star. Thank you for your generosity, Ms Thornton!'

Amy paid for the weirdest clothes she'd ever bought, smiling shyly as the organizers of Lemon Aid gushed over her, telling her she was the next big thing, what an honour it was to meet her and what a natural beauty she was. Rosay hung back the whole time, smiling to herself and looking like she was on another planet.

At last it was time to leave. In fact, Amy was a lot later than she'd meant to be. Damien would be at home waiting for her by now. As she stood with Rosay in the taxi queue outside the hotel, she wrote him a quick text to say she was on her way. But before she could send it, Rosay took the phone out of her hand.

'Trust me,' Rosay said, as Amy reached for it. She held it away from Amy, madly pressing buttons. 'There. I've told him you're out with the girls tonight and not to wait up.'

'Rosay! You can't do that!' Amy and Damien had a date! They hadn't actually arranged anything, but she knew that he'd have a plan. He always did, these days. He wouldn't be happy about her going out.

'Too late. It's sent.' Rosay laughed and slipped the phone into her bag. 'Don't worry, I put lots of soppy love stuff at the end. He'll forgive you. He'd forgive anything from you.' She laughed. 'I have it on good authority.'

'I don't know what you're talking about.' Amy made a face at her. 'But you'd better not ever do that again!'

'It depends whether I ever need to.' Rosay shrugged. 'I've been thinking of doing this for a few days now, but the stuff I saw tonight made me sure. This is an intervention, Amy.'

'A what?'

Rosay laughed, moving forward as another taxi pulled away. 'You know when people are, like, drug addicts and stuff and their friends have to be cruel to be kind? So they step in and drag them away and make them face their problem? I've seen it on films.'

'Now you're really not making sense. I'm not a drug addict.' Amy swung her purchases in her hands. For the first time, the thought crossed her mind that she might be addicted to *shopping*, though. Every time she felt down or stressed these days, she headed straight for the shops. Somehow it calmed her down, even though it was actually contributing to her problems.

But that was different, wasn't it? All girls liked shopping, especially style experts on daytime television! Hopefully Spencer could get her another job she could do from Stanleydale – maybe a magazine column like Coleen Rooney – and then she'd definitely be able to pay her dad back.

Anyway, Rosay was the one who'd got her buying all the strange clothes tonight. It couldn't possibly be what she was talking about now.

'Here's our car!'

Rosay allowed the uniformed porter to open the car door for her, turning and posing for a couple of nearby straggling photographers before she climbed in with a swish of her skirt. Amy ignored the paps and got in beside her, just missing Rosay's instructions to the driver.

Rosay turned to Amy as the car pulled away from the hotel.

'OK, I know you're not a drug addict,' she said. 'But there is *something* going on with you and I'm going to get to the bottom of it.'

Amy opened her mouth to say something but Rosay jumped in quickly.

'Don't argue! You need this. You've been skulking around those television studios, barely cracking a smile except when the camera's on you, and even then it looks forced.'

Amy gave her a horrified look.

'Yeah, a bit like that!' Rosay exclaimed. 'And then there was that stuff with Josh just now. OK, he looked at you like he wanted to eat you for dinner, but I bet you get that a lot from boys. What I'm worried about is the way you looked at him like you felt *guilty* or something.' Rosay shook her head. 'And I know you. I know you didn't do anything with Josh.'

'I didn't,' Amy said miserably. Rosay was too good at this. Now she was tempted just to tell her everything – it sounded like she would guess it anyway. But telling her anything about this could land Rosay right back in trouble with Claudette.

'Look at you! I'm so right – you need this intervention, badly! OK, here we are.' They pulled up outside a building with a large neon sign that said 'Shadows'. There was a massive, snaking queue outside but Rosay ignored it and strolled straight to the front in her spectacular dress, posing again for a few photographers by the door. Just like what happened with Damien at Monty's the other night, the bouncer lifted the barrier and waved them through. 'Lovely to see you, Ms Sands,' he said politely as they walked in. Amy was sure he gave her an uncertain look as she swept past, but he didn't say anything.

Inside, Shadows was almost the exact opposite of Monty's. This club was showy and new-looking and everything glowed. The thumping beat of the music was pretty similar, though, and Amy thought she spotted the same It Girl as she had at Monty's, throwing back slammers at the bar with two girls Amy recognized from *Heat* magazine as minor royals.

'I thought you wanted to talk to me!' Amy shouted over the music as Rosay dragged her on to the dance floor, which was heaving with bodies.

'Yeah, yeah. Let's dance first and talk later!' She threw herself into the beat, looking completely in her element.

Amy tried to loosen up but couldn't help thinking that the whole of Shadows was amazingly crowded considering it was still early evening. 'Why is it so busy?' she shouted to Rosay.

'It's a twenty-four-hour club,' Rosay called back. 'Some of these people haven't been home for days. They haven't got a clue what time it is!' She laughed. 'We should stay all night. They do a fantastic breakfast!'

'I've got to be at the studio at six tomorrow!' Usually Amy loved dancing and the music at Shadows was great, but tonight she just wasn't in the mood.

'All the more reason!' Rosay shouted. Then she stopped dancing and looked at Amy pointedly. 'You just can't relax, can you? Never mind, let's go straight to phase two.' She took Amy's elbow and started to weave her way through the crowds. Amy followed unsteadily, feeling out of her depth as she pushed past film and television stars and famous singers. She really hoped no one knew who she was, or more importantly how old she was.

The club was huge. Rosay led Amy up a clear Perspex staircase where another bouncer was waiting. He opened a door as soon as he saw them and Amy stepped into a large glass-fronted room. It overlooked the club below, but the music was muffled now and the sounds of laughter and chatter filled the air instead.

'See, Amy? Even VIP clubs have VIP areas. We're *very, very* important persons!' Rosay laughed, settling on a plush sofa and putting her bag on a coffee table that was lit neon blue.

Amy looked around. Apart from a few minutes in Monty's,

most of which looked more like a school than a club anyway, she'd never been anywhere as posh and star-studded as this in her life. But she'd managed to get into a few normal clubs in Leeds with Asha and Susi, and she decided she wasn't going to feel intimidated.

'Can I get you a drink?' she asked Rosay confidently.

'Frankie will bring drinks and snacks over in a sec – he knows what I like, and I know you'll like them too.' She smiled at Amy. 'So all you need to worry about is telling me everything.'

Amy looked at her hands. Should she do that? Where would she even begin?

'No, you go first,' she said. 'Tell me about you and Scott.'

Rosay slouched back on the sofa, still managing to look elegant. 'You're not getting out of it that easily! OK, I will, but it will only take ten seconds and then it's your turn.'

A skinny boy with a half-unbuttoned shirt leant over them, placing green drinks in long-stemmed glasses on the table, together with a delicate silver dish of salted almonds.

'Emerald Cities for you, beautiful girls,' he said.

Rosay beamed at him. 'Thanks, Frankie, you're wonderful. How's Barney?'

'Good.' The boy had a thick foreign accent that Amy couldn't place. 'We're still both at the love shack, you know?' He raised his eyebrows suggestively and smirked at Amy.

'Oh, is that another club?' she asked.

'In a way.' Rosay smiled at Frankie. 'I bet your flat's a bit like this place.'

'Yeah, we *wish*. It's really a lot more like Zone Two.'

'*That*'s a club,' Rosay added for Amy's sake. 'In Camden.'

Frankie gave Amy a long look. 'Wow, you're every bit as cute as you look on the telly. I never miss *The Morning Show*.' He turned to Rosay. 'And you, Ms Sands, are *fabulous* on *Bandwagon*. Me and B are voting for you all the way! You're the best one there.'

'Oh, shut up,' Rosay laughed. 'You know you're getting a massive tip from me anyway!'

The boy made a hurt face. 'I'm not in it for the money! It's the truth!' He counted on his fingers. 'The little blonde starlet is good, but she's losing her marbles and it's not pretty to watch. The Brazilian beauty makes my ears bleed. The chavvy one looks and sounds plastic. And I've already forgotten about the redhead who mysteriously left. But you – you're pure talent.'

'Yeah, yeah. You can go now. Say hi to the B-boy from me!' Rosay blew him a kiss as he left. 'I love him. And his boy-friend. They used to slip me free drinks when I had no money, you know, when they were still at Jasper's. They risked their jobs for me.'

'Sounds great.' Amy nudged her. 'But now I think *you're* trying to get out of it. So tell me about Scott.'

Rosay laughed and leant back. 'OK, well, I know I don't have to ask you not to tell anyone – I trust you.'

Amy tried not to think about that.

Rosay sipped her cocktail. 'Anyway, it really is simple. We're teaching Scott a lesson.'

'What do you mean?'

'Scott thinks he can have any girl he wants and treat them however he likes. So, well, we're playing him at his own game. The plan is: he falls for me big-time, then I dump him. We think it's time someone broke *his* heart.'

'Who's *we*?'

Rosay looked sheepish. 'Me and Trina. I kept in touch with her a bit, you know, after the whole mess last year. I know she's kind of . . . abrasive, but we were in the same boat, in a way – we both had our lives ruined by Paige's affair with Scott. So we make a good team.' She looked serious. 'I'll tell you what, though, we would have involved Paige in this too, if we thought she'd understand. It could do her good, getting some revenge. But tonight has proved that could never happen.'

'You mean at the fashion show?'

Rosay nodded. 'She heard me talking to Scott in the foyer, before I noticed her. I suppose it must've sounded pretty bad because . . .' She bit her lip. 'Because I'm trying hard to make it convincing with Scott – making it sound like I'm totally into him, you know. But I wish I could explain to Paige that it's *him* we're trying to hurt, not her. Even if I don't like her much.'

Amy thought that was a bit of an understatement. Although, now she thought about it, Rosay seemed to have mellowed a bit lately where it came to Paige. She even bordered on being *nice* to her on set.

'But how is Trina involved?' Amy asked.

'Well, she's behind it all. I mean, obviously I'm the one going out with him – he'd never have got back with her. But she knows him inside out and she's telling me exactly what to say and do to impress him. And it's totally working. Honestly, it's amazing.' She smiled. 'I swear I haven't even kissed him yet, and you should see the way he is with me. You should *hear* him! I never knew a guy could be that romantic, especially one like Scott, who has girls falling over him and doesn't even have to try.'

Rosay was speaking really fast and not meeting Amy's eyes.

'So how long has this been going on?'

'Well, the photos of me and him before Paige dumped him – they were a set-up, before any of this started. It's what gave Trina the idea. Frances got a PR agency to work on it for the launch of *Bandwagon*.'

'So that *was* you – that picture of the so-called Miss X with Scott?'

'Yeah, but it was just a friendly hug, you know. I think all I said first was "Hi, great to see you" and then I put my arms around him. I knew exactly where the cameras where and how to make it look worse without showing my face. But we weren't, you know, doing anything.'

Amy thought it sounded a bit like the picture of her and Josh.

'Then when all that was over and Paige publicly dumped him, I bumped into Scott in Monty's and we talked for hours.' She sighed. 'It's weird. I've known him for years and he's been out with both of my ex-flatmates, but it was like we suddenly, I don't know, *noticed* each other or something.' She swallowed hard. 'Er, I mean, *he* noticed *me*.'

Amy looked closely at her friend. 'Rosay, are you sure you know what you're doing?' She hesitated before adding, 'Because you sound a bit like you're into him, too.'

Rosay made a horrified face. 'Rubbish. I could never fall for someone like Scott! I am *done* with footballers.' She stared at her drink. 'But I'm glad it's convincing. So far, I've denied everything to the press, which Trina thinks makes Scott look a total idiot, because he's done the opposite. He's been spouting on about me to anyone who'll listen – hopefully except Paige.' She sighed. 'But I've decided it's time to be seen with him in public, and soon Trina and I can decide the best way to dump him for maximum heartbreak.' She gave a hollow laugh. 'Isn't it a great plan?'

Amy shook her head. 'I don't know. It all sounds a bit . . . horrible, playing with people's feelings like that.'

Rosay shook her head. 'It's not horrible *enough*. That's what he's done to everyone he's ever dated. Believe me, he deserves this. Trina said she knows some awful things about when he used to go out with –'

Amy's phone started ringing and she remembered too late that Rosay still had it.

'Claudette!' Rosay exclaimed, staring at Amy's caller display. 'Oh my God, I don't believe it!'

Amy tried to keep her voice even. 'Can I have my phone?'

She looked around, working out where she could take the call. How could she move away without making Rosay suspicious? 'I'll just go . . . over there, because . . .'

Rosay gasped. 'No, you won't! Because now I've worked out *exactly* what's going on with you! And *I'll* take the call, if you don't mind.'

Amy did mind. 'Rosay . . .' She reached for her phone, wishing she'd got it back sooner.

Rosay pulled away from her. 'Hi, Claudette? No, it's Rosay. Yes, she's with me. No, I won't put her on.' There was a pause. 'She didn't tell me anything. She didn't have to, because I know you, remember? I should have known it was something like this. I bet you've got her reporting gossip for you, now I'm not playing any more. Well, neither is she. So that's it. Goodbye.'

She hung up and nodded, satisfied, holding Amy's phone out to her. 'I'm right, aren't I?'

Looking at Amy seemed to give Rosay all the confirmation she needed.

'OK, well, you're going out with a millionaire boy wonder, so I know you're not doing it for money. Besides, you're too sweet for that. So how did she talk you into it? What's she got on you?'

Amy stared at her drink.

'Tell me, Amy,' Rosay commanded.

'A photo,' Amy mumbled. Her heart pounded, though it felt good to tell someone at last. 'Of me . . . with Josh.'

'Oh,' Rosay said. Her eyes widened in surprise. '*Oh*.'

'There was nothing going on,' Amy said quickly. 'It was like the one you told me about of you and Scott – it looked worse than it was. Some random person caught us on a phone camera and tried to sell the picture.' She looked at the ceiling, trying to stop the tears that threatened to fall as she thought about what would happen now. 'Claudette's made up a story to go with it. She says it won't only affect my relationship with Damien. It could be a scandal for your step-dad too, for employing Josh. And he might have to resign and . . . and Damien's career . . .' Amy stopped. She didn't want to think about it, let alone say it.

Rosay stared at her for a long moment. But she didn't seem remotely worried, which was weird.

'God, Amy, why didn't you tell me?' Rosay said at last.

'Claudette said she'd –'

'Yeah, yeah, I'm sure she threatened you good and proper. But still, you should have told me. If anyone can sort this out,

I can! Don't forget that my dad owns one of the biggest picture agencies in England, and I've got him wrapped round my little finger. I'll get him on the case.'

Amy tried to smile, but she was still worried. 'But it's no good – she's got that PR guy on her side. I know he works with your dad sometimes, but he's really close to Claudette.'

'You're right, he is.' Rosay smirked. 'In fact, that gives me an idea . . . Maybe Scott's not the only one we can play at his own game. Maybe we can get some evidence of Claudette and Spencer, you know, *together*. Let's see how *she* likes it! I have contacts in the pap world, you know. I could make this happen like – that!' She clicked her fingers.

'Do you really think there's something going on between Claudette and Spencer?' Amy still didn't think so, but she was starting to doubt that anything in this world was exactly how it seemed.

'Who cares? Since when has lack of truth stopped the gossip machine?' Rosay looked thoughtful. 'Listen, Amy, don't you worry about a thing. You keep doing your job at the television studio, make sure Spencer Greene doesn't suspect anything's wrong. I bet Claudette won't say anything – in fact, I bet she hasn't even told him exactly what's going on with you. She'll be hoping you get scared and go crawling back to her.'

Amy didn't say that she was already thinking of phoning Claudette to apologize.

'And leave it with me. Everything's going to be fine, I promise.' She gave Amy a bossy look. 'Now – it's time for phase three. Where does Asha live?'

Amy was startled by the sudden change of subject. 'With her uncle. Why?'

'What's the address?'

'It's in a text on my phone.' As Amy looked it up and told her, Rosay plucked her own phone out of her tiny clutch bag and repeated it into the mouthpiece.

Then she said to Amy, 'OK, there's a car waiting for you outside with strict orders to take you to Asha's house. She'll be there – there's no way that date with Josh ended anything other than disastrously. So. You're going to explain everything to her – and I mean *everything*! And you're not leaving until you two are friends again.'

'But she won't want to speak to me.' Amy panicked at the thought. 'Seriously, Rosay!'

'Rubbish! Is it any wonder she's getting upset with you when you're shutting her out of your life? You've got to tell your friends what's going on, Amy. That's what we're for!'

'But I can't speak to Asha *tonight*! At least let me leave it a few days and . . .'

Rosay shook her head firmly. 'No way! You're doing it right now! In fact . . .' She called Frankie over and whispered in his ear.

He smiled at Amy and said, 'Sure.'

Rosay said, 'Great. Frankie's escorting you to the car so that you can't escape. And I'm not hearing any arguments. Besides, you might want to go now anyway, because my date's arrived.'

Amy looked round. Scott White was striding towards them, leaving a trail of whispering, staring women in his wake. He acknowledged Amy briefly, but his eyes lit up when he saw Rosay. In an instant, his whole body language changed from 'total sex god' to 'nervous schoolboy'. He ran a hand through his famous haircut and hesitated before leaning in and kissing Rosay on the cheek. Rosay giggled. He touched her arm and said something. She blushed. He laced his fingers with hers and they didn't once take their eyes off each other.

Amy left Shadows with Frankie making sweet and funny small talk beside her. She tried not to worry about the conversation she was about to have, or the fact that Rosay didn't seem to be acting with Scott at all.

16

Rosay was right. It took some initial persuasion by Susi and half an hour of pleading by Amy, but Asha eventually agreed to talk to her. Susi left them to it, saying she needed an early night and she'd get all the details from her sister the next day. She'd been asked to go in early and spend the morning updating the supplier database while Asha manned the shop floor, but she said she could easily talk Mr Mishra into letting her and Asha take an extra-long lunch together.

Asha asked Amy a ton of questions, demanding to know every last detail of what had been going on, and Amy found herself blurting out everything, including the recent awkwardness between her and Damien, his proposal, the terrible GCSE results and the credit-card debt.

'You mean I've been madly jealous all this time and your life's actually a total mess?' Asha laughed. 'Wait till I tell Susi all of this. At least you've given us plenty to talk about tomorrow at lunch!'

Before long Asha was hugging Amy and saying she was sorry. She said she couldn't promise never to feel any more jealousy over Amy's glamorous life – were there any vacancies at *The Morning Show* for her, and could Amy get her into

Shadows or Monty's some time, please? But she'd definitely never let a boy come between them again. Especially not a total loser like Josh.

'Although I still think he's fit,' Asha added. 'And I did agree to go to the *Bandwagon* final party with him.'

'You're joking, Ash!'

She shrugged. 'Well, you know how lads always flock to girls with boyfriends? I thought I could use him to attract someone better! Also, I figure he owes me another A-list event.' She laughed. 'May as well make the most of it while he's still in with the right people. He's leaving his job, did you know?'

'No!' Amy said.

'Ha, I knew two weren't really that close! Not that anyone will believe it if the photo comes out. What are we going to do about that?'

Amy secretly glowed at the way Asha said 'we' – it was such a relief that the problem – among others – wasn't entirely hers any more. She couldn't believe she'd had all this bottled up inside for so long. It was like a huge weight had been lifted off her shoulders, even though she knew she still had to deal with it all. Not to mention telling Damien and her dad.

'Rosay's got contacts. She's sorting it out,' she told Asha.

And she tried hard to believe it, but for the whole of the next morning she was a nervous wreck, listening out for gossip on the set and using every spare minute to leaf through the latest newspapers and magazines, which had pictures of her being 'escorted out of Shadows by a staff member', but nothing more incriminating than that. At least she wouldn't have to explain this photo to Damien. He hadn't seemed to mind at all about her last-minute night out with Rosay and had been asleep when she'd got in. This morning they'd had a quiet ride in the car to work, with her almost dozing on Damien's shoulder.

Amy's interview on *The Morning Show* went brilliantly. She was almost starting to relax when she switched her phone on in the dressing room and found nine missed calls from unknown numbers, a message from her dad asking her to call, and a message from Susi and Asha saying her dad had called *them* and she really should call him. She nearly chewed her entire manicure off thinking about it.

Was this it? Had the photo got out? She'd heard all about the way the press hounded people in the midst of a scandal. And maybe her friends and family were trying to warn her – or they were being pursued too . . .

Her heart thumped as her phone rang again with another unknown number and she answered it.

It was Spencer, saying he'd been dying to reach her all morning, and he'd been asking Lauren to call her too. It turned out he'd received a flood of offers for her and went into dizzying detail about them all. He advised her to accept at least one of the requests for a magazine column – 'It needn't take up much of your time, Amy, and we can easily find a ghost writer for you if you prefer' – and to try to fit in the shopping centre opening in a month's time, plus a couple of charity events. 'And there's another proposal which I think you should seriously consider – that fitness DVD Frances mentioned a while ago – but I'll get back to you when I have firmer details. Plus the perfume people have been on to Miranda again,' he said. 'Can't you see if you can talk Damien into it? It could be very lucrative for both of you, and good for your profiles, but the deal is really for you as a couple. They really want to tap into the teenage market and you two would be perfect. It's an opportunity that won't be around forever either.'

Amy was pretty sure Damien wouldn't go for it, and he probably wouldn't be very impressed about her doing the other publicity things, either. That's if she could do them, what with going back to Stanleydale at the weekend.

'I'll speak to him,' she promised anyway.

'Good, you should. You're just such a hot couple right now – everyone wants to cash in,' Spencer said. 'And you're definitely rising as a star in your own right, Amy. If you carry on charming the nation like this, we'll both be able to retire soon!' He laughed.

Amy hoped this all meant she'd earn enough to cover her dad's credit-card bill. And then she worried again about the photo. If it got out, it would be an end to all the offers, she was sure. And Spencer really didn't seem to know about it, otherwise he surely would have mentioned it by now.

Amy almost considered asking him directly, but then he seemed so close to Claudette that he'd probably do anything that Claudette wanted, including releasing a damaging photo of Amy. How could she stop them?

Amy gripped the phone. Rosay's offer to play Claudette at her own game suddenly seemed tempting. Maybe she should tell Rosay to go ahead with starting a rumour about Spencer and Claudette.

'And another thing, Amy,' Spencer was saying, his voice warm. 'My little girl keeps nagging me to ask for a signed photo of you.'

'Oh, I didn't know you had a little girl.'

'Yes, and she's a huge fan of yours. I've got a girl and a boy. Molly's seven and Tom's four. My wife's good friends with Claudette, you know. Claudette used to live in the same town we do, in Essex. I still commute – I'm not a proper Londoner like her! But between you and me, I think she visits my office a lot to get that touch of home, even though she rarely comes back to Diston!' He laughed. 'Though she's there at the moment, of course. Anyway, Molly would be thrilled if you could sign a photo for her.'

'Oh my God, well, yes of course I will,' Amy stuttered, snapping back to reality. She couldn't believe she'd actually contemplated trying to spread a vicious rumour about Claudette and Spencer. He had a young family! And what about hurting the lovely Danny Harris? What was the *matter* with her?

'Great. Well, Lauren's still at lunch. When she gets back, I'll have her arrange a photo shoot. You need some press pictures anyway, and not just for Molly. It's Lauren's last day tomorrow – she's asked to leave a day early, so we don't have admin cover on Friday. But it's no problem. If she can't sort it out on time, I'll have Emily tell you the arrangements next week instead,' Spencer said.

'I'm going back to Stanleydale this weekend,' Amy said, realizing with a churn of her stomach that her summer in London really was nearly over. There were just days left.

That's if she was going home. Did she want to give up this life? It seemed like a crazy thing to do, in exchange for living with her parents in Stanleydale and going back to school.

'Really? Oh, what a shame. Still, I'm sure it's temporary. Who could resist the lure of this world? I know I can't! Well,

I've just had a thought. Would you like to come for dinner before you leave? My wife would love to meet you, and you'd make Molly's month!'

'Oh. That's kind of you, but I don't know . . .' Amy thought about how curious she was to see Claudette's hometown. Maybe she could even find out more about what Claudette was up to – something different that Rosay could use against her. 'Though it sounds great.'

'Great! How about tomorrow?'

'Oh, I can't. Damien's got a match.' And he was already descending into dark moods whenever Amy mentioned it.

'Of course, of course. Well, you'll probably be busy with the *Bandwagon* after-party on Friday, and then you're going back, is that right? Tell you what – why don't you come before the match and just have an early bite to eat with us? I'm off work tomorrow afternoon and Molly goes to bed at seven anyway. I can arrange a car for you, and my driver can take you back to Stadium Gardens in time for the game.'

'Er . . . OK. Sure.' It seemed impossible to turn down the offer, especially when Spencer could end up being the answer to her money worries.

'Good! Oh, and, Amy, well done for the way you've been reporting to Claudette. I know it was an unfortunate business with Marie Brown, and I did have some work to do to keep Johann and Kylie's party disaster out of the gossip columns. But you did the right thing.' Spencer hesitated. 'I wouldn't normally discuss other clients, but, well, Marie isn't a client. She approached me about going to the press and building a career for herself out of it, but frankly I don't think I can represent her. I think it'll pay to keep on the right side of

Frances Kemp, and we'll do well out of that revelation you made. Frances loves you, you know! You could really have a great career in television. Congratulations – it's going so well!'

Amy's stomach ached at the thought that her gossip had ruined Marie's chance and now Spencer was telling her she'd have a career out of it. She'd been enjoying working in television but she'd never thought of it as a long-term thing. Then again, with her GCSE results maybe she should give up on school altogether. Maybe she'd just tell everyone she'd changed her mind about what she wanted to do with her life. Would her mum and dad mind? And what would Damien say? He thought all the media stuff was a load of rubbish. But if she stayed in London, she could live with him – maybe even get engaged to him after all. Could her priorities really have changed this much in just four weeks? It seemed just about every thing else had.

When Spencer had gone, Amy thought for ages. She had to sort this mess out somehow. She had to work out what she really wanted, and then she had to tell the truth to people like Damien and her parents, and hope they'd understand.

She sent her dad another text stalling for time, and promised herself it would be the last one. Next time, she'd talk to him properly.

When Damien came home, they made pre-match pasta and chatted about nothing much. She decided not to tell him about the endorsement offers – it just wasn't the right time. He was in one of his subdued moods, probably worrying about the match again.

They settled down and watched the final heat of *Bandwagon*, which wasn't exactly ideal for cheering anyone up.

Paige Young forgot a complete verse of the Mariah Carey song and stood, frozen in the spotlight, horror-stricken. The camera panned over The Miss Exes and even Trina looked like she felt sorry for her. The Miss Exes won the heat despite a hefty sympathy vote for Paige. In the post-vote programme, Trina said she spoke on behalf of the whole group when she said they loved Paige and wished her well, despite having had some differences in the past.

When the interviewer turned to Paige for a reaction, she ripped off her microphone and stormed off the set shouting that she knew Trina was up to something and she didn't want any part in it. There was a stunned silence in the live studio for a few seconds before the interviewer turned professionally to Courtney and got her talking about her hopes and dreams and promising future as a singer, and how proud Steve was of her and how they were the perfect couple.

Amy laughed and nearly made a comment to Damien about Steve lapping up Lauren's attention at the launch party, but then she stopped herself quickly, remembering the fight that it had started. Maybe she should tell Damien now about the Josh thing, and everything – maybe it was time to come clean. After all, she'd felt so much better since telling her friends.

She glanced over at him, but he was asleep, snoring softly with his head on the arm of the sofa.

17

The next day, Amy got away from work much earlier than usual and found herself at home with lots of time to kill before Spencer's car was due to collect her and drive her to Essex. She spent ages choosing an outfit that would do for tea at Spencer's followed by an evening match, and eventually settled on a pair of Seven for All Mankind jeans, a floaty top from Kate Moss's Topshop range and a pair of sandals from her shoe spree at Office.

She thought about tonight's match, hoping she'd see Damien play this time. But when she'd tentatively asked him about it yesterday, he'd totally clammed up and acted all weird again. And she hadn't seen Damien all day – she'd been on a 'late' at the studio so she'd missed him in the morning, and Damien had texted her to say that Big Carl was keeping the whole team for talks until the match.

There was no sign of Paige cleaning outside her room, which made Amy breathe a small sigh of relief. She hadn't spoken to her properly since Tuesday and she really wasn't looking forward to the conversation about Rosay and Scott. Although maybe Paige wouldn't ask any more, now that she'd overheard Rosay on the phone talking to him.

Amy was just deciding which of her new bags to use when a message from her dad came through: 'We saw you on television yesterday. You look very healthy and happy but wrap up warmer or you'll catch a cold. Call us, Amy – if that envelope doesn't arrive tomorrow we'll have words with the school on Monday! Your mother sends love and misses you.'

Well, at least he didn't seem to expect a reply today. The searing guilt from thinking like this about talking to her dad made her cheeks feel hot, and she started to feel the pull of the shops. After all, she needed something new for the final *Bandwagon* party tomorrow, which was sure to be a glamorous affair, complete with photo calls and paps hanging around outside.

But Asha had made her promise the other day that she wouldn't do this any more – go shopping every time she felt stressed. And Amy had promised her that she wouldn't. It was simple. It was only shopping – how hard could it be not to do it?

Then again, tomorrow was a special occasion. She couldn't just wear any old thing. A quick trip to Orange County wouldn't hurt, and Asha didn't have to know about it.

She was on her way out when she remembered that she hadn't checked the gossip sites since yesterday. She'd almost forgotten to worry about the Josh thing today. But not quite. It was still there in the back of her mind, together with all the other worries she still had to sort out.

She turned back to look for Damien's laptop, but as she passed the open door to Paige's room Amy noticed her computer switched on in a corner of the room, a fancy football screensaver bouncing in Royal Boroughs colours across the monitor. Surely Paige wouldn't mind if Amy checked it quickly?

Amy crept into the room and sat on the office chair at Paige's tidy desk. She opened a web browser. She only had to type three letters of the main gossip site into the search box before the computer suggested the complete site name. Obviously it must be a site that Paige visited regularly too. Amy wondered if Paige had been checking for Scott gossip. She really wouldn't put it past Paige to cyber-stalk Scott.

The site was filled with pictures and stories. Amy scrolled through quickly. There was nothing about her, but towards the bottom of the page she spotted a grainy shot of Rosay leaving Shadows nightclub arm-in-arm with Scott. Amy wondered whether Paige had seen it. There was a link, so Amy clicked on it.

The page that opened was in Royal Boroughs colours and headed: *'My Secret Scandalous WAG Blog!'* Amy vaguely remembered Susi mentioning it.

It had the same photo of Rosay and Scott as the one on the other page. And she could see various mentions of Claudette, Courtney and some other girlfriends of Boroughs footballers.

Whose blog was this? Amy clicked on the profile information but it just said: *'I am someone in the KNOW! P.S. Nightclub promoters and fans of me, pleez leave me a comment with ur email addy and I will get back 2 u!!!'*

Amy frowned – it didn't mean much to her. She went back to the main page.

The post at the very top said: *'Watch this space for the JUICIEST stuff – yes, I've been holding out, but soon I can tell you EVERYTHING!'*

Below was a post about Claudette, which said, '*She's disappeared mysteriously to her hometown – probably having some secret plastic surgery at the Diston Clinic!!! Claudette could use a boob job, if you know what I mean!!!*' Then there was a huge photo of Claudette at a recent film premiere, not looking remotely in any need of surgery. The blog declared that her boob job would be '*a double surprise for hubby Danny!*' Amy stared at it, wondering if it could be true. She could somehow imagine it more easily than Claudette doing something kind and normal like visiting her mum and looking after her brother. It would be just like Claudette to keep her plastic surgery a secret – she'd probably tell everyone her increased chest was natural. And maybe the way Claudette could only use her phone at certain times was because she was in hospital? It would also explain why she hadn't wanted Danny to visit her.

Amy was just about to click the browser shut when something struck her as odd. The story about the boob job was the first bit of slightly negative gossip Amy had seen about Claudette. Ever.

Claudette prided herself on the way the devoted Spencer kept everything out of the papers and gossip columns. What was going on?

Amy decided to investigate further. She thought she'd start with a quick search to see whether there was really a Diston Clinic in Claudette's hometown, but as soon as she typed the first two letters into the toolbar, the search offered a strange completed term – a word Amy had never seen before. And something about it made Amy stop in her tracks.

'Diabulimia'.

And underneath were a list of similar searches, including 'diabulimia + safe', 'diabetic bulimia' and 'diabetic weight loss'.

Diabetic bulimia? Why was Paige reading about this stuff? Amy clicked on the top result.

When the page came up, she instantly forgot all about Claudette. She read page after page of information about an eating disorder that was 'on the increase' and was 'said to affect an incredibly high percentage of young women diagnosed with diabetes'. She didn't have to read long to find out that girls with diabetes found that skipping insulin was 'an incredibly effective way to lose weight and regain control over their lives'. '*When the focus is already so intensely on food intake, it's a simple step to take,*' she read. One of the other articles ended with the words 'complications include kidney damage, liver damage, blindness, coma and death'. *Death?* Amy stared at it in horror.

The voice from behind her made Amy jump a mile.

'What are you reading?'

Paige stood by her bed, unsmiling, looking tired and thin. *Incredibly* thin. Amy couldn't believe she'd never thought of it before. But Paige had talked a lot recently about eating and drinking whatever she liked – it wasn't like she'd shown any signs of an eating disorder.

Except that she *had* talked a lot about food. And not needing insulin so much any more, and regaining control over her life.

'I was just . . . checking some blogs,' Amy said. She wondered whether she should tell the truth about what she'd read, and confront Paige about it. It was serious stuff. 'I'm really

188

sorry. I meant to use Damien's laptop, but I saw your computer on and didn't think you'd mind. I know I should have asked –'

'No, it's fine, don't worry. Are they gossip sites? Is there anything about Scott today?' Paige moved closer, looking straight at the screen and taking the decision out of Amy's hands. The diabulimia site filled the screen. 'Oh. I see.'

Amy bit her lip.

'Why on earth would you read about that, Amy? How did you hear about it? I found out through trial and error, myself. Mostly error.' She gave a hollow laugh and looked Amy up and down, not all that kindly. 'But you can't do it, you know. You need to be diabetic for it to work. I don't blame you for wanting to, though. It really works.'

Amy decided to ignore the jibe. She didn't ever want to be as thin as her flatmate anyway. She looked ill. She *was* ill.

'It's fantastic,' her flatmate continued. 'You don't even need the kind of willpower you need for anorexia.'

She was making it sound like anorexia was a *good* thing.

'Paige, have you read it properly? Did you see the side effects?'

'It doesn't apply to me.' Paige waved her hand dismissively. 'I've looked into it and sometimes I chat online to other girls who do it. We have a kind of support network going, and we're very careful. We do it just enough, you know, so that it's safe but we keep our health. We're not stupid.'

Amy looked at her. 'But you don't *look* healthy, Paige,' she said carefully.

'Oh, now you sound like Kylie!' Paige laughed. 'Honestly, it's really sweet of you to worry, but I'm fine.'

'Does Kylie know about this?'

'Of course! Well, more or less – she got suspicious a while ago. I asked her not to tell anyone what I was doing, and she said she wouldn't as long as I stopped doing it. So it's fine.'

'But you didn't stop doing it,' Amy said with certainty, 'did you?'

'Amy, I swear, I'm in control. In fact, I don't think I've ever been so in control in my life. It's brilliant!' She paused. 'You won't tell anyone either, will you?' It sounded more like a statement than a question. She gazed at Amy with wide, heavy-lidded eyes.

'Are you going to stop doing it?'

Paige laughed. 'You and Kylie are so alike sometimes. Now. Can I have my computer back? I'd like to see if there's anything about Rosay and Scott. Did she tell you anything? Because I overheard her on the phone to him, you know, and I think they really are together, no matter how much she denies it. She probably told you but I kind of lost it at Lemon Aid on Tuesday and had a real go at her. But she deserves it – I can't believe she'd do this to me! What did she tell you about it? She's been avoiding me as much as possible at the studio.'

'Um,' Amy said, feeling weird about the change of subject, and the fact that Paige hadn't promised anything. 'I think . . . You know, Rosay's not trying to hurt you. But about the . . . insulin thing, Paige. Have you spoken to a doctor about it?'

'Yes, yes! Don't worry. I speak to doctors all the time. Too much. Listen, will you drop it, because you're starting to upset me. I'm not sure I want to live with a complete nag, if you know what I mean. I know you're leaving soon, but if you go on like this, it might have to be sooner.'

Amy stared at her. Paige always gave the impression of being easy-going, but she wasn't really. Not at all. She wanted everything exactly her own way.

And was she *threatening* her now?

Paige continued as if she hadn't said anything unusual. 'So tell me more about Rosay and Scott,' she said breezily.

Amy sighed. 'I told you everything I know. Really,' she lied. It was all going to come out soon anyway, now that Rosay was being seen with Scott in public. Amy didn't see why she had to get involved.

Suddenly she felt as tired as Paige looked. She wished she could skip the whole Spencer thing and just be at Stadium Gardens, cheering for her boyfriend as he set up a brilliant goal in his Premiership debut.

'I'm not going to the match tonight,' Paige said as if she'd read her mind. 'I need my beauty sleep for the final tomorrow. Trina's not going either, and I will not be beaten by *her*.'

Amy glanced at the clock on the computer. She'd spent ages reading the sites, and didn't really have time for shopping now. Though Asha would say it was just as well. 'OK, well, I have to go out, so good luck for tomorrow,' she told Paige. 'And see you then. Sorry about using your computer.'

She grabbed her bag and left quickly, still seriously worried about Paige, but also not wanting to stick around to witness her reaction when she saw the picture of Rosay with Scott outside Shadows.

18

As the sleek black car sent by Spencer cruised through the suburban streets of Diston, Amy managed to put Paige out of her mind and started worrying about Claudette instead. It hadn't taken them long, even in afternoon city traffic, to reach this town, and Amy could see why Spencer commuted to work. But she wondered why Claudette didn't go home more often, and why, according to Danny, she rarely took her husband with her. Unless it was all to do with secret plastic surgery – maybe Claudette had had other treatments at the clinic?

Then Amy wondered if they could be driving past Claudette's house. It was obvious that Diston was a town of two halves. First the car twisted through narrow streets with rows of terraced houses, many of which were boarded up or run down and scruffy-looking. And then, after a long stretch of dual carriageway, they turned into a wide road that reminded Amy of the boulevards of Paris. The houses here were far away from each other, and had lots of parts to them, like gables, carports and extensions. They were surrounded large, leafy gardens.

The car pulled into one of the larger houses and pulled to a stop on a gravel path.

Immediately, a little girl with elaborate cornrows in her hair appeared at the side of the car and waved at the dark-tinted window as the driver opened Amy's door and waited politely.

'Hi, I'm Amy,' Amy said as she climbed out of the car.

The little girl smiled, showing her missing front teeth and the cutest dimples Amy had ever seen. Then she giggled. 'I *know*!'

'And are you Miss Greene?'

'Not really! I'm just Molly!' The girl nearly doubled up with laughter.

Spencer appeared at the doorway and said sternly, 'Molly, what did I tell you about not running out on to the driveway?' His voice softened. 'Come on, inside!' He turned to Amy. 'Great to see you! Well, you've already met Molly. And this is my wife Dee, and Tom, the baby of the family.'

A strikingly willowy woman appeared behind Spencer with a large red-faced boy in her arms. 'Hi, Amy,' she said, wincing as Tom pulled at her hair. 'I'm really glad you could come – Molly's so happy. I've heard a lot about you from Spencer, and Claudette too.' Tom screamed in her ear and Amy could see Dee was trying not to react. 'Look, I'm afraid we're in the middle of a major tantrum here. So much for Terrible Twos – he's four and he still hasn't grown out of it! I'm going to put him in his room so he can calm down.' The wailing got louder. 'Yes, I am! And Spencer's putting the tea together – it's only simple I'm afraid, but . . . anyway, maybe you could wait in there . . .' She pointed to a large room where a television was blaring CBeebies.

'Can I take Amy to my room instead?' Molly said, jumping up and down. 'Can I show her my *High School Musical* dressing-up clothes and Hannah Montana microphone?'

Dee rolled her eyes. 'I'm sure Amy would prefer to sit in there.'

'Oh no, I don't mind,' Amy smiled. She was warming to Molly's enthusiasm.

The little girl chattered non-stop all the way up the stairs and into her large bedroom, which was top-to-toe pink and contained a mixture of Hannah Montana, *High School Musical* and Royal Boroughs posters, toys and bedding.

'You can sit there if you like,' Molly said, pointing to an *HSM* inflatable chair in a corner of the room. 'And I'll show you my things. Would you like to see my dressing-up clothes?'

'OK,' said Amy, suddenly really enjoying herself. It felt refreshing and cosy to be in a family home again – even if it was ten times the size of the one she'd grown up in.

Molly opened a wardrobe the size of Paige's, filled with cheerleading outfits and princess and fairy dresses, hung neatly on hangers and colour-coded so that they ran left to right in a rainbow-like spectrum.

'Here they are. I don't want to try them on now. I put my best clothes on because you were coming,' Molly explained. She pointed to her cute tweed pinafore dress, which looked to Amy like miniature Burberry. 'But I've got lots of pictures of me being a princess. Want to see them?'

'Sure.' Amy smiled.

Molly switched on a gorgeous pink laptop in the corner of her room – and Amy thought about how she'd never had anything like *that* in her room at home either – and clicked expertly around until she brought up a slideshow of photos of herself dressed up as Gabriella, complete with microphone.

'I can do all the words,' she said. 'To all the songs from all the films, not just the first one.'

'Wow,' Amy said, and she wasn't just pretending to be impressed.

'Yeah, I can. I'll sing one for you in a minute if you like. You know Auntie Claudette?'

Amy nodded, although it felt really weird to hear someone like Claudette described as 'Auntie'.

'She said she can maybe take me to see the next film that has Corbin Bleu in it the first day it ever comes out! Auntie Claudette is *amazing*!'

Amy wondered if they were talking about the same Claudette. 'Wow, that's nice of her to take you to a premiere.'

'I *know*! She's so nice and so beautiful – just like you!' Molly beamed, showing her gappy teeth. 'I want to be like you or her when I grow up. Do you want to see pictures of Auntie Claudette with my mum when they were young?'

'Oh. Yeah, OK.' Amy was suddenly overcome with curiosity about what Claudette might have been like as a child. Was she drop-dead glamorous then? Probably, Amy decided. She probably grew up like Molly, as close to being an actual princess as Amy could imagine.

She moved over and stood behind Molly as the little girl clicked through various screens and on to a site called *YourPhotosSafeWithUs.com*.

'Mummy and Daddy keep some of their favourite pictures on a special webby-site so we can't lose them in a fire,' she explained. 'But it's all a-crypted, so no one else would ever, ever be able to see. I'm allowed to look, though, because I love the photos of baby me and baby Tom. It's easy, I have a bookmark here.' She showed Amy the site's login screen, which displayed the username 'SGreeneDGreene'.

'And I just have to write in "MollyTom1234". I can spell it all by myself, easy peasy.' Molly typed it in and a series of folders popped up.

Amy wondered if she should ask Spencer about looking at the photos if they were private family ones, but then she didn't want Claudette to hear about it. In the end curiosity got the better of her, and she decided just to tell him that he might want to update the password now Molly had told her what it was.

Molly opened a folder named after her and spent ages chatting to Amy about each cute picture. Then she opened the one labelled 'Tom – baby photos'.

'This one has Auntie Claudette in it! She met Mummy in hospital and they made friends,' Molly was explaining, bringing up a photo of a happy-but-tired Dee holding a tiny baby in her arms. 'That's Tom. He screamed a bit less then, but only a bit, and only because he wasn't at home yet so it was quiet.' She rolled her eyes, looking just like her mother. 'And this one has Mummy with Auntie Claudette and her little brother George. I'm not a-sposed to show anyone these photos, you know, but you're special and I know you'd like them.' She smiled. 'And anyway, you're Auntie Claudette's friend. Mummy said so.'

Amy tried to smile at that, but she couldn't. Instead she looked at the picture, and then she stifled a gasp and looked again.

There was Dee with Tom again, clearly in a hospital ward.

And next to her was an extremely tired-looking, make-up-free, entirely unglamorous but still recognizable Claudette, also holding a tiny baby in her arms.

'George and Tom are like twins, except with different mummies,' Molly said. Then she frowned. 'I mean, they have the same birthday. I think that's why Mummy made friends with Auntie Claudette, because my brother and Auntie Claudette's brother are twins. I wish I was a twin. Even though George and Tom sometimes hit each other at nursery, Mummy said.'

'But . . .' Amy was sure this couldn't be what it looked like. 'Where's George's mummy?' she asked, not quite believing she was having this conversation with a seven-year-old.

'Oh, she's at home with George and Auntie Claudette. They live in a little house on the other side of town, though Auntie Claudette is usually in London,' Molly said. 'But George's mummy has broken her leg and can't move much and Auntie Claudette is looking after them for a bit because she's so kind. Oh, wait, do you mean in the pictures?' She looked confused. 'She wasn't there. I've got a photo of her, though. Wait – I'll find it.' She clicked past another photo of Claudette and Dee holding babies, with similar tired, proud expressions on their faces, although Claudette looked about ten years younger than Dee.

'I think Auntie Claudette stayed in the hospital with her baby brother. I didn't do that with Tom – no one even asked me to, though I think I would have said no! But maybe it's because I was so little.' Molly shrugged and scrolled through the photos, chatting away. And Amy kept a smile on her face, but she was completely distracted.

Molly's explanations made no sense. And the photos couldn't lie.

Claudette had a baby. No, she had a four-year-old – a boy she described as her brother to everyone. Maybe everyone including Danny Harris, the footballer she'd married two years ago. Amy thought about everything Danny had said to her, and it really did seem that way.

Maybe even Danny didn't know.

Amy made it through the rest of the afternoon at Spencer's by smiling politely and pretending everything was fine, even though her mind was reeling with theories about what she'd discovered.

Molly had said the babies were twins. For a moment Amy wondered whether this could mean that Spencer was the father, and the rumours she'd heard about Spencer and Claudette were true. But it made no sense – what about Dee? Amy watched as Spencer and his wife wrestled with their kids and smiled at each other, looking like a wonderful couple, and she quickly dismissed that crazy idea.

Anyway, when Amy thought about it, the way Spencer acted with Claudette was protective and fatherly, as if he was looking after her. Maybe Spencer and Dee had felt sorry for the teenage mum they met in hospital. Perhaps they wanted to help Claudette protect her secret now that her life had taken a different turn, and Spencer was just the person to do it.

When Amy said goodbye, Molly gave her a big hug and told her to come back again soon. Spencer had to go and put Tom to bed, but Dee and Molly stood and waved Amy off as the car swept away from the grand property, heading towards the smaller houses on the other side of town. Amy realized it was probably the area Claudette had grown up in, if what Molly said was true. She gazed out of the window, half expecting to see Claudette holding a pre-schooler's hand, or pushing a swing in the playground – an image that would have seemed impossible a few hours ago.

Then Amy's thoughts took a different direction. She considered all the time she'd spent worrying herself sick about the Josh photo getting out, and the way Claudette's threats had totally changed her life and her relationships with friends, and with Damien. She thought about the horrible way Claudette called her 'baby' and made her feel small and useless. Suddenly she was filled with anger. Claudette's secret was much more scandalous than an altered photo of Amy in a kiss that hadn't even happened. Claudette's secret could threaten her marriage and her status – and the papers would *love* it!

Before she could think about it any more, or lose her nerve, she picked up the phone and dialled Claudette's number.

'Baby!' Claudette answered, making Amy's blood boil. 'I thought I'd never hear from you again! I was just about to release that photo into the wild, you know, but I thought I'd give you one more day. I knew you'd come crawling back to me!'

'Claudette,' Amy said, trying to keep her voice even through her anger. 'Don't call me *baby*.' She piled as much meaning as possible into the final word.

Claudette laughed lightly but she sounded distracted. Amy made out a screaming noise in the background and it occurred to her that she'd heard the sound in several previous conversations between them. But she recognized it now. It sounded a lot like when Spencer's son Tom was having a tantrum.

'Is that George?' Amy asked, hoping her voice didn't sound like it was shaking.

'Yes! I keep thinking he's gone for the night and then he wakes up crying minutes later –' Claudette stopped. 'Hold on, what do you know about my brother?'

'Nothing,' Amy said, as the crying died down. 'I don't know anything about your brother. Because I don't think you *have* a brother.' She took a deep breath. 'You have a son.'

The silence then seemed to go on forever.

Claudette's voice wavered. 'Amy, have you lost your mind? Honestly, I do worry about you sometimes.' There was a pause in which neither of them spoke. 'OK, I get it, what has Trina been saying? You were supposed to report everything Trina said straight to me! Bloody Rosay, interfering like that.' She took a deep breath. 'Trina *lies*, Amy! She makes stuff up! Anyway, she was supposed to stay away! She wasn't supposed to come back from Brazil! No one even *warned* me she was coming, and I worked so hard at gossip control. And I haven't managed to dig up a single thing on her – not a thing! It's like she really is a saint now, and I know that can't be true.' She paused, as if she was getting herself together. 'What exactly did that *liar* say?'

'Trina didn't say anything, Claudette,' Amy said calmly, feeling more and more confident. 'And don't try to get out of this because I know it's true. I even have proof, and unlike yours mine is *genuine.*'

'Amy,' Claudette said with a rising note of panic. 'Amy, who have you told? You haven't . . . you haven't said anything about this to Danny, have you?'

'I haven't told anyone.'

Claudette breathed out. 'Of course, because it's clearly nonsense,' she said slowly. 'Everyone knows George is my brother. What kind of "proof" could you possibly have?'

'Well,' said Amy, 'I have access to a photo.'

'Trina has a photo?' Claudette's voice was tiny. 'Wait, what sort of photo?'

'A photo of you in hospital, holding a newborn baby.' Amy waited a second to let it sink in. 'It looks pretty obvious the baby's yours, Claudette.'

'I don't believe you. That's impossible!'

'Maybe not.'

There was another silence. Then Claudette sounded defeated. 'OK, so you know George is mine and you have evidence. So what do you want from me?' The last bit was exactly what Amy herself had said all those days ago, when Claudette had threatened *her*.

And Amy couldn't believe Claudette had actually just admitted the truth. She realized with a start that this was what it had all been about – the way Claudette had bribed Rosay, and then her. The close relationship with Spencer, who was obviously helping her cover it up. The lack of negative publicity. Claudette had been carefully protecting her secret – and it must have been an incredibly stressful full-time job.

Especially because it sounded like Trina knew something about it all, and Claudette had guessed that. It explained why she seemed so intent on getting rid of Trina.

And no wonder Claudette was holding on to the photo of Amy and Josh. She needed it to get Amy to listen out for gossip – but she also needed it in case Amy heard anything. Claudette had said, 'Everyone trusts you, Amy'. If she *had* heard something from Trina, Claudette would have used the photo to make Amy publicly back up claims that Trina was talking nonsense, or something similar.

But now Amy had a photo too.

Claudette had made Amy – and so many others – feel terrible, and now Amy could do the same to her. And she could ruin Claudette's life in one phone call – two, if you counted asking Rosay for her dad's phone number. All she had to do was call Matt Sands and tell him how to access the photos. After that, she was sure the media circus would start in an instant.

But she couldn't. It would be wrong. What about little Molly, who had been so sweet and trusting – what if she got blamed for showing Amy the photo? What about Claudette's mother, who was bringing up George as her own son? What about George himself? How would this change his little life?

Claudette's voice rose, as if she sensed Amy's hesitation. 'You can't do this to me, you know. I'm in control here. I'll get to you first, and you'll be sorry.'

Claudette deserved this, Amy thought. She was still threatening her, even now!

And revealing this story could solve quite a few of her problems. Money, for one. Hadn't Claudette herself said that the only way to get past Spencer was with a big-money scandal? This kind of revelation about an England player's wife had to be worth a lot. How much money would Amy get from being its source?

Enough to completely cover her dad's credit-card bill? Probably.

'Amy? Are you there? Did you hear me? Aren't you worried

that I'll get to you first? And your friends! I can get to all of you!'

'No, not really,' Amy said truthfully. 'I don't think you'd dare. Not now.'

Sure enough, all the confidence drained from Claudette's voice. 'So tell me what you want from me!'

'Nothing. I want nothing more to do with you, Claudette.'

Amy's hand shook as she hung up.

19

Amy arrived at Stadium Gardens flustered and ten minutes late, her head crammed with questions and problems. Had she done the right thing about the Claudette scandal? Then there was Paige's secret, which seemed too dangerous to keep. And, at the back of her mind, her own worries lurked – all the stuff she hadn't yet told her dad. Or Damien.

It felt like a huge mess. She was going to have to deal with it all sooner rather than later, especially the things that Rosay, Asha and Susi now knew.

She thought she should probably sleep on it, and decide what to do in the morning, if there was time before all the madness of being on *The Morning Show* started. But, right now, there was a match to watch.

The box at Stadium Gardens was fairly quiet, with many of the wives and girlfriends gearing up for *Bandwagon* the next day. Even those who weren't starring in it had been invited to the after-show party, which was sure to be a grand affair, and there had been general murmurings about extra facials and spa sessions and early nights.

Amy saw Rosay sitting on her own at the far end. She sat down next to her, immediately scouring the pitch for Damien.

'He's not playing,' Rosay said, watching her. 'Neither is Scott.'

'Oh. Are you sure?'

'Yes.' Rosay frowned, looking utterly miserable.

'So are they on the bench?'

'I don't think so.' Rosay sighed. 'My step-dad's been on the warpath lately, but I've ignored him as usual. But on the way here, my driver had this phone-in on the radio. And I heard all these guys moaning about the Boroughs' manager letting personal feelings get in the way of football.' She gulped. 'All the callers were livid, but that's not going to make any difference. Not if Carlo has issues with him. He's been dropped.'

Amy's heart thumped. What was going on? 'Damien's been dropped?'

'I meant Scott,' Rosay said, and Amy tried not to breathe a sigh of relief.

'No way! That has to be rubbish. Isn't Scott a top goal-scorer?'

'Yeah. But my step-dad always says there's more to it than that. I've heard him loads of times, complaining that Scott's not a team player. Carlo's never really liked him, but he gets a lot of pressure from the chairman to play him, because Scott's a crowd-pleaser.'

'Then why . . . ?'

'Because of me, Amy!' Rosay looked like she was trying not to cry. 'Because I let the rumours get out. And I think Carlo's gone crazy! I knew he'd be upset but I didn't think he'd do anything like that! Refusing to play his best striker like this – it's madness!' Rosay stared at the pitch. 'Although the radio presenters didn't say anything about me. They said that Scott has been off his game. Which has kind of been true . . . Oh God, what if it's my fault! Because of what I'm doing to him!'

A chant lifted from the away side of the crowd: 'Watch out, watch out, Scott White's about!'

Rosay covered her eyes with her hand. 'And that is *not* going to help,' she moaned.

Amy spotted Big Carl at the side of the pitch, pretending to ignore the chants but getting increasingly heated with his shouting at the players.

'Trina's going to love this!' Courtney said loudly to her sister at the other side of the box. 'She'll be in such a good mood about all the Scott-bashing – now I'm even more certain we'll beat Paige tomorrow!'

She laughed hard until her sister, who'd come in matching clothes again, hit her arm and said, 'Ssh, you sound like a proper mentalist.'

'Don't speak to me like that – I'm a star in the making!' Courtney laughed again and crooned '*Scott White is a Creep*'. Then she called over, 'Isn't that right, Rosay? Trina told me what you pair were up to! Fan-bloody-tastic, I say! It's about time footballers learnt they can't just get away with everything they want. Course, my Steve's not like that.'

'Not *much*!' her sister snorted.

'Who asked you, anyway? You're lucky I still talk to you, now I'm a rising *star*!'

As the sisters kept bickering, Amy nudged Rosay. 'She's got a point, though,' she said. 'What do you care if Scott gets dropped? Weren't you about to dump him – and didn't you say that wasn't even horrible *enough*?'

Rosay gave her a look that was pure misery. 'Bloody hell,' she said very quietly. 'I can't pretend any more.' She sighed. 'Amy, I am *madly* in love with Scott. I have never felt like this before for anyone, not even Marc, I swear. It's the works – I can't eat, I can't sleep, I can't breathe. I think about him all the time.' She put her head in her hands. 'Trina's going to kill me, Carlo's going to disown me, and that's not even the reason I'm in big, big trouble.'

Amy and Rosay watched the rest of the game in silence, as Steve let in three goals in quick succession and even Courtney stopped smiling. Royal Boroughs lost 3–0 and, as Rosay suspected, there was no sign of Scott on the pitch or on the subs bench. There was no sign of Damien, either.

The girls trooped out and Courtney's sister tried desperately to cheer everyone up. She suggested that they all go for post-match drinks without the lads. 'They're all going to be a mopey bunch of miseries and who needs that the night before your big day?' she argued.

Amy sent a quick message to Damien to say she'd see him later, and followed the girls to dinner in a cosy French restaurant where they sat around looking as mournful as the lads probably did, even though Courtney's sister kept trying to build up enthusiasm for the *Bandwagon* final.

As they left, Courtney put her arm around her sister and said miserably, 'Thanks, hun, you can really be OK sometimes after all.'

Rosay asked Amy to wait for her a minute as the sisters got in a taxi together. Then she said, 'Please don't tell anyone what I told you. Oh, which reminds me. I've been meaning to tell you something but I got so distracted with Scott and . . .' She went into a daydream.

'What, Rosay?'

'Oh, sorry. It's about the photo. You know, the one of you and Josh outside that restaurant? I asked my dad to put out feelers and he did – he's very good. Knows everyone in the business. And guess what?'

'What?'

'It's nothing. The photo, I mean. Dad's seen it. Apparently it looks completely innocent. It looks like Josh gave you a friendly kiss on the cheek.'

'He did!'

Rosay smiled knowingly. 'They would have had a job talking that up. No one would have bought it.'

'You're joking!'

'I'm not. I told you that you should have asked me sooner. Claudette stitched you up, Amy.' Rosay smirked. 'Don't worry. I'm sure we'll find a way to get our own back on her.'

Amy crept into the flat, knowing that Paige was asleep. But the whole of Spooky Towers was eerily quiet anyway, and there was no sign of Damien. He'd left his laptop on the coffee table by the sofa, though, with the lid open, so it looked like he'd been home. Weird. Had he come home and then gone to Monty's, or somewhere like that? She checked her phone, but there was no message from him. She went to her room to kick her shoes off as she tapped in a message asking him where he was.

Then she froze. There was a note on her pillow, just like the ones Damien used to leave on the fridge for her back at Caseydene.

Except that this one wasn't friendly.

The writing was a scrawl, as if he'd written it in a hurry. Or as if he was really angry when he wrote it.

It said: 'Amy. Am staying away for a few days to get my head together. At least now I know the score. Goodbye.'

There were no kisses, no 'love from Damien'. Amy's stomach lurched as she stared at the note in confusion. Damien was going away for *a few days*? But Amy only had another full day in London herself!

She tried to call Damien but it went to voicemail. She started typing him another text but she didn't know what to say. What was going on? Why did Damien need to *get his head together*? She knew now that this couldn't be about the Josh thing. She couldn't believe she'd worried so much for no reason. But what *was* it about?

Something made her go back to the laptop. Other than the note, it was the only thing that seemed out of place in the spotless flat. She'd never seen it on the coffee table before.

She wiggled the mouse and the screen instantly lit up with the blog page she'd been looking up earlier on Paige's computer: *My Secret Scandalous WAG Blog!*

Amy noticed immediately that it had been updated. She looked closer.

There were no photos but Amy's name jumped out at her over and over again. The latest post was entirely about Amy: how Amy had run up a huge credit-card bill, how Amy had practically failed her GCSEs and hadn't told her parents, how Amy had struggled to hide a photo of herself and Josh kissing, and, almost worse than that . . . how Amy wanted to turn down Damien's proposal of marriage, but didn't know how.

'*Poor little Amy. Don't we wish we all had "problems" like these!*' the blogger had sneered. '*All she has to do is marry Damien and use his money to pay off the debt! Then she can have that fit student as a bit on the side, and as for the exams . . . well, be honest, girls, would you really care? I know I wouldn't! She has it MADE! I wish I was Amy Thornton!!!*'

Amy wanted to shut her eyes and pretend the words weren't there, but she forced herself to read it all again, although after the first three words she felt like smashing the laptop to pieces.

But even if she did that, it wouldn't make any difference. It was there, and by tomorrow it would be everywhere. And even if it wasn't – even if she could stop it somehow – it was too late.

Damien had obviously seen it.

Who could have done this to her?

Amy read it again. Who even *knew* this stuff about her?

She narrowed it down to a list of three, but it only made her feel a million times worse. The list went: Rosay, Susi and Asha. It made no sense, but there it was. It was impossible, though! Her friends would never want to hurt her. But maybe . . . maybe someone had got to one of them somehow?

Then she thought about the people who definitely *would* want to hurt her. Amy had never had enemies before she came to London, but now she could list at least three people who had it in for her.

Firstly, there was Paige. When Amy glanced at the blog again, she saw an icon in the top left-hand corner that said: 'User=PaigeLovesScotty'. So Paige was logged in on Damien's computer. It must have been her who had shown Damien the blog. Maybe she thought it was a way of getting Amy off her back now that Amy knew her secret. But she couldn't have written it – could she?

Then there was Marie Brown. Amy had even admitted to her that she was responsible for what happened with Will. Maybe the sprinkler incident hadn't been enough for Marie – or maybe she'd decided that Kylie really wasn't the one she wanted to get revenge on after all. But how could she have found out all this information about Amy?

And lastly, most obviously, there was Claudette. Claudette, who had blackmailed Amy over an innocent photo, and said that she – and Spencer – were experts at digging up dirt and using it wisely.

But Claudette should be scared of Amy right now. And Spencer had been so friendly. She'd been to his house and met his wife and kids! Could he really turn on her like this?

She didn't know what to do. It turned out she had at least three enemies, and maybe she couldn't trust any of her friends. There was blog post online and it was full of terrible things about her. And they were all true.

But – worst of all – Damien had left her.

20

Amy slept fitfully, worrying about everything but not making any decisions. She was awake well before she was due to leave, even though it was an 'early' day: her last interview with Julia Lightman. She almost wanted to give up on the whole thing, but she needed the money. And maybe she'd find time to speak to Rosay and find out whether she knew anything.

She hesitated outside Paige's bedroom door, wondering whether to wake up her flatmate and find out what exactly had happened with Damien last night. But then she remembered how tired Paige had been, and Paige wasn't due at the studio for another couple of hours. She should let her sleep.

She checked outside in case Damien's car was waiting for her at the usual time, but it wasn't, of course. Her heart felt heavy as she rang a taxi to take her to the studio. Then she remembered that he would definitely be up already. She tried his phone five times, which was pretty useless really since his phone was obviously turned off, or he was rejecting her calls.

All morning at the studios, Amy was waiting for people to look at her strangely or talk about breaking news from the blog. But everything went on exactly as normal. She held her breath for Julia Lightman's non-scripted questions, half-expecting something like, *You hid your GCSE results from your family and Damien – what was that like for you?* But instead, she was asked some easy questions about today's final and what she thought the girls would be wearing to the after-party. Amy managed to smile and chatter away about fashion while her insides churned.

After the interview, she went back to her dressing room to try ringing Damien again, which was even more pointless than before as he would be at training now. But there was nothing else she wanted to do.

As she picked up her phone, it rang. Was this it? Had her story gone public? In her panic, she couldn't even bring herself to look at the caller display. She answered the phone with her heart in her mouth.

'Hi, Amy! So did you see it?' came a voice. It was female and chirpy, and vaguely familiar. 'Was it weird to see your secrets splashed all over my blog?'

Amy's stomach turned over. 'What? Who is this?'

'Only the next Victoria Beckham or Coleen Rooney!' The girl laughed. Then she said more seriously, 'Oh, of course you don't recognize me. You think I'm a total nobody. I saw it in your eyes, even before you said anything.' She sounded bitter. 'Well, you're wrong. Because I've done it. I'm in! I'm snaring myself a footballer! And I certainly won't mind being called a WAG!'

Realization swept over Amy. 'Oh my God! Lauren?'

'Yeah, who else?' The voice – Lauren, Spencer's assistant – gave a dry laugh. 'My book said if you want to be a WAG, you have to be prepared to get a bit devious and think on your feet.

"*Plenty of people want what you want. You have to use tricks to beat them to it.*" So that's what I've done.'

Amy felt sick. She'd been wrong not to report Lauren before. 'You mean the blog?' she asked. 'Did *you* write that?'

'Yep, that's me! I get loads of hits, you know. I knew I was getting famous when Paige Young started emailing me after my first Scott White piece! Though I did chat to her at the party as well. She's totally nice, unlike *some* WAGs.' She tutted. 'You know, I started the blog so that promoters might put me on their lists to get into the exclusive clubs and stuff. But it didn't exactly work.' She sighed. 'Maybe because I didn't know any proper gossip. I was kind of, you know, making it up, to be honest, from bits and pieces I got at the office. Like, I knew that Claudette was away but I didn't know why. It was fun to make guesses, though. Don't you think she could do with a boob job?'

She laughed, but Amy didn't answer.

'Some of it was true, of course. Like the thing Scott White said about Rosay. I heard that at the party you invited me to.'

'I didn't invite you,' Amy couldn't stop herself blurting out. 'You stole my invitation. And I didn't report you!'

'Oh, aren't you generous,' said Lauren, her voice full of sarcasm.

Amy frowned. 'I don't get it. Why would you do this to me?'

'Do what? Post things that are *true*?'

Lauren was making Amy want to scream! 'But how . . . how could you even know those things? Paige didn't know –'

'No, she didn't! Poor her, with a flatmate who thinks she's all that, and tells her nothing. Anyway, I have other sources.'

She laughed. 'Coffee Coffee at lunchtime is *the* place to spot celebrities, though I don't always manage it. But on Wednesday I discovered the next best thing. Celebrity gossip!' She raised her voice. 'Your northern friends talk so *loudly* – don't they care about your privacy? Some friends! Though one of them shushed the other one a few times, but I still heard every word of what they were talking about. Or rather, *who*. You, Amy. It was gold dust gossip! I knew it would come in useful.'

Amy's heart raced. It was true, Asha did have a habit of talking loudly in public. And she'd had a lot to tell Susi on the day after Lemon Aid, and Amy knew they'd gone for lunch together. Her heart sank.

'What do you mean, "come in useful"?' Amy said dully. Lauren had posted it now. The damage was done. Why were they even having this conversation?

'I mean, because I'm holding it over you. You know, like a threat. The post is friends-only, as I'm sure you noticed.' She sighed. 'Paige is *such* a good friend. Well, and kind of my only blog friend. But when I emailed her about it, she jumped at the chance! She left that page open for you, just like I asked her to. She said you'd definitely see it when you got in.' She paused. 'So . . . here it is. I'll make that post public – the whole world will see it – if you don't help me out.' Her voice turned nasty. 'Because *I need help*, don't I, Amy?'

Amy's head was spinning. 'What are you talking about?' she asked.

'I'm talking about tonight's party, of course. I want to go, and I tried every way I could think of but nothing worked. And then last night I decided to use *this*, thanks to Paige. So, what do you think?'

Now Amy didn't know whether to laugh or cry. 'You went to all these lengths – wrote all that damaging stuff about me – just to get into a party?'

'Well, yeah. Amy, I *have* to go to that party. I know that goalie fancies me – and I'm *way* better-looking than Courtney! Also one of the other footballers has . . . The thing is, I am totally going to be a WAG! Do you get it?'

There was a silence. Amy couldn't believe what Lauren had done.

'Listen, do you get it?' Lauren repeated. 'All you have to do is get me in and I'll take the post down instead of making it public. It's simple!'

Amy only had to think about it for a second.

She'd had enough of being blackmailed.

'Get lost, Lauren,' she said.

'What? You can't be serious? You don't mind if everyone sees it?'

'It's too late,' Amy said. 'Do what you like.'

'I don't believe you!' Lauren's voice grew high-pitched with desperation. 'Well, will you get me into the party anyway? I have to go!'

Something suddenly occurred to Amy. 'Lauren, if you and Paige are friends, why don't you just ask her to get you in?'

'Oh, I tried that *first*, of course,' Lauren said. 'But she said she wasn't going. You have to actually arrive with an invited person to –'

'Hold on, Paige isn't going?' Amy interrupted her. Paige was part of the *Bandwagon* cast. She had to go! 'When did she say that?'

'Last night, of course.'

'She said *last night* that she wasn't going to a party . . . today?'

'Yeah! I suppose she needs to sleep off a shed-load of booze, or whatever. At least she managed to do me that favour with the computer before she dozed off.'

Amy put a hand over her mouth.

'She sounded well out of it!' Lauren continued. 'She said she was so tired that all she wanted to do was sleep forever. So I said –'

Amy hung up on Lauren and raced out into the corridor, instantly forgetting all her own troubles.

She saw Trina, Courtney and Rosay on set, being fussed with by some make-up artists. Further down, the crew were in a huddle, arguing among themselves. She heard one of them say, 'I tried five times!'

'Is Paige here?' she called to anyone and everyone. 'Has anyone seen Paige?'

'You as well, sweetheart?' said a man with a clipboard and a headset. 'We've been calling her all morning. She answered the fifth time we called, saying we'd woken her up. Then she fell asleep again during the call.' He rolled his eyes. 'I've got a pair of runners on their way to drag her out of bed and give her whatever she needs so she can make it through today.'

'I'm her flatmate,' Amy explained. 'I know what's wrong with her!'

'I bet. Heavy night last night, was it?'

'No, it's not like that! It's . . . Can I go with them?'

He shrugged. 'Suit yourself, love. They're getting in a cab right now.'

21

Once Amy started telling secrets, she couldn't seem to stop.

The first one she told was to the doctor at the hospital. She and the runners had found Paige in a terrible state but thankfully still conscious. At Amy's insistence, they'd managed to get her into the taxi to take her to the private hospital that Amy knew Paige had been treated at before, when Damien had rushed her there. They hadn't managed to avoid the paparazzi outside the flat, but there wasn't much Amy could do about that. It looked like there would be more pictures of 'Paige the alkie' in the papers tomorrow.

While Paige was in a small white room being treated, Amy stood outside the door listening to the doctor ranting to a nurse about Paige's condition. 'She was well on her way to lapsing into a diabetic coma,' he boomed. 'Highly irresponsible. It's as if her diabetes has been left completely untreated! Someone needs to check whose patient she is.'

She walked into the room. 'Um, can I say something?' she said.

The doctor looked up with barely disguised impatience. 'Are you a relative?'

'No, I'm her flatmate. I, er, brought her in —'

'Then, sorry, but you shouldn't even be here.'

And Amy would have loved to turn and run. But instead she stood her ground and insisted that she needed to speak to him. She told him everything she knew about Paige and her diabulimia.

His expression softened slightly, but he muttered, 'Stupid girl. The consequences of something like this are *extremely* serious!' Then he said, 'You did the right thing, telling us. Miss Young needs specialist treatment. I'll talk to her parents when they arrive.' And, when he thought Amy had left the room, she heard him tell the nurse, 'We need to send for a psychiatric assessment.'

She sat in a plush waiting room for a while with the runners, who thoughtfully brought her tea. 'Don't mention it, that's what we do,' the boy shrugged when she thanked him.

Then the girl, who'd been outside the main doors talking on her phone for half an hour, added, 'I don't know if you're interested in the news from the front, but I may as well tell you. Take your mind off things. Apparently, they're not cancelling *Bandwagon*. The show is going on.' She glanced at her colleague. 'And they want us back there.'

He made a face at her and groaned.

'But how can they go on without Paige?' Amy said.

The runners looked at each other.

'They're going to say it's laryngitis,' the girl said. 'Although everyone's going to assume it's alcohol poisoning and she's in rehab or something. *Is* it alcohol? She didn't smell like –'

'But I mean how can they do the final without Paige?' Amy asked quickly. She hadn't told them anything about Paige's condition.

'They've changed the line-up and started the voting from zero again. The Miss Exes only have two members now.'

'Didn't I say! Didn't I say she's the best!' the boy grinned.

'Who is?' Amy asked.

'Rosay Sands, of course. She's going to sing on her own. And I bet she'll win, too! Ooh! My friends all *love* her – she's like the new Kylie Minogue, even if she looks more like Dannii! Oh, except now she's changed her hair . . .'

'Poor Paige,' the girl said. 'Rosay gets Paige's recording contract *and* her boyfriend.'

'Scott White is not Rosay's boyfriend and he was never Paige's either.' The boy winked dramatically. 'I swear, that guy is *anyone*'s!'

The next secret was even harder to tell, because it was Amy's own. But it had to be done. And not because of the blog. Even if that stuff with Lauren hadn't happened – even if Lauren hadn't made that post public – Amy knew this phone call was long overdue. She leant on the wall outside the hospital and dialled the number.

'Hi, Dad,' she said, listening as he sounded surprised and then happy to hear from her, and knowing she was about to shatter his mood for good, or at least for a *very* long time.

'No, things aren't going so well,' she said. 'There are some things I need to tell you.'

She told him about the credit card.

And the worst thing was, just as Amy had suspected, he didn't go crazy with fury and shout at her and demand his money back. Instead he went very quiet for a very long time and said, 'How much? How much debt am I in?' He sounded like he was arranging a funeral.

'*I'm* in debt, Dad, not you!' Amy said, gripping the phone and trying not to cry. '*I* spent the money. I haven't even worn half of the clothes I bought!'

'How much, Amy?'

She couldn't tell him she wasn't even sure. She came up with a figure that was possibly about right, or slightly under.

He gasped.

'When does the bill arrive?' she asked him, closing her eyes and not wanting to hear the answer.

'I can't remember,' he said in a shocked voice. 'There's never anything on it.' He seemed to recover slightly. 'I think it's the end of the month – any day now. Amy, listen, I'd like you to cut up that card.' He sounded calm now. 'And I won't tell your mother any of this. I don't want to upset her. She's out at the hairdresser's now – probably at a fraction of what you've been paying for all your glamorous hairdos.'

She bit her lip to stop herself crying. 'I can pay it back! Well, most of it, I think. I've been working!'

'I think that's part of the problem, Amy,' her dad said sadly. 'That television thing isn't proper work. You've been buying into all the glamour. You need to come home and do an honest day's labour. I'm sure Water World will have you back.' He paused as if he was thinking hard. 'OK, this is what I'd like you to do. No, in fact this is what you *will* do. You're due home this weekend anyway, otherwise I'd have said you should come home right this minute. You know, Amy, you never told us when you were arriving and your mother's been asking, but I've said, leave her alone, let Amy have some fun . . .' He sighed. 'So what time is your ticket booked for?'

'I haven't got one. Damien got me a one-way flight before. He was going to buy me a ticket back, but . . .' She realized that she and Damien hadn't even talked about it.

He scoffed. 'A flight! I bet you were expecting to fly business class, too!'

She didn't reply, because she had been.

'What's happened to you, Amy? Look, you can take the train with your friends. Susi and Asha are travelling tomorrow, aren't they? That's the last thing I'll let you pay for on the card before we destroy it, and I'll cover the cost. But get the cheapest ticket you can.'

'OK, Dad,' Amy said, knowing she was going to have to put up with comments like this for a very long while. And she deserved them, too.

'And you can use your remaining time to return any of the things you've bought and haven't worn. And when you get home and start working, you're to give all your earnings to me, and I'll give you an allowance. A small one. I'm sorry, Amy, but you've proved you can't look after yourself. You need to come back down to earth and get started on those A-level courses of yours –'

So then Amy had told him her other secret. He took that calmly too, as if nothing could shock him now. But she felt the disappointment in his voice increase until she could hardly bear to listen to him as he talked about the local college and re-takes, and possible evening classes that left her with more time to work.

By the time she hung up, she felt wrung out.

Back inside the hospital, she checked on Paige and was told by a nurse that she could leave now. Paige's parents were on their way, on the long drive from her family home. Her condition was stable, which is more than could be said for Amy's.

Amy wished she could ring Damien, but there was no point in even trying. She decided to ring Asha or Susi. But the phone rang in her hand before she'd entered the first digit.

It was Spencer.

'Listen, Amy, I'll get straight to the point. I've heard some disturbing news from Claudette.' He sounded business-like and brisk, and nowhere near as friendly as he'd been the last time she'd seen him.

She couldn't believe how stupid she'd been not to think that Claudette would run to Spencer with Amy's threat. Her heart sank. How much more could she take today?

'I'm sorry,' she said quickly, meaning it. She realized it didn't matter how awful Claudette had been to her. Two wrongs didn't make a right. She shouldn't have played Claudette at her own game.

'What for?' Spencer said, sounding hurried. 'Do you have to go? Well, so do I, but I'll keep it quick, I promise. Listen, I'm afraid to say that Claudette's discovered a website that my temp started, one that's full of lies about her. I feel terrible about it! Lauren wrote most of it at work but I had no idea. The IT guy unlocked the account for me today and I see that she's even made something up about a worrying photo of you with that boy who used to be a sports psychologist at Royal Boroughs. I mean, I did see a photo a while ago, but nothing like what she was talking about! We all pretty much ignored it.'

So Spencer had never known about Claudette's schemes. Amy felt bad for having been unsure about that.

'Don't worry, Amy, the post was a draft and it's been deleted. To think of the kind of damaging gossip Lauren could have released!' Spencer continued, 'I've been considering prosecution.'

'Oh. No, don't do that! Lauren is just . . . really messed up,' Amy said. Something about her dad's disappointment in her made her suddenly want to protect everyone, even Lauren who had ruined her life – by telling the truth.

'Well, unfortunately it's more complicated than that. We're having to buy her off instead, with a fairly hefty payoff – there are some lawyers taking care of it right now.'

'Because of the site?'

'No, another matter – a threatened kiss-and-tell on one of Miranda's clients.' He sighed. 'But I just want to let you know that the site has been shut down and we're keeping it out of the press. Anyway, Amy, I hope you're considering those endorsement offers . . .'

'I, er . . . No, I have to go home and get a proper job. My dad said.' She felt like the baby Claudette always said she was.

'Nonsense. I can assure you this *is* proper work, and very lucrative too. Would you like me to speak to your father for you?'

'No!' she almost shouted. 'Um, no, no, it's OK.'

'OK, but if you do, just say the word. Any time. Right, I must go. There's a big story that's about to break for one of my dearest clients. We need to discuss exactly how to play it for the weekend papers. See you later, Amy.'

Amy felt like she was walking in slow motion as she left the hospital grounds. She was absolutely desperate to see Damien.

She blinked away the tears and headed for Mishra's Office Supplies instead.

22

Asha's plan for making Amy feel better involved forcing her sister to take the rest of the afternoon off work.

'It's your turn, Susi. Plus Amy needs to be with a friend who's not a total blabbermouth,' she'd said. Amy had told them all about Lauren, and Asha had been horrified that she'd had a part to play in Damien leaving. 'Though don't go to Coffee Coffee, just in case.'

'It's not your fault. It's mine. I should have told Damien everything before,' Amy said, realizing with a sinking feeling that it was true. 'I don't know when I stopped telling him stuff.'

Susi took charge and accompanied Amy to the flat, which Amy and the runners had left in a mess earlier. Paige would have hated the state the place was in. As they tidied, Amy told Susi the truth about her flatmate. She didn't want to keep any secrets from her friends any more.

Then Susi helped Amy gather up armfuls of clothes that still had tags on them, carefully setting aside the dress Damien had bought for Amy in Paris. 'Though I wouldn't mind popping over there to take it back,' Susi joked, and Amy tried to smile.

Going round the shops returning things was embarrassing, and Amy felt hot with shame. Susi noticed and started making up elaborate excuses like: 'I didn't like the colour. It clashes with my Tibetan Terrier called FooFoo.' Amy had to stifle a laugh when Susi actually said those words to the snooty assistant at Orange County.

'What?' Susi shrugged afterwards. 'I've been enjoying being more like Asha lately. Besides, you know Kylie Kemp really would take something back for that reason.'

Amy finally managed a smile. Her friends were great.

She felt all wrong going to the live *Bandwagon* broadcast with Asha later, considering she was in such trouble with her dad, but Asha talked her into it. 'Your dad hasn't grounded you *yet*,' she said. 'You've got another night before you become a stop-at-home slave-worker. Besides, you're doing me a favour. Josh can't make it to the party until later and I need to arrive with an officially invited guest, and that's you.'

So Amy had popped over to Caseydene and picked up her old suitcase from Barbie's housekeeper, because it would have felt wrong to wear anything new after what she'd admitted to her dad. She took it back to the empty flat, selected one of her year-old Primark dresses, put it on and sighed.

'You look fantastic,' Asha said. 'We both do. Come on, Amy, let's knock 'em dead with our Stanleydale style.'

The *Bandwagon* performances were fantastic, both by The Miss Exes, now a duo, and Rosay Sands, singing solo. Trina, in her bizarre new 'Be Nice To Paige' phase, had made a point of choosing songs that suited a solo artist. They all ended up warbling old Leona Lewis numbers. They would have sounded great sung by Paige, but they suited Rosay's deeper, more soulful voice even better.

The final votes were close, but Rosay was declared the overall winner of *Bandwagon*. Trina gave her a hug and looked genuinely happy for her. Courtney didn't, but in the after-show the presenter said that all three of them were set to become stars, and she cheered right up, especially when a staged-sounding call came through from a music company executive who said he wanted to sign The Miss Exes.

The after-party was full of television stars, staff, press and Frances Kemp's friends, including Barbie di Rossi, who was beside herself with pride at her daughter's win. A table of footballers and their mates were laughing raucously, challenging each other to loud dares, like downing their drinks in one. Kylie was sitting with them, next to Johann, alternately laughing and saying light-heartedly, 'You lot are like animals!' Scott White wasn't with them, and there was no sign of Danny Harris either . . . or Damien, Amy noted with a heavy heart. After a while, she spotted Scott with Rosay in a corner of the room, out of sight of Barbie. They looked completely involved in each other. *Well, good for them*, she thought. Maybe Scott had changed – who knew? She hoped Paige wouldn't get to hear about it until she felt stronger, though.

Amy left Asha talking animatedly to a group of *Bandwagon* staff members to find a quiet place to make a call. She stood outside the main party room with her phone in her hand. She tried Damien three times, but again his mobile went to voicemail.

Where *was* he? Why wouldn't he at least *talk* to her?

'Uh, hi,' came a voice next to her.

She looked up. It was Josh. She looked down at her phone again.

'Hello.' She didn't mean to sound so cold but she really didn't want to see him. 'Asha's in there.' She pointed.

'OK, thanks.'

She waited for him to leave, but he didn't.

'Amy . . .'

'What?' She wasn't going to look up again in case he gave her another of those smouldering looks. She had enough trouble and confusion in her life right now.

He sighed. 'Look, I swear I'm not harassing you. I know now that it's never going to happen between us . . .'

She couldn't resist rolling her eyes. Josh's habit of wanting to talk about everything was *not* normal and it was really getting on her nerves right now.

'Asha's in there,' she repeated pointedly. And Amy sincerely hoped she was in there chatting up some other, more deserving lad.

Josh was *still* standing around. 'I know. And it's never going to happen between me and Asha either, but I don't think she really cares.' He smiled. 'No, what I wanted to say was, well . . . About everything that's happened . . .'

Amy stared at her phone and wished he'd get to the point.

He took a deep breath. 'Look, as you've probably heard, I've decided to leave my job with Carlo di Rossi and do other things. And our paths might cross professionally, but I hope we can also stay friends. So I want you to know that I really didn't mean to drive a wedge between you and Damien. And, in case this is what you're thinking, I honestly wasn't behind him being dropped – all the arguments were between Damien and Carlo. I even tried to intervene, but –'

'What?' Amy had barely been listening but she looked up then. 'Damien was dropped?'

Josh stared at her, obviously struggling not to say something like, *Didn't you know?*

'You mean, just for those first two matches?' Amy continued, conscious that she was sounding nervous. 'I know he didn't play those. I was there. But is it more than that? Is it serious? What's it about?'

Josh looked flustered. 'Look, I don't really know the full story. Amy, I think you should talk to *him*,' he said, and finally left her alone.

Amy wanted to scream. As if that wasn't what she was *trying* to do! Though now she realized that she wasn't the only one who had been hiding things. Damien was guilty of that, too. He hadn't told her anything about arguments with his manager – he'd just grumbled generally about training. He should have told her he was having problems!

But if Damien wouldn't talk to her, what could she do about it?

The door to the main party room burst open and Rosay rushed out.

'Amy, hurry up, it's all kicking off again, just like what happens at every party Trina ever goes to! She's standing on the table and going on about making a big announcement in a minute, after she's sung a song. Wonder what she's going to come out with *this* time!'

'It's all about me, of course,' drawled a voice behind them.

Amy and Rosay turned and saw Claudette, looking utterly

glamorous in a shimmering gold-and-black dress that was cut in a way that proved she hadn't recently had – and didn't need – a boob job.

'Excuse me, baby, I'm needed inside,' Claudette said.

Amy stared at her, but it was hard to tell what was going on behind Claudette's designer sunglasses.

'Oh, and don't tell me not to call you "baby" – I'll call you whatever I like.' Claudette took her glasses off and gave Amy one of her best condescending looks. 'You might think you've won now, you and all your little friends who rally round you.' She put the sunglasses back on. 'But you don't scare me – you *or* Trina. You have nothing on me. I've taken control and I know exactly how to play this and come up smelling of roses. Though I won't forget your part in it.' She held her head high. 'And yes, that's a threat.'

As Claudette swept past them, Amy noticed that her walk wasn't as much of a swagger as usual. She might be pretending to be fine, but Claudette was nervous – Amy was sure of it.

'What does she mean by "your part in it"? What's going on?' Rosay asked Amy after the door swung shut.

'I don't really know,' Amy mumbled. Well, she could make a guess. But she hadn't told anyone about the photo – except Claudette herself.

Rosay looked thoughtful. 'She probably means you're the reason Trina's got something up her sleeve. It's weird – Trina usually holds back when it comes to Claudette. But you should have seen her face when I told her about you and the Josh photo – she was all *"right, that's enough now"*.' She sighed. 'To tell you the truth, I'm relieved it's not about me and Scott. Trina's been funny with me ever since we went public, even though it was her idea and she couldn't possibly know I'm not acting! Come on, let's find out what she's up to.'

Inside, Trina was just reaching the end of a slightly out-of-tune ballad.

Claudette was standing in the darkness of the doorway when Rosay and Amy walked in. Rosay went to join Scott, who was waiting for her by the other footballers. He put his arm around her as the room erupted into over-the-top applause for Trina. Amy stood near them.

'Thank you, thank you!' Trina called from the table she was standing on. 'Even if my good friend Rosay won the competition, in a way we're *all* winners tonight!'

Scott gave Rosay a passionate kiss. There was no doubt about it: they definitely looked like a couple now. Amy glanced over at Barbie, but she was grinning from ear to ear, obviously not sharing her husband's misgivings about Scott White.

'And a special mention for my good friend Paige, who is hopefully in rehab now getting the help she needs!' Trina smiled angelically. 'It's all thanks to me that she has reformed. I've been a good influence on her, and very kind to her despite the way she's treated me.' She looked pointedly at some of the journalists in the room as they scribbled furiously in their notebooks.

Amy sighed. So maybe Trina hadn't forgiven Paige after all. She'd just decided to use her to score points and improve her own image.

Trina continued loudly to her audience, 'And now for a special announcement. I'd like to say welcome back to an old friend who's been away for a while! I was going to make this announcement without her, but when I warned her about it, she decided to come here and be in the thick of it. She's nothing if not brave!' Trina laughed. 'Isn't that right, Claudette darling?'

The room fell silent as everyone turned to stare at Claudette.

But, weirdly, Claudette didn't respond with her usual confidence. She pushed her shades further on to her nose and moved closer to Trina, muttering, 'God, can you just get it over with, please? And I *won't* forget this.'

'Of course you won't, honey,' Trina said to her in a soft, caring voice, as if there wasn't a whole roomful of people listening to her. 'But I'm doing you a favour. You'll get a clean slate. Believe me, it's *cleansing*. I'm an expert at it. At last, you can stop being terrified of me, because the worst will have happened.' She laughed. 'As if I'd have said anything before. I knew how bad it could be for you, and I have a lot of *heart*, you know. But you just kept playing your tricks on innocent friends.' She looked at Amy. 'And I think I've let you get away with it too long. It's time. Besides, it goes really well with something else I was going to announce tonight anyway.'

Then she addressed the room.

'OK, ladies, gentlemen . . . and footballers,' Trina said, laughing at her own old joke. 'I have an announcement to make and it's a bit of a shocker, but I'm doing this as a favour to a friend. In fact, several friends, and girls all over the world. Because, as we all know . . . Scott White is a creep!'

Rosay shifted uncomfortably and said, 'Trina, what are you doing?'

Beside her, Scott laughed good-naturedly. 'Hey! Can you give it a rest now, Trina?'

'I haven't even started, *Scott*. Because it's time everyone heard what you told me that night all those years ago when you were drunk – the thing you swore me to secrecy on. You probably don't even remember telling me, do you? Well, I kept it quiet for Claudette's sake, because no matter how she treated us, I knew this wasn't just about her.'

Amy couldn't believe what she was hearing – or seeing. Claudette looked like she was cowering in Trina's shadow.

'Well, things have changed and Claudette actually *wants* you all to know this now. *Damage limitation*, is that what the PR guy said? He also said something about me having some photo and I played along.' She laughed, looking at Claudette. 'Well, I don't know anything about any photo, but I do know the truth and I'm perfectly happy to announce it for you. Ladies and gentlemen . . . Claudette wants you all to know this . . .'

A few people were getting restless now, but most were still staring at Trina.

'Claudette wants you all to know that . . . she has a son! She had a baby four years ago, a boy called George. She'll thank you guys in the press to stay out of his life, though . . .'

The room erupted into gasps and buzzing conversation.

'Where's Harris?' one of the footballers said loudly. 'He's a dark horse!'

'He only met her a couple of years ago,' the boy beside him pointed out.

'Oh,' said the first boy. 'Oh, *right*!'

From the other side of the room, a woman remarked, 'I thought George was her brother. Is he really her son?'

Claudette said nothing. She kept her dark glasses on and stood still as the questions continued.

'Yes, George is Claudette's son,' Trina announced, interrupting the gossip. 'But before you kind members of the press start having a go at her, she'd like you to note that she's done her best for him all these years, even missing the opportunity to help out at *Bandwagon* to look after him, and selflessly handing him to her mother for a stable upbringing. Which is more than we can say for the baby's father, who didn't even want to know.' She paused for long enough to cause an even more frantic buzz in the room. Then she added sweetly, 'Isn't that right, Scott?'

After that, it was pandemonium. Frances must have allowed the press to call for reinforcements because suddenly there were photographers climbing over each other to take photos of Claudette, and reporters shoving voice recorders at her as she said in a quiet voice, 'It's all true. Me and Scott were at school together . . . That's how I met Danny, when I moved to London and went to see Scott, although Danny didn't know about . . . No, Scott didn't want to know, and what choice did I have? I wanted to do the right thing . . .' Claudette looked like she was struggling to hold her head high, but her voice cracked slightly when she answered a reporter's question about Danny. 'He's left. . . he'll be . . . Excuse me, but I really don't want to talk about my husband . . . No, I'm staying at my mum's right now. She's been wonderful and I only wanted the best for my baby, unlike Scott . . .'

Meanwhile the press were also hounding Scott. 'It wasn't like that!' he was saying, his brow furrowed defensively as if he'd just been accused of fouling another player. He clutched at Rosay, explaining to her and the reporters at the same time, 'She said she didn't want anything more to do with me. It was just a teenage fling! She said it was all taken care of!'

Then Trina shouted loudly from the table she was still standing on, 'And one more thing, everyone! Scott, Rosay has something to say to you. Isn't that right, Rosay?' She laughed.

Scott glared at Trina and tightened his grip on Rosay's shoulder. 'Trina, OK, you've had your fun and ruined some lives – *again* – but don't drag her into this. OK?'

'Too right, babe!' Barbie called in the distance. 'Them pair are in love.'

Trina shot Scott a disdainful look. 'Yeah, that's what we wanted you to think.' She laughed at Scott. 'She's not stupid – unlike you! She only went out with you to play you at your own game! And now he's dumped, isn't he, Rosay?'

'You're wrong!' Scott shook his head. Then he said gently, 'Rosay, tell her she's wrong about us.'

Rosay's face was pure misery as she shook her head and whispered, 'No. She's right.'

Scott let go of her as if he'd been burned. He kicked a table, swore loudly at the entire room and slammed out.

In the brief silence that followed, Asha turned to Josh, who'd just got her a drink. 'Oh by the way, you're chucked and all.'

23

After all the drama, Amy found the thought of going back to the empty flat even more depressing than before. So when Rosay asked her if she wanted to stay overnight in her old room at Caseydene, she jumped at the chance.

They stayed up half the night, eating vegetable crisps in the kitchen while Rosay seemed to forget all about having just won a major recording contract. Instead she poured her heart out about how madly in love she was with Scott and how horrible this whole situation was, but she knew she'd done the right thing. That didn't stop her asking Amy a hundred times what Amy would have done in her shoes. Amy kept saying she was really not someone to ask about relationships, since she'd clearly messed up her own excellent one with Damien, but Rosay wasn't really listening. She mostly just wanted to talk non-stop, which suited Amy.

The next day they got up late and had a long, luxurious breakfast. Then Amy phoned Asha and Susi to check what time they were getting their train.

'I'd better go back and pack,' she told Rosay when she hung up. 'I haven't got long before I have to head back to real life.'

'Want me to come with you to the flat?'

'Would you? That would be great.' She tried to sound less pathetic. 'You should probably take back all those cases you let me borrow. I'm just taking my big old one home.'

Rosay gave her a long, sympathetic look. 'Aw, Amy, don't worry. I've been there, remember? I thought I'd lost everything, too, last year, and look how I bounced back!' She gave a sad smile. 'Oh, OK, I'm not a good example, but you'll do it better! And you'd better visit, by the way, or I'll come up there and kidnap you myself! Not that I've ever been to those far-flung corners of England before. Is Leeds on the end of the Northern Line?'

Amy smiled a tiny bit. As if Rosay even knew how to find the Northern Line. Come to think of it, Amy didn't either. Asha and Susi were seasoned tube travellers by now, but Amy had got used to taking taxis everywhere.

She took her final chauffeured car journey to meet Asha and Susi at the station, said goodbye to Rosay and donned her sunglasses as a half-hearted disguise before joining the queue for tickets. She couldn't help thinking about how much had happened since the last time she'd been at King's Cross station with her friends nearly two weeks ago, when they had surprised her by saying they were staying longer.

There was a train every half hour, but Susi and Asha were being met by their mum at the station and they'd promised to be on the four thirty. The twins met Amy at the ticket office, but it took so long for Amy to get her ticket that Asha groaned, 'We've got no time for shopping!' and Susi nudged her hard.

'Ow! What?' Asha looked at Amy. 'Oh, right. Sorry. I keep forgetting. We looked your thing up at work yesterday, by the way – your compulsive shopping disorder, or whatever it's called. There was a fancy Greek word for it on the site – not "shopaholic", but something to do with manic onions or something.'

'Oniomania,' Susi said.

'Yeah, whatever. Apparently it's treated the same way as eating disorders are, because you can't stop shopping altogether any more than you can stop eating.' Asha sighed longingly. 'Too right! Anyway, maybe you and Paige can get counselling together.'

Susi nudged her even harder. 'Ash, come on! Now is *not* the time.'

'I wasn't even supposed to tell Susi about the diabulimia thing,' Amy muttered, suddenly worrying about Paige and hoping she was OK. She'd rung the hospital this morning, but they wouldn't tell her anything because she wasn't family. The staff must have bent some rules to tell her what they had yesterday.

'Course you were supposed to tell us! Friends need to know what's going on in each other's lives,' Asha declared. 'Surely you know that by now. We just have to keep a closer eye on who's listening in.' She looked around dramatically, regarding random passers-by with suspicion.

'Never mind all that!' Susi moaned. 'We've got a train to catch!'

'Isn't that . . . ?' Asha asked, staring hard into the distance. 'No, it can't be. Never mind.'

'Ash! Stop eyeing up strangers and hurry up!'

Susi wheeled her case towards the row of ticket barriers, behind which their train was already waiting on the platform.

There was a larger barrier at the side where a member of the station staff was standing, checking tickets and waving people with pushchairs through. Amy thought they'd be using that one, but when Susi and Asha headed for the smaller barriers, she followed them, dragging her monster case along behind her. Her friends, who were used to a daily commute on the Tube to work from Uncle Dinesh's house, expertly inserted their tickets, shoved their cases past the barrier and scooted to the other side. Amy put her ticket in the slot, turned and hesitated, tilting her case and worrying that it was too thick to fit through the gap.

She heard a clunking sound and took a step forwards just in time to clear the barrier. But the metal arms locked around her suitcase and jammed. An alarm sounded and what seemed like a hundred people behind her tutted loudly and muttered rude things about tourists.

She tugged at her case, but it was well and truly stuck.

The guard at the large barrier looked over, rolled his eyes and called, 'I'll be there in a second.'

An announcement blared about her train and all the stations it would stop at, and the fact that the doors would lock before departure for everyone's safety. Amy thought they still had at least five minutes before that could happen, but Susi gave her a thoroughly panicked look from where she and Asha had stopped.

'You go ahead! I'll catch up with you,' Amy called to them, barely glancing back as another annoyed commuter approached the barrier and shoved at her case.

'Don't you think I've tried that?' Amy snapped at the person behind her, now feeling totally stressed.

'You were pulling. I'm pushing. It's a different action. Anyway, Ames, I was only trying to help!'

Amy did a double-take at the sound of the voice.

'Damien?'

She turned round.

It was him. Damien stood on the other side of the barrier, wearing a cap, sports shirt and jeans and no trace of Armani. He looked totally like the guy she'd said goodbye to in Stanleydale all those weeks ago. And also completely gorgeous – something that had never changed. Her heart leapt.

He'd come to the station. Why? Had he come to see her to make sure she was leaving? She felt the blood rush to her head and a pounding in her ears.

'What are you doing here?'

'Trying to help *you*! Yeah, like the idiot I am. I should have known you'd rather shut me out completely than accept any help from *me*!'

He glared at her and it was obvious he wasn't talking about a stuck suitcase.

She felt a surge of anger. How dare he stand there accusing her when he'd been just as bad? 'Yeah? Well, you didn't let *me* in on anything that was going on at the club. You never said anything about arguments with Big Carl and being dropped from the team!'

He looked shocked for a second then smirked. 'I should have known *Josh* would tell you about that! By the way, nice touch, using my own laptop to tell me about you two.' His voice oozed sarcasm. 'Thanks a lot, Amy – that really made my day, coming home to *that* after a terrible match, while you were supposedly out with the girls!'

'I *was* out with the girls!' Amy pulled at her case in frustration, wishing she could make a run for it. 'God, Damien, there is nothing going on between me and Josh, and there never was, and you *know* it! That photo you read about – in the blog that *Paige* left out for you to read – was a fake! And you should trust me, the same way I trusted you with Paige!'

He scoffed. 'Yeah, in the *end*! Honestly, Amy, it's one rule for you . . .'

'You're one to talk! Or rather, *not* talk!'

He stared at her for ages, as if he was deciding whether or not to say something. 'Look, I didn't tell you what was going on because the arguments were about *you*!' He sighed. 'About you and Josh! And I didn't want to tell you because . . . it was too much like the way you got upset about me and Paige. And after the way I went on at you before . . . I felt like a complete hypocrite.'

'What are you talking about?'

He shrugged and mumbled, 'I couldn't get it out of my head that you and Josh . . . you know. Though you told me there was nothing going on and I knew I should believe you. But Josh has been winding me up something chronic these last two weeks. He told Big Carl about the row I had with him at the *Bandwagon* party, you know. So then Big Carl said I needed anger management sessions. But I wasn't going to have them with *Josh*!'

'That's nothing to do with me.' Amy put her hands on her hips.

'Maybe not, but he was still after you! There was that night that I told the lads I was taking you to Monty's, and when I got there *he* was there! And he *never* goes out with us! He was only there because he must've heard you'd be there!'

Two girls stared as they passed through the barriers. 'I recognize them off the telly,' one of them said to her friend.

Damien continued, ignoring them. 'Anyway, that night I told Josh to stay away from you, and I didn't even raise my voice, but he went blabbing to Big Carl, saying I was being *abusive* again!' He ran an exasperated hand through his hair. 'And our manager treats us like school kids. It's driving me crazy! He keeps me behind all the time and lectures me for hours because Josh makes him worry about my "attitude". He even kept me behind on the night of Johann's party – it's like being in detention! It's not just me! He dropped Scott in the last game just because of some gossip about his step-daughter – I mean, you know I don't exactly rate Scott *or* Rosay, but still. It's nothing to do with football! No wonder there are rumours about Scott looking for a transfer.'

Amy watched him clench and unclench his fists.

'So Big Carl said I wouldn't be played until I apologized to Josh,' he continued. 'I mean, did you ever hear anything so *stupid*? Josh should be apologizing to *me*!'

Damien took out his frustration on the case, giving it another hard shove. To Amy's annoyance, it cleared the barriers and landed with a loud thud on her left foot.

'Ouch!' Amy cried, pulling up her injured foot and hopping around.

'God, sorry, Ames,' Damien said, his voice softening.

The guard, who'd been finally on his way over, shrugged and went back to his post.

'That's OK,' Amy mumbled, wondering if she'd been too hard on him just now. He sounded like he'd been through a lot with the whole Josh thing. And he sounded like he was ready to forgive her, too, for not telling him all that stuff. Maybe they could work things out after all.

But then he ruined it by adding, 'Is your case extra heavy because it's full of all that stuff you told me you got *free*?'

She glared at him. So he still wanted to have a go at her after all!

'Yeah, that was another surprise! Why didn't you tell me you were in trouble with money? I could have helped!'

Amy felt herself suddenly snap. She thought of Asha shouting at her about how she was letting Damien pay for everything. She thought of Lauren suggesting that Damien was the answer to all her money problems. She thought about how she didn't want to be *that* girl – and Damien knew that! Or at least he *used* to know. Before he became a Premiership footballer, and everything changed. *He* changed.

Now her blood was really boiling. 'I don't need your money!' She picked up her case. 'If you must know, I took most of the stuff back! And I'm going to work to pay back the rest. And you know what, Damien Taylor? If you think I'm after your money, you don't know me at all! And we are *finished*!'

She picked up her case and walked away as fast as she could, blinking back tears. Had she really been dying to talk to Damien? Right now, she never wanted to see him again in her life! The train was about to leave anyway, to take her hundreds of miles away from him. Asha and Susi would be wondering where she was. Sure enough, another announcement blared and a guard started working his way up the train, slamming doors.

Amy reached the second-class section of the train before she glanced back.

To her surprise, Damien had cleared the barriers and was covering the ground between them with all the speed of a Premiership footballer.

He stopped in front of her and spoke through gritted teeth, not remotely out of breath. 'God, Amy! Will you *stop* it! I wasn't offering you my money! I was offering my *help*.' He dropped his holdall at his feet. 'You know what? You really can't deal with my new life, can you? That's why you went all weird when I asked you to marry me.'

Amy glared at him. Her phone started ringing in her bag but she ignored it – whoever it was, she needed to say this first.

She said coldly, 'Of course I can deal with your new life. But I don't want to. Because you have *changed*, Damien!'

'Maybe, but I don't think so. I think *you* have. Because from the moment I got signed you went to pieces and failed your GCSEs!'

She couldn't believe he'd said that! 'I told you we're finished! I honestly never want to see you again, and I mean it!'

She jumped on the train. It probably wasn't the carriage Asha and Susi were in but she didn't care – she just wanted to get away from Damien.

He was still standing there, so she called down, 'Anyway, I didn't *fail*! And why would you think that had anything to do with *you*? And the reason I don't want to marry you is nothing to do with your life. It's because I've got my *own* life!'

'As if I ever thought you hadn't!' His eyes blazed as he looked up, stepping towards the train. 'You knew I meant getting married in the future, not right now! I've never thought for a minute that you should give up everything – or *anything* – and follow me. I even told you that at Kylie's party. And I said I wouldn't mention it again, and it was fine! It was a spur-of-the-moment thing, and maybe I shouldn't have said it, and I know that now. But you were obviously still talking to your friends about it – and not to *me* – as if it was some big *problem*, when all I was ever really saying is that I want to be with you forever –'

The door next to them slammed and the guard appeared in front of them. 'Are you two on, or off?' he said gruffly. 'We're locking the doors now.'

'I'm on, he's *off*!' Amy said pointedly.

'She's wrong,' Damien said, hopping on to the train. 'I'm not leaving her.'

The guard sighed, slammed the door behind them and moved on.

Amy suddenly realized that Damien would have needed a ticket to clear the barrier. And his holdall was at his feet.

'Damien, what's going on?' She put her annoyance aside as the realization surged through her. 'You didn't come to the station to see me, did you?'

'I was pretty sure you'd be here, if that's what you mean. I found out when I went to talk to Big Carl this afternoon. Barbie told me.'

A whistle blew in the distance and the train started to pull away.

'But really I'm here because I'm going home.'

He shrugged at her as if he hadn't just dropped a huge bombshell.

'Damien!' Amy couldn't disguise her horror. 'You can't!'

'Why not?'

'You just can't! Any more than I would give up my life to stay here with you – even if it means retaking my GCSEs and travelling backwards and forwards every weekend to see you and worrying about what you get up to when I'm not around.' She reached over to him, gripping his shoulders, not even realizing her anger had flooded away. 'Even if it means us getting back to normal, even if I'd love to see you all the time . . . you can't give up football!'

He looked surprised. 'But didn't you just finish with me?'

'Yes . . . But . . .'

'So there's really still a chance for us?' He sounded so hopeful that she felt her insides melt. The truth was, she loved him, no matter how infuriating he was. What she felt for him was never going anywhere, and she knew it. They were just so right together.

Her heart galloped as he looked deep into her eyes and said seriously, 'You know, Ames, after I saw that website, I went to stay with Johann because I needed some time to think. But I realized I wasn't really angry with you, especially when Kylie told me about how you'd helped Paige. I should have been there, Amy – I shouldn't have stormed off and left you like that. I'm sorry. And Paige told Kylie to tell you she was sorry too. I didn't know what she was talking about then, but I think I get it now. Paige was behind the blog thing, yeah?'

'Kind of,' Amy muttered. 'It's a long story.'

'Anyway, I knew there would be an explanation and you'd make it all OK. I'd just like you to *tell* me stuff, that's all, so I don't have to find out about your life online like that.'

She muttered, 'I know. I'm sorry too. But you're as bad as me!'

'I know. You're right. Listen . . . If I promise to tell you everything, and you do the same for me – so we always know the score – can we try again, Ames?'

'Maybe,' she said slowly. 'But you are *not* giving up football. You should ring Big Carl right now and take back your resignation.'

The shadow of a smile crossed his lips. 'Amy, that's not what I talked to Big Carl about today.'

'Oh?'

'No. I went to tell him I'd apologize to Josh. I realized I had to swallow my pride, because Big Carl might be treating me like a school kid, but I was behaving like one too.'

'You've apologized to Josh?'

'I will when I get a chance – and *he's* just resigned, so I'll have to find him first! But I promised Big Carl, so I'll do it.' He made a face and sighed. 'And I'm on the team for the away game tomorrow. It's in York, and the coach is stopping for me on its way up. Apparently I'm a special case. Big Carl said it was OK if I went to see my mum and Stephen for a bit first.'

Damien smiled at her shyly. 'And you too, of course, gorgeous girl-next-door. Maybe you can even come to the match and watch me set up my first Premiership goal.' His eyes sparkled.

'God, Day, you'll be lucky!' Amy laughed as he put his arms around her and pulled her closer. 'I mean not about the goal – I know you'll do that! But about me going. I think I'm grounded for the rest of my life!'

He shrugged, holding her tightly. 'We'll get through it,' he mumbled as he touched the heart pendant she hadn't taken off, even when she thought they might have split up for good. 'We can get through anything, me and you.'

His mouth was so close to hers now that she'd only have to move her head a tiny amount to make their lips lock deliciously.

But then the train lurched, throwing them together, and they did more than kiss. They sank into the corner of the gangway, entwined and totally lost in each other as if they'd never been apart. As if they were already home.

'Oh, here you are, Amy! Susi's been worried about you,' came a voice from above them.

Only Asha could be so shameless.

'Hi, Ash,' Amy mumbled, her mouth buried in Damien's shoulder.

Asha rolled her eyes. 'Yeah, well, I'm not going to ask what *he's* doing here, or why you're all over each other in the middle of a train, because I know by now that you two can't ever keep your hands off each other for long, no matter what,' Asha said lightly. 'But Amy, can I talk to you alone a sec?'

Amy stifled a groan, but Damien said, 'It's OK, Ames. I'll wait for you.' He gave her a short but meaningful kiss.

'That's sweet,' said Asha when she'd dragged her into the carriage and the door had hissed to an automatic close behind them. 'But you have to listen to this, Amy! We have just had the offer of a lifetime! And I mean *we*!'

Amy laughed at the intensity on Asha's face. 'What are you talking about?'

'Well, I have just been speaking to your agent!' Asha said. 'Or PR guru, or whatever he's called. God knows where he got my number – although it could have been Josh, I suppose, who is about as ungodlike as you can get. Anyway, this guy said he'd tried you first but there was no answer.'

The train swayed and Amy gripped on to a luggage rack, waiting for Asha to get to the point.

'So here it is!' said Asha dramatically. 'You and me and Susi are starring in a fitness DVD that they want to sell in time for New Year's resolutions. Some people I met at that party thought we'd be perfect for it! And can you guess who's going to be our so-called personal trainer for the routine?'

Amy shook her head, feeling dazed.

'Only *Josh*, that's who! So we can really make him suffer! And we can do it all at the weekends from sixth form! In London, so you can see Damien! And it pays *loads*! And we are going to be *massive*! And I've already said yes, and Spencer said he'd talk your dad round, and he'll probably have to work on my mum, too.'

Asha beamed at her friend.

'So what do you think of *that*, Amy Thornton. Fancy being a footballer's girlfriend and celebrity with your *own* goals?'